The Ninth Vibration

L. Adams Beck

Contents

THE NINTH VIBRATION

BY

L. Adams Beck

THE NINTH VIBRATION

There is a place uplifted nine thousand feet in purest air where one of the most ancient tracks in the world runs from India into Tibet. It leaves Simla of the Imperial councils by a stately road; it passes beyond, but now narrowing, climbing higher beside the khuds or steep drops to the precipitous valleys beneath, and the rumor of Simla grows distant and the way is quiet, for, owing to the danger of driving horses above the khuds, such baggage as you own must be carried by coolies, and you yourself must either ride on horseback or in the little horseless carriage of the Orient, here drawn and pushed by four men. And presently the deodars darken the way with a solemn presence, for-

> These are the Friars of the wood,
> The Brethren of the Solitude
> Hooded and grave-"

-their breath most austerely pure in the gradually chilling air. Their companies increase and now the way is through a great wood where it has become a trail and no more, and still it climbs for many miles and finally a rambling bungalow, small and low, is sighted in the deeps of the trees, a mountain stream from unknown heights falling beside it. And this is known as the House in the Woods. Very few people are permitted to go there, for the owner has no care for money and makes no provision for guests. You must take your own servant and the khansamah will cook you such simple food as men expect in the wilds, and that is all. You stay as long as you please and when you leave not even a gift to the khansamah is permitted.

I had been staying in Ranipur of the plains while I considered the question of getting to Upper Kashmir by the route from Simla along the old way to Chinese

Tibet where I would touch Shipki in the Dalai Lama's territory and then pass on to Zanskar and so down to Kashmir - a tremendous route through the Himalaya and a crowning experience of the mightiest mountain scenery in the world. I was at Ranipur for the purpose of consulting my old friend Olesen, now an irrigation official in the Rampur district - a man who had made this journey and nearly lost his life in doing it. It is not now perhaps so dangerous as it was, and my life was of no particular value to any one but myself, and the plan interested me.

I pass over the long discussions of ways and means in the blinding heat of Ranipur. Olesen put all his knowledge at my service and never uttered a word of the envy that must have filled him as he looked at the distant snows cool and luminous in blue air, and, shrugging good-natured shoulders, spoke of the work that lay before him on the burning plains until the terrible summer should drag itself to a close. We had vanquished the details and were smoking in comparative silence one night on the veranda, when he said in his slow reflective way;

"You don't like the average hotel, Ormond, and you'll like it still less up Simla way with all the Simla crowd of grass-widows and fellows out for as good a time as they can cram into the hot weather. I wonder if I could get you a permit for The House in the Woods while you re waiting to fix up your men and route for Shipki."

He explained and of course I jumped at the chance. It belonged, he said, to a man named Rup Singh, a pandit, or learned man of Ranipur. He had always spent the summer there, but age and failing health made this impossible now, and under certain conditions he would occasionally allow people known to friends of his own to put up there.

"And Rup Singh and I are very good friends," Olesen said; "I won his heart by discovering the lost Sukh Mandir, or Hall of Pleasure, built many centuries ago by a Maharao of Ranipur for a summer retreat in the great woods far beyond Simla. There are lots of legends about it here in Ranipur. They call it The House of Beauty. Rup Singh's ancestor had been a close friend of the Maharao and was with him to the end, and that's why he himself sets such store on the place. You have a good chance if I ask for a permit.

He told me the story and since it is the heart of my own I give it briefly. Many centuries ago the Ranipur Kingdom was ruled by the Maharao Rai Singh a prince of the great lunar house of the Rajputs. Expecting a bride from some far away king-dom (the name of this is unrecorded) he built the Hall of Pleasure as a summer palace, a house of rare and costly beauty. A certain great chamber he lined with carved figures of the Gods and their stories, almost unsurpassed for truth and life. So, with the pine trees whispering about it the secret they sigh to tell, he hoped to create an earthly Paradise with this Queen in whom all loveliness was perfected. And then some mysterious tragedy ended all his hopes. It was rumoured that when the Princess came to his court, she was, by some terrible mistake, received with insult and offered the position only of one of his women. After that nothing was known. Certain only is it that he fled to the hills, to the home of his broken hope, and there ended his days in solitude, save for the attendance of two faithful friends who would not abandon him even in the ghostly quiet of the winter when the pine boughs were heavy with snow and a spectral moon stared at the panthers shuffling through the white wastes beneath. Of these two Rup Singh's ancestor was one. And in his thirty fifth year the Maharao died and his beauty and strength passed into legend and his kingdom was taken by another and the jungle crept silently over his Hall of Pleasure and the story ended.

"There was not a memory of the place up there," Olesen went on. "Certainly I never heard anything of it when I went up to the Shipki in 1904. But I had been able to be useful to Rup Singh and he gave me a permit for The House in the Woods, and I stopped there for a few days' shooting. I remember that day so well. I was wandering in the dense woods while my men got their midday grub, and I missed the trail somehow and found myself in a part where the trees were dark and thick and the silence heavy as lead. It was as if the trees were on guard - they stood shoulder to shoulder and stopped the way. Well, I halted, and had a notion there was something beyond that made me doubt whether to go on. I must have stood there five minutes hesitating. Then I pushed on, bruising the thick ferns under my shooting boots and stooping under the knotted boughs. Suddenly I tramped out of the jungle into a clearing, and lo and behold a ruined House, with blocks of marble lying all about it, and carved pillars and a great roof all being slowly smothered by the jungle. The weirdest thing you ever saw. I climbed some fallen columns to get a better look, and as I did I saw a face flash by at the arch of a broken window. I sang out in Hindustani, but no answer: only the echo from the woods. Somehow that dampened my ardour, and I didn't go in to what seemed like a great ruined hall for the place was so eerie and lonely, and looked mighty snaky into the bargain. So I came ingloriously away and told Rup Singh. And his whole face changed. 'That is The House of Beauty,' he said. 'All my life have I sought it and in vain. For, friend of my soul, a man must lose himself that he may find himself and what lies beyond, and the trodden path has ever been my doom. And you who have not sought have seen. Most strange are the way of the Gods'. Later on I knew this was why he had always gone up yearly, thinking and dreaming God knows what. He and I tried for the place together, but in vain and the whole thing is like a dream. Twice he has let friends of mine stay at The House in the Woods, and I think he won't refuse now."

"Did he ever tell you the story?"

"Never. I only know what I've picked up here. Some horrible mistake about the Rani that drove the man almost mad with remorse. I've heard bits here and there. There's nothing so vital as tradition in India."

"I wonder'. what really happened."

"That we shall never know. I got a little old picture of the Maharao - said to be painted by a Pahari artist. It's not likely to be authentic, but you never can tell. A Brahman sold it to me that he might complete his daughter's dowry, and hated doing it."

"May I see it?"

"Why certainly. Not a very good light, but - can do, as the Chinks say.

He brought it out rolled in silk stuff and I carried it under the hanging lamp. A beautiful young man indeed, with the air of race these people have beyond all others;- a cold haughty face, immovably dignified. He sat with his hands resting lightly on the arms of his chair of State. A crescent of rubies clasped the folds of the turban and from this sprang an aigrette scattering splendours. The magnificent hilt of a sword was ready beside him. The face was not only beautiful but arresting.

"A strange picture," I said. "The artist has captured the man himself. I can see him trampling on any one who opposed him, and suffering in the same cold secret way. It ought to he authentic if it isn't. Don't you know any more?"

"Nothing. Well - to bed, and tomorrow I'll see Rup Singh."

I was glad when he returned with the permission. I was to be very careful, he said, to make no allusion to the lost palace, for two women were staying at the House in the Woods - a mother and daughter to whom Rup Singh had granted hospitality because of an obligation he must honor. But with true Oriental distrust of women he had thought fit to make no confidence to them. I promised and asked Olesen if he knew them.

"Slightly. Canadians of Danish blood like my own. Their name is Ingmar. Some people think the daughter good-looking. The mother is supposed to be clever; keen on occult subjects which she came back to India to study. The husband was a great naturalist and the kindest of men. He almost lived in the jungle and the natives had all sorts of rumours about his powers. You know what they are. They said the birds and beasts followed him about. Any old thing starts a legend."

"What was the connection with Rup Singh?"

"He was in difficulties and undeservedly, and Ingmar generously lent him money at a critical time, trusting to his honour for repayment. Like most Orientals he never forgets a good turn and would do anything for any of the family - except trust the women with any secret he valued. The father is long dead. By the way Rup Singh gave me a queer message for you. He said; 'Tell the Sahib these words - "Let him who finds water in the desert share his cup with him who dies of thirst." He is certainly getting very old. I don't suppose he knew himself what he meant."

I certainly did not. However my way was thus smoothed for me and I took the upward road, leaving Olesen to the long ungrateful toil of the man who devotes his life to India without sufficient time or knowledge to make his way to the inner chambers of her beauty. There is no harder mistress unless you hold the pass-key to her mysteries, there is none of whom so little can be told in words but who kindles so deep a passion. Necessity sometimes takes me from that enchanted land, but when the latest dawns are shining in my skies I shall make my feeble way back to her and die at her worshipped feet. So I went up from Kalka.

I have never liked Simla. It is beautiful enough - eight thousand feet up in the grip of the great hills looking toward the snows, the famous summer home of the Indian Government. Much diplomacy is whispered on Observatory Hill and many are the lighter diversions of which Mr. Kipling and lesser men have written. But Simla is also a gateway to many things - to the mighty deodar forests that clothe the foot-hills of the mountains, to Kulu, to the eternal snows, to the old, old bridle way that leads up to the Shipki Pass and the mysteries of Tibet - and to the strange things told in this story. So I passed through with scarcely a glance at the busy gayety of the little streets and the tiny shops where the pretty ladies buy their rouge and powder. I was attended by my servant Ali Khan, a Mohammedan from Nagpur, sent up with me by Olesen with strong recommendation. He was a stout walker, so too am I, and an inveterate dislike to the man-drawn carriage whenever my own legs would serve me decided me to walk the sixteen miles to the House in the Woods, sending on the baggage. Ali Khan despatched it and prepared to follow me, the fine cool air of the hills giving us a zest.

"Subhan Alla! (Praise be to God!) the air is sweet!" he said, stepping out behind me. "What time does the Sahib look to reach the House?"

"About five or six. Now, Ali Khan, strike out of the road. You know the way."

So we struck up into the glorious pine woods, mountains all about us. Here and there as we climbed higher was a little bank of forgotten snow, but spring had triumphed and everywhere was the waving grace of maiden-hair ferns, banks of violets and strangely beautiful little wild flowers. These woods are full of panthers, but in day time the only precaution necessary is to take no dog, - a dainty they cannot resist. The air was exquisite with the sun-warm scent of pines, and here and there the trees broke away disclosing mighty ranges of hills covered with rich blue shadows like the bloom on a plum, - the clouds chasing the sunshine over the mountain sides and the dark green velvet of the robe of pines. I looked across ravines that did not seem gigantic and yet the villages on the other side were like a handful of peas, so tremendous was the scale. I stood now and then to see the rhododendrons, forest trees here with great trunks and massive boughs glowing with blood-red blossom, and time went by and I took no count of it, so glorious was the climb.

It must have been hours later when it struck me that the sun was getting low and that by now we should be nearing The House in the Woods. I said as much to Ali Khan. He looked perplexed and agreed. We had reached a comparatively level place, the trail faint but apparent, and it surprised me that we heard no sound of life from the dense wood where our goal must be.

"I know not, Presence," he said. "May his face be blackened that directed me. I thought surely I could not miss the way, and yet-"

We cast back and could see no trail forking from the one we were on. There was nothing for it but to trust to luck and push on. But I began to be uneasy and so was the man. I had stupidly forgotten to unpack my revolver, and worse, we had no food, and the mountain air is an appetiser, and at night the woods have their dangers, apart from being absolutely trackless. We had not met a living being since we left the road and there seemed no likelihood of asking for directions. I stopped no longer for views but went steadily on, Ali Khan keeping up a running fire of low-voiced invocations and lamentations. And now it was dusk and the position decidely unpleasant.

It was at that moment I saw a woman before us walking lightly and steadily under the pines. She must have struck into the trail from the side for she never could have kept before us all the way. A native woman, but wearing the all-concealing boorka, more like a town dweller than a woman of the hills. I put on speed and Ali Khan, now very tired, toiled on behind me as I came up with her and courteously asked the way. Her face was entirely hidden, but the answering voice was clear and sweet. I made up my mind she was young, for it had the bird-like thrill of youth.

"If the Presence continues to follow this path he will arrive. It is not far. They wait for him."

That was all. It left me with a desire to see the veiled face. We passed on and Ali Khan looked fearfully back.

"Ajaib! (Wonderful!) A strange place to meet one of the purdah-nashin (veiled women)" he muttered. "What would she be doing up here in the heights? She walked like a Khanam (khan's wife) and I saw the gleam of gold under the boorka."

I turned with some curiosity as he spoke, and lo! there was no human being in sight. She had disappeared from the track behind us and it was impossible to say where. The darkening trees were beginning to hold the dusk and it seemed unimaginable that a woman should leave the way and take to the dangers of the woods.

"Puna-i-Khoda - God protect us!" said Ali Khan in a shuddering whisper. "She was a devil of the wilds. Press on, Sahib. We should not be here in the dark."

There was nothing else to do. We made the best speed we could, and the trees grew more dense and the trail fainter between the close trunks, and so the night came bewildering with the expectation that we must pass the night unfed and unarmed in the cold of the heights. They might send out a search party from The House in the Woods - that was still a hope, if there were no other. And then, very gradually and wonderfully the moon dawned over the tree tops and flooded the wood with mysterious silver lights and about her rolled the majesty of the stars. We pressed on into the heart of the night. From the dense black depths we emerged at last. An open glade lay before us - the trees falling back to right and left to disclose - what?

A long low house of marble, unlit, silent, bathed in pale splendour and shadow. About it stood great deodars, clothed in clouds of the white blossoming clematis, ghostly and still. Acacias hung motionless trails of heavily scented bloom as if carved in ivory. It was all silent as death. A flight of nobly sculptured steps led up to a broad veranda and a wide open door with darkness behind it. Nothing more.

I forced myself to shout in Hindustani - the cry seeming a brutal outrage upon the night, and an echo came back numbed in the black woods. I tried once more and in vain. We stood absorbed also into the silence.

"Ya Alla! it is a house of the dead!" whispered Ali Khan, shuddering at my shoulder, - and even as the words left his lips I understood where we were. "It is the Sukh Mandir." I said. "It is the House of the Maharao of Ranipur."

It was impossible to be in Ranipur and hear nothing of the dead house of the forest and Ali Khan had heard - God only knows what tales. In his terror all discipline, all the inborn respect of the native forsook him, and without word or sign he turned and fled along the track, crashing through the forest blind and mad with fear. It would have been insanity to follow him, and in India the first rule of life is that the Sahib shows no fear, so I left him to his fate whatever it might be, believing at the same time that a little reflection and dread of the lonely forest would bring him to heel quickly.

I stood there and the stillness flowed like water about me. It was as though I floated upon it - bathed in quiet. My thoughts adjusted themselves. Possibly it was not the Sukh Mandir. Olesen had spoken of ruin. I could see none. At least it was shelter from the chill which is always present at these heights when the sun sets, - and it was beautiful as a house not made with hands. There was a sense of awe but no fear as I went slowly up the great steps and into the gloom beyond and so gained the hall.

The moon went with me and from a carven arch filled with marble tracery rained radiance that revealed and hid. Pillars stood about me, wonderful with horses ramping forward as in the Siva Temple at Vellore. They appeared to spring from the pillars into the gloom urged by invisible riders, the effect barbarously rich and strange - motion arrested, struck dumb in a violent gesture, and behind them impenetrable darkness. I could not see the end of this hall - for the moon did not reach it, but looking up I beheld the walls fretted in great panels into the utmost splendour of sculpture, encircling the stories of the Gods amid a twining and under-weaving of leaves and flowers. It was more like a temple than a dwelling. Siva, as Nataraja the Cosmic Dancer, the Rhythm of the Universe, danced before me, flinging out his arms in the passion of creation. Kama, the Indian Eros, bore his bow strung with honey-sweet black bees that typify the heart's desire. Krishna the Beloved smiled above the herd-maidens adoring at his feet. Ganesha the Elephant-Headed, sat in massive calm, wreathing his wise trunk about him. And many more. But all these so far as I could see tended to one centre panel larger than any, representing two life-size figures of a dim beauty. At first I could scarcely distinguish one from the other in the upward-reflected light, and then, even as I stood, the moving moon revealed the two as if floating in vapor. At once I recognized the subject - I had seen it already in the ruined temple of Ranipur, though the details differed. Parvati, the Divine Daughter of the Himalaya, the Emanation of the mighty mountains, seated upon a throne, listening to a girl who played on a Pan pipe before her. The goddess sat, her chin leaned upon her hand, her shoulders slightly inclined in a pose of gentle sweetness, looking down upon the girl at her feet, absorbed in the music of the hills and lonely places. A band of jewels, richly wrought, clasped the veil on her brows, and below the bare bosom a glorious girdle clothed her with loops and strings and tassels of jewels that fell to her knees - her only garment.

The girl was a lovely image of young womanhood, the proud swell of the breast tapering to the slim waist and long limbs easily folded as she half reclined at the divine feet, her lips pressed to the pipe. Its silent music mysteriously banished fear. The sleep must be sweet indeed that would come under the guardianship of these two fair creatures - their gracious influence was dewy in the air. I resolved that I would spend the night beside them. Now with the march of the moon dim vistas of the walls beyond sprang into being. Strange mythologies - the incarnations of Vishnu the Preserver, the Pastoral of Krishna the Beautiful. I promised myself that next day I would sketch some of the loveliness about me. But the moon was passing on her way - I folded the coat I carried into a pillow and lay down at the feet of the goddess and her nymph. Then a moonlit quiet I slept in a dream of peace.

Sleep annihilates time. Was it long or short when I woke like a man floating up to the surface from tranquil deeps? That I cannot tell, but once more I possessed myself and every sense was on guard.

My hearing first. Bare feet were coming, falling softly as leaves, but unmistakable. There was a dim whispering but I could hear no word. I rose on my elbow and looked down the long hall. Nothing. The moonlight lay in pools of light and seas of shadow on the floor, and the feet drew nearer. Was I afraid? I cannot tell, but a deep expectation possessed me as the sound grew like the rustle of grasses parted in a fluttering breeze, and now a girl came swiftly up the steps, irradiate in the moonlight, and passing up the hall stood beside me. I could see her robe, her feet bare from the jungle, but her face wavered and changed and re- united like the face of a dream woman. I could not fix it for one moment, yet knew this was the messenger for whom I had waited all my life - for whom one strange experience, not to be told at present, had prepared me in early manhood. Words came, and I said:

"Is this a dream?"

"No. We meet in the Ninth Vibration. All here is true."

"Is a dream never true?"

"Sometimes it is the echo of the Ninth Vibration and therefore a harmonic of truth. You are awake now. It is the day-time that is the sleep of the soul. You are in the Lower Perception, wherein the truth behind the veil of what men call Reality is perceived."

"Can I ascend?"

"I cannot tell. That is for you, not me.

"What do I perceive tonight?"

"The Present as it is in the Eternal. Say no more. Come with me."

She stretched her hand and took mine with the assurance of a goddess, and we went up the hall where the night had been deepest between the great pillars.

Now it is very clear to me that in every land men, when the doors of perception are opened, will see what we call the Supernatural clothed in the image in which that country has accepted it. Blake, the mighty mystic, will see the Angels of the Revelation, driving their terrible way above Lambeth - it is not common nor

unclean. The fisherman, plying his coracle on the Thames will behold the conse-
cration of the great new Abbey of Westminster celebrated with mass and chant
and awful lights in the dead mid-noon of night by that Apostle who is the Rock of
the Church. Before him who wanders in Thessaly Pan will brush the dewy lawns
and slim-girt Artemis pursue the flying hart. In the pale gold of Egyptian sands the
heavy brows of Osiris crowned with the pshent will brood above the seer and the
veil of Isis tremble to the lifting. For all this is the rhythm to which the souls of men
are attuned and in that vibration they will see, and no other, since in this the very
mountains and trees of the land are rooted. So here, where our remote ancestors
worshipped the Gods of Nature, we must needs stand before the Mystic Mother of
India, the divine daughter of the Himalaya.

How shall I describe the world we entered? The carvings upon the walls had
taken life - they had descended. It was a gathering of the dreams men have dreamed
here of the Gods, yet most real and actual. They watched in a serenity that set them
apart in an atmosphere of their own - forms of indistinct majesty and august beauty,
absolute, simple, and everlasting. I saw them as one sees reflections in rippled water
- no more. But all faces turned to the place where now a green and flowering leafage enshrined and partly hid the living Nature Goddess, as she listened to a voice
that was not dumb to me. I saw her face only in glimpses of an indescribable sweetness, but an influence came from her presence like the scent of rainy pine forests,
the coolness that breathes from great rivers, the passion of Spring when she breaks
on the world with a wave of flowers. Healing and life flowed from it. Understanding also. It seemed I could interpret the very silence of the trees outside into the
expression of their inner life, the running of the green life-blood in their veins, the
delicate trembling of their finger-tips.

My companion and I were not heeded. We stood hand in hand like children
who have innocently strayed into a palace, gazing in wonderment. The august life
went its way upon its own occasions, and, if we would, we might watch. Then the
voice, clear and cold, proceeding, as it were, with some story begun before we had
strayed into the Presence, the whole assembly listening in silence.

"- and as it has been so it will be, for the Law will have the blind soul carried
into a body which is a record of the sins it has committed, and will not suffer that
soul to escape from rebirth into bodies until it has seen the truth -"

And even as this was said and I listened, knowing myself on the verge of some great knowledge, I felt sleep beginning to weigh upon my eyelids. The sound blurred, flowed unsyllabled as a stream, the girl's hand grew light in mine; she was fading, becoming unreal; I saw her eyes like faint stars in a mist. They were gone. Arms seemed to receive me - to lay me to sleep and I sank below consciousness, and the night took me.

When I awoke the radiant arrows of the morning were shooting into the long hall where I lay, but as I rose and looked about me, strange - most strange, ruin encircled me everywhere. The blue sky was the roof. What I had thought a palace lost in the jungle, fit to receive its King should he enter, was now a broken hall of State; the shattered pillars were festooned with waving weeds, the many coloured lantana grew between the fallen blocks of marble. Even the sculptures on the walls were difficult to decipher. Faintly I could trace a hand, a foot, the orb of a woman's bosom, the gracious outline of some young God, standing above a crouching worshipper. No more. Yes, and now I saw above me as the dawn touched it the form of the Dweller in the Windhya Hills, Parvati the Beautiful, leaning softly over something breathing music at her feet. Yet I knew I could trace the almost obliterated sculpture only because I had already seen it defined in perfect beauty. A deep crack ran across the marble; it was weathered and stained by many rains, and little ferns grew in the crevices, but I could reconstruct every line from my own knowledge. And how? The Parvati of Ranipur differed in many important details. She stood, bending forward, wheras this sweet Lady sat. Her attendants were small satyr-like spirits of the wilds, piping and fluting, in place of the reclining maiden. The sweeping scrolls of a great halo encircled her whole person. Then how could I tell what this neary obliterated carving had been? I groped for the answer and could not find it. I doubted-

"Were such things here as we do speak about?   Or have we eaten of the insane root   That takes the reason captive?"

Memory rushed over me like the sea over dry sands. A girl - there had been a girl - we had stood with clasped hands to hear a strange music, but in spite of the spiritual intimacy of those moments I could not recall her face. I saw it cloudy against a background of night and dream, the eyes remote as stars, and so it eluded me. Only her presence and her words sur- vived; "We meet in the Ninth Vibration.

All here is true." But the Ninth Vibration itself was dream-land. I had never heard the phrase - I could not tell what was meant, nor whether my apprehension was true or false. I knew only that the night had taken her and the dawn denied her, and that, dream or no dream, I stood there with a pang of loss that even now leaves me wordless.

A bird sang outside in the acacias, clear and shrill for day, and this awakened my senses and lowered me to the plane where I became aware of cold and hunger, and was chilled with dew. I passed down the tumbled steps that had been a stately ascent the night before and made my way into the jungle by the trail, small and lost in fern, by which we had come. Again I wandered, and it was high noon before I heard mule bells at a distance, and, thus guided, struck down through the green tangle to find myself, wearied but safe, upon the bridle way that leads to Fagu and the far Shipki. Two coolies then directed me to The House in the Woods.

All was anxiety there. Ali Khan had arrived in the night, having found his way under the guidance of blind flight and fear. He had brought the news that I was lost in the jungle and amid the dwellings of demons. It was, of course, hopeless to search in the dark, though the khansamah and his man had gone as far as they dared with lanterns and shouting, and with the daylight they tried again and were even now away. It was useless to reproach the man even if I had cared to do so. His ready plea was that as far as men were concerned he was as brave as any (which was true enough as I had reason to know later) but that when it came to devilry the Twelve Imaums themselves would think twice before facing it.

"Inshalla ta-Alla! (If the sublime God wills!) this unworthy one will one day show the Protector of the poor, that he is a respectable person and no coward, but it is only the Sahibs who laugh in the face of devils."

He went off to prepare me some food, consumed with curiosity as to my adventures, and when I had eaten I found my tiny whitewashed cell, for the room was little more, and slept for hours.

Late in the afternoon I waked and looked out. A, low but glowing sunlight suffused the wild garden reclaimed from the strangle-hold of the jungle and hemmed in with rocks and forest. A few simple flowers had been planted here and there, but its chief beauty was a mountain stream, brown and clear as the eyes of a dog, that fell from a crag above into a rocky basin, maidenhair ferns growing in such masses about it that it was henceforward scarcely more than a woodland voice. Beside it two great deodars spread their canopies, and there a woman sat in a low chair, a girl beside her reading aloud. She had thrown her hat off and the sunshine turned her massed dark hair to bronze. That was all I could see. I went out and joined them, taking the note of introduction which Olesen had given me.

I pass over the unessentials of my story; their friendly greetings and sympathy for my adventure. It set us at ease at once and I knew my stay would be the happier for their presence though it is not every woman one would choose as a companion in the great mountain country. But what is germane to my purpose must be told, and of this a part is the per- sonality of Brynhild Ingmar. That she was beautiful I never doubted, though I have heard it disputed and smiled inwardly as the disputants urged lip and cheek and shades of rose and lily, weighing and appraising. Let me describe her as I saw her or, rather, as I can, adding that even without all this she must still have been beautiful because of the deep significance to those who had eyes to see or feel some mysterious element which mingled itself with her presence comparable only to the delight which the power and spiritual essence of Nature inspires in all but the dullest minds. I know I cannot hope to convey this in words. It means little if I say I thought of all quiet lovely solitary things when I looked into her calm eyes, - that when she moved it was like clear springs renewed by flowing, that she seemed the perfect flowering of a day in June, for these are phrases. Does Nature know her wonders when she shines in her strength? Does a woman know the infinite meanings her beauty may have for the beholder? I cannot tell. Nor can I tell if I saw this girl as she may have seemed to those who read only the letter of the book and are blind to its spirit, or in the deepest sense as she really was in the sight of That which created her and of which she was a part. Surely it is a proof of the divinity of love that in and for a moment it lifts the veil of so-called reality and shows each to the other mysteriously perfect and inspiring as the world will never see them, but as they exist in the Eternal, and in the sight of those who have learnt that the material is but the dream, and the vision of love the truth.

I will say then, for the alphabet of what I knew but cannot tell, that she had the low broad brows of a Greek Nature Goddess, the hair swept back wing-like from the temples and massed with a noble luxuriance. It lay like rippled bronze, suggesting something strong and serene in its essence. Her eyes were clear and gray as water, the mouth sweetly curved above a resolute chin. It was a face which recalled a mod-elling in marble rather than the charming pastel and aquarelle of a young woman's colouring, and somehow I thought of it less as the beauty of a woman than as some sexless emanation of natural things, and this impression was strengthened by her height and the long limbs, slender and strong as those of some youth trained in the pentathlon, subject to the severest discipline until all that was superfluous was fined away and the perfect form expressing the true being emerged. The body was thus more beautiful than the face, and I may note in passing that this is often the case, because the face is more directly the index of the restless and unhappy soul within and can attain true beauty only when the soul is in harmony with its source.

She was a little like her pale and wearied mother. She might resemble her still more when the sorrow of this world that worketh death should have had its will of her. I had yet to learn that this would never be - that she had found the open door of escape.

We three spent much time together in the days that followed. I never tired of their company and I think they did not tire of mine, for my wanderings through the world and my studies in the ancient Indian literatures and faiths with the Pan-dit Devaswami were of interest to them both though in entirely different ways. Mrs. Ingmar was a woman who centred all her interests in books and chiefly in the scientific forms of occult research. She was no believer in anything outside the range of what she called human experience. The evidences had convinced her of nothing but a force as yet unclassified in the scientific categories and all her interest lay in the undeveloped powers of brain which might be discovered in the course of ignorant and credulous experiment. We met therefore on the common ground of rejection of the so-called occultism of the day, though I knew even then, and how infinitely better now, that her constructions were wholly misleading.

Nearly all day she would lie in her chair under the deodars by the delicate splash and ripple of the stream. Living imprisoned in the crystal sphere of the intel-lect she saw the world outside, painted in few but distinct colours, small, compre-hensible, moving on a logical orbit. I never knew her posed for an explanation. She had the contented atheism of a certain type of French mind and found as much ease in it as another kind of sweet woman does in her rosary and confessional.

"I cannot interest Brynhild," she said, when I knew her better. "She has no affinity with science. She is simply a nature worshipper, and in such places as this she seems to draw life from the inanimate life about her. I have sometimes wondered whether she might not be developed into a kind of bridge between the articulate and the inarticulate, so well does she understand trees and flowers. Her father was like that - he had all sorts of strange power with animals and plants, and thought he had more than he had. He could never realize that the energy of nature is merely mechanical."

"You think all energy is mechanical?"

"Certainly. We shall lay our finger on the mainspring one day and the mystery will disappear. But as for Brynhild - I gave her the best education possible and yet she has never understood the conception of a universe moving on mathematical laws to which we must submit in body and mind. She has the oddest ideas. I would not willingly say of a child of mine that she is a mystic, and yet -"

She shook her head compassionately. But I scarcely heard. My eyes were fixed on Brynhild, who stood apart, looking steadily out over the snows. It was a glorious sunset, the west vibrating with gorgeous colour spilt over in torrents that flooded the sky, Terrible splendours - hues for which we have no thought - no name. I had not thought of it as music until I saw her face but she listened as well as saw, and her expression changed as it changes when the pomp of a great orchestra breaks upon the silence. It flashed to the chords of blood-red and gold that was burning fire. It softened through the fugue of woven crimson gold and flame, to the melancholy minor of ashes-of-roses and paling green, and so through all the dying glories that faded slowly to a tranquil grey and left the world to the silver melody of one sole star that dawned above the ineffable heights of the snows. Then she listened as a child does to a bird, entranced, with a smile like a butterfly on her parted lips. I never saw such a power of quiet.

She and I were walking next day among the forest ways, the pine-scented sunshine dappling the dropped frondage. We had been speaking of her mother. "It is such a misfortune for her," she said thoughtfully, "that I am not clever. She should have had a daughter who could have shared her thoughts. She analyses everything, reasons about everything, and that is quite out of my reach."

She moved beside me with her wonderful light step - the poise and balance of a nymph in the Parthenon frieze.

"How do you see things?"

"See? That is the right word. I see things - I never reason about them. They are. For her they move like figures in a sum. For me every one of them is a window through which one may look to what is beyond."

"To where?"

"To what they really are - not what they seem."

I looked at her with interest.

"Did you ever hear of the double vision?"

For this is a subject on which the spiritually learned men of India, like the great mystics of all the faiths, have much to say. I had listened with bewilderment and doubt to the expositions of my Pandit on this very head. Her simple words seemed for a moment the echo of his deep and searching thought. Yet it surely could not be. Impossible.

"Never. What does it mean?" She raised clear unveiled eyes. "You must forgive me for being so stupid, but it is my mother who is at home with all these scientific phrases. I know none of them."

"It means that for some people the material universe - the things we see with our eyes - is only a mirage, or say, a symbol, which either hides or shadows forth the eternal truth. And in that sense they see things as they really are, not as they seem to the rest of us. And whether this is the statement of a truth or the wildest of dreams, I cannot tell."

She did not answer for a moment; then said;

"Are there people who believe this - know it?"

"Certainly. There are people who believe that thought is the only real thing - that the whole universe is thought made visible. That we create with our thoughts the very body by which we shall re-act on the universe in lives to be.

"Do you believe it?"

"I don't know. Do you?"

She paused; looked at me, and then went on:

"You see, I don't think things out. I only feel. But this cannot interest you."

I felt she was eluding the question. She began to interest me more than any one I had ever known. She had extraordinary power of a sort. Once, in the woods, where I was reading in so deep a shade that she never saw me, I had an amazing vision of her. She stood in a glade with the sunlight and shade about her; she had no hat and a sunbeam turned her hair to pale bronze. A small bright April shower was falling through the sun, and she stood in pure light that reflected itself in every leaf and grass-blade. But it was nothing of all this that arrested me, beautiful as it was. She stood as though life were for the moment suspended;- then, very softly, she made a low musical sound, infinitely wooing, from scarcely parted lips, and instantly I saw a bird of azure plumage flutter down and settle on her shoulder, pluming himself there in happy security. Again she called softly and another followed the first. Two flew to her feet, two more to her breast and hand. They caressed her, clung to her, drew some joyous influence from her presence. She stood in the glittering rain like Spring with her birds about her - a wonderful sight. Then, raising one hand gently with the fingers thrown back she uttered a different note, perfectly sweet and intimate, and the branches parted and a young deer with full bright eyes fixed on her advanced and pushed a soft muzzle into her hand.

In my astonishment I moved, however slightly, and the picture broke up. The deer sprang back into the trees, the birds fluttered up in a hurry of feathers, and she turned calm eyes upon me, as unstartled as if she had known all the time that I was there.

"You should not have breathed," she said smiling. "They must have utter quiet."

I rose up and joined her.

"It is a marvel. I can scarcely believe my eyes. How do you do it?"

"My father taught me. They come. How can I tell?"

She turned away and left me. I thought long over this episode. I recalled words heard in the place of my studies - words I had dismissed without any care at the moment. "To those who see, nothing is alien. They move in the same vibration with all that has life, be it in bird or flower. And in the Uttermost also, for all things are One. For such there is no death."

That was beyond me still, but I watched her with profound interest. She recalled also words I had half forgotten-

"There was nought above me and nought below,   My childhood had not learnt to know;   For what are the voices of birds,   Aye, and of beasts, but words, our words, -   Only so much more sweet."

That might have been written of her. And more.

She had found one day in the woods a flower of a sort I had once seen in the warm damp forests below Darjiling - ivory white and shaped like a dove in flight. She wore it that evening on her bosom. A week later she wore what I took to be another.

"You have had luck," I said; "I never heard of such a thing being seen so high up, and you have found it twice."

"No, it is the same."

"The same? Impossible. You found it more than a week ago." "I know. It is ten days. Flowers don't die when one understands them - not as most people think."

Her mother looked up and said fretfully:

"Since she was a child Brynhild has had that odd idea. That flower is dead and withered. Throw it away, child. It looks hideous."

Was it glamour? What was it? I saw the flower dewy fresh in her bosom She smiled and turned away.

It was that very evening she left the veranda where we were sitting in the subdued light of a little lamp and passed beyond where the ray cut the darkness. She went down the perspective of trees to the edge of he clearing and I rose to follow for it seemed absolutely unsafe that she should be on the verge of the panther-haunted woods alone. Mrs. Ingmar turned a page of her book serenely;

"She will not like it if you go. I cannot imagine that she should come to harm. She always goes her own way - light or dark."

I returned to my seat and watched steadfastly. At first I could see nothing but as my sight adjusted itself I saw her a long way down the clearing that opened the snows, and quite certainly also I saw something like a huge dog detach itself from the woods and bound to her feet. It mingled with her dark dress and I lost it. Mrs. Ingmar said, seeing my anxiety but nothing else; "Her father was just the same; - he had no fear of anything that lives. No doubt some people have that power. I have never seen her attract birds and beasts as he certainly did, but she is quite as fond of them."

I could not understand her blindness - what I myself had seen raised questions I found unanswerable, and her mother saw nothing! Which of us was right? presently she came back slowly and I ventured no word.

A woodland sorcery, innocent as the dawn, hovered about her. What was it? Did the mere love of these creatures make a bond between her soul and theirs, or was the ancient dream true and could she at times move in the same vibration? I thought of her as a wood-spirit sometimes, an expression herself of some passion of beauty in Nature, a thought of snows and starry nights and flowing rivers made visible in flesh. It is surely when seized with the urge of some primeval yearning which in man is merely sexual that Nature conceives her fair forms and manifests them, for there is a correspondence that runs through all creation.

Here I ask myself - Did I love her? In a sense, yes, deeply, but not in the common reading of the phrase. I have trembled with delight before the wild and terrible splendour of the Himalayan heights-; low golden moons have steeped my soul longing, but I did not think of these things as mine in any narrow sense, nor so desire them. They were Angels of the Evangel of beauty. So too was she. She had none of the "silken nets and traps of adamant," she was no sister of the "girls of mild silver or of furious gold"; - but fair, strong, and her own, a dweller in the House of Quiet. I did not covet her. I loved her.

Days passed. There came a night when the winds were loosed - no moon, the stars flickering like blown tapers through driven clouds, the trees swaying and lamenting.

"There will be rain tomorrow." Mrs. Ingmar said, as we parted for the night. I closed my door. Some great cat of the woods was crying harshly outside my window, the sound receding towards the bridle way. I slept in a dream of tossing seas and ships labouring among them.

With the sense of a summons I waked - I cannot tell when. Unmistakable, as if I were called by name. I rose and dressed, and heard distinctly bare feet passing my door. I opened it noiselessly and looked out into the little passage way that made for the entry, and saw nothing but pools of darkness and a dim light from the square of the window at the end. But the wind had swept the sky clear with its flying bosom and was sleeping now in its high places and the air was filled with a mild moony radiance and a great stillness.

Now let me speak with restraint and exactness. I was not afraid but felt as I imagine a dog feels in the presence of his master, conscious of a purpose, a will entirely above his own and incomprehensible, yet to be obeyed without question.

I followed my reading of the command, bewildered but docile, and understanding nothing but that I was called.

The lights were out. The house dead silent; the familiar veranda ghostly in the night. And now I saw a white figure at the head of the steps - Brynhild. She turned and looked over her shoulder, her face pale in the moon, and made the same gesture with which she summoned her birds. I knew her meaning, for now we were moving in the same rhythm, and followed as she took the lead. How shall I describe that strange night in the jungle. There were fire-flies or dancing points of light that recalled them. Perhaps she was only thinking them - only thinking the moon and the quiet, for we were in the world where thought is the one reality. But they went with us in a cloud and faintly lighted our way. There were exquisite wafts of perfume from hidden flowers breathing their dreams to the night. Here and there a drowsy bird stirred and chirped from the roof of darkness, a low note of content that greeted her passing. It was a path intricate and winding and how long we went, and where, I cannot tell. But at last she stooped and parting the boughs before her we stepped into an open space, and before us - I knew it - I knew it! - The House of Beauty.

She paused at the foot of the great marble steps and looked at me.

"We have met here already."

I did not wonder - I could not. In the Ninth vibration surprise had ceased to be. Why had I not recognized her before - O dull of heart! That was my only thought. We walk blindfold through the profound darkness of material nature, the blinder because we believe we see it. It is only when the doors of the material are closed that the world appears to man as it exists in the eternal truth.

"Did you know this?" I asked, trembling before mystery.

"I knew it, because I am awake. You forgot it in the dull sleep which we call daily life. But we were here and THEY began the story of the King who made this house. Tonight we shall hear it. It he story of Beauty wandering through the world and the world received her not. We hear it in this place because here he agonized for what he knew too late."

"Was that our only meeting?"

"We meet every night, but you forget when the day brings the sleep of the soul. - You do not sink deep enough into rest to remember. You float on the surface where the little bubbles of foolish dream are about you and I cannot reach you then."

"How can I compel myself to the deeps?"

"You cannot. It will come. But when you have passed up the bridle way and beyond the Shipki, stop at Gyumur. There is the Monastery of Tashigong, and there one will meet you-

"His name?"

"Stephen Clifden. He will tell you what you desire to know. Continue on then with him to Yarkhand. There in the Ninth Vibration we shall meet again. It is a long journey but you will be content."

"Do you certainly know that we shall meet again?"

"When you have learnt, we can meet when we will. He will teach you the Laya Yoga. You should not linger here in the woods any longer. You should go on. In three days it will be possible."

"But how have you learnt - a girl and young?"

"Through a close union with Nature - that is one of the three roads. But I know little as yet. Now take my hand and come.

"One last question. Is this house ruined and abject as I have seen it in the day-light, or royal and the house of Gods as we see it now? Which is truth?"

"In the day you saw it in the empty illusion of blind thought. Tonight, eternally lovely as in the thought of the man who made it. Nothing that is beautiful is lost, though in the sight of the unwise it seems to die. Death is in the eyes we look through - when they are cleansed we see Life only. Now take my hand and come. Delay no more."

She caught my hand and we entered the dim magnificence of the great hall. The moon entered with us.

Instantly I had the feeling of supernatural presence. Yet I only write this in deference to common use, for it was absolutely natural - more so than any I have met in the state called daily life. It was a thing in which I had a part, and if this was supernatural so also was I.

Again I saw the Dark One, the Beloved, the young Krishna, above the women who loved him. He motioned with his hand as we passed, as though he waved us smiling on our way. Again the dancers moved in a rhythmic tread to the feet of the mountain Goddess - again we followed to where she bent to hear. But now, solemn listening faces crowded in the shadows about her, grave eyes fixed immovably upon what lay at her feet - a man, submerged in the pure light that fell from her presence, his dark face stark and fine, lips locked, eyes shut, arms flung out cross-wise in utter abandonment, like a figure of grief invisibly crucified upon his shame. I stopped a few feet from him, arrested by a barrier I could not pass. Was it sleep or death or some mysterious state that partook of both? Not sleep, for there was no flutter of breath. Not death - no rigid immobility struck chill into the air. It was the state of subjection where the spirit set free lies tranced in the mighty influences which surround us invisibly until we have entered, though but for a moment, the Ninth Vibration.

And now, with these Listeners about us, a clear voice began and stirred the air with music. I have since been asked in what tongue it spoke and could only answer that it reached my ears in the words of my childhood, and that I know whatever that language had been it would so have reached me.

"Great Lady, hear the story of this man's fall, for it is the story of man. Be pitiful to the blind eyes and give them light."

There was long since in Ranipur a mighty King and at his birth the wise men declared that unless he cast aside all passions that debase the soul, relinquishing the lower desires for the higher until a Princess laden with great gifts should come to be his bride, he would experience great and terrible misfortunes. And his royal parents did what they could to possess him with this belief, but they died before he reached manhood. Behold him then, a young King in his palace, surrounded with splendour. How should he withstand the passionate crying of the flesh or believe that through pleasure comes satiety and the loss of that in the spirit whereby alone pleasure can be enjoyed? For his gift was that he could win all hearts. They swarmed round him like hiving bees and hovered about him like butterflies. Sometimes he brushed them off. Often he caressed them, and when this happened, each thought proudly "I am the Royal Favourite. There is none other than me."

Also the Princess delayed who would be the crest-jewel of the crown, bringing with her all good and the blessing of the High Gods, and in consequence of all these things the King took such pleasures as he could, and they were many, not knowing they darken the inner eye whereby what is royal is known through disguises.

(Most pitiful to see, beneath the close-shut lids of the man at the feet of the Dweller in the Heights, tears forced themselves, as though a corpse dead to all else lived only to anguish. They flowed like blood-drops upon his face as he lay enduring, and the voice proceeded.) What was the charm of the King? Was it his stately height and strength? Or his faithless gayety? Or his voice, deep and soft as the sitar when it sings of love? His women said - some one thing, some another, but none of these ladies were of royal blood, and therefore they knew not.

Now one day, the all-privileged jester of the King, said, laughing harshly:

"Maharaj, you divert yourself. But how if, while we feast and play, the Far Away Princess glided past and was gone, unknown and unwelcomed?"

And the King replied:

"Fool, content yourself. I shall know my Princess, but she delays so long that I weary.

Now in a far away country was a Princess, daughter of the Greatest, and her Father hesitated to give her in marriage to such a King for all reported that he was faithless of heart, but having seen his portrait she loved him and fled in disguise from the palaces of her Father, and being captured she was brought before the King in Ranipur.

He sat upon a cloth of gold and about him was the game he had killed in hunting, in great masses of ruffled fur and plumage, and he turned the beauty of his face carelessly upon her, and as the Princess looked upon him, her heart yearned to him, and he said in his voice that was like the male string of the sitar:

"Little slave, what is your desire?"

Then she saw that the long journey had scarred her feet and dimmed her hair with dust, and that the King's eyes, worn with days and nights of pleasure did not pierce her disguise. Now in her land it is a custom that the blood royal must not proclaim itself, so she folded her hands and said gently:

"A place in the household of the King." And he, hearing that the Waiting slave of his chief favorite Jayashri was dead, gave her that place. So the Princess attended on those ladies, courteous and obedient to all authority as beseemed her royalty, and she braided her bright hair so that it hid the little crowns which the Princesses of her House must wear always in token of their rank, and every day her patience strengthened.

Sometimes the King, carelessly desiring her laughing face and sad eyes, would send for her to wile away an hour, and he would say; "Dance, little slave, and tell me stories of the far countries. You quite unlike my Women, doubtless because you are a slave."

And she thought - "No, but because I am a Princess," - but this she did not say. She laughed and told him the most marvellous stories in the world until he laid his head upon her warm bosom, dreaming awake.

There were stories of the great Himalayan solitudes where in the winter nights the white tiger stares at the witches' dance of the Northern Lights dazzled by the hurtling of their myriad spears. And she told how the King-eagle, hanging motionless over the peaks of Gaurisankar, watches with golden eyes for his prey, and falling like a plummet strikes its life out with his clawed heel and, screaming with triumph, bears it to his fierce mate in her cranny of the rocks.

"A gallant story!" the King would say. "More!" Then she told of the tropical heats and the stealthy deadly creatures of forest and jungle, and the blue lotus of Buddha swaying on the still lagoon,- And she spoke of loves of men and women, their passion and pain and joy. And when she told of their fidelity and valour and honour that death cannot quench, her voice was like the song of a minstrel, for she had read all the stories of the ages and the heart of a Princess told her the rest. And the King listened unwearying though he believed this was but a slave.

(The face of the man at the feet of the Dweller in the Heights twitched in a white agony. Pearls of sweat were distilled upon his brows, but he moved neither hand nor foot, enduring as in a flame of fire. And the voice continued.)

So one day, in the misty green of the Spring, while she rested at his feet in the garden Pavilion, he said to her:

"Little slave, why do you love me?"

And she answered proudly:

"Because you have the heart of a King."

He replied slowly;

"Of the women who have loved me none gave this reason, though they gave many."

She laid her cheek on his hand.

"That is the true reason."

But he drew it away and was vaguely troubled, for her words, he knew not why, reminded him of the Far Away Princess and of things he had long forgotten, and he said; "What does a slave know of the hearts of Kings?" And that night he slept or waked alone.

Winter was at hand with its blue and cloudless days, and she was commanded to meet the King where the lake lay still and shining like an ecstasy of bliss, and she waited with her chin dropped into the cup of her hands, looking over the water with eyes that did not see, for her whole soul said; "How long 0 my Sovereign Lord, how long before you know the truth and we enter together into our Kingdom?"

As she sat she heard the King's step, and the colour stole up into her face in a flush like the earliest sunrise. "He is coming," she said; and again; "He loves me."

So he came beside the water, walking slowly. But the King was not alone. His arm embraced the latest-come beauty from Samarkhand, and, with his head bent, he whispered in her willing ear.

Then clasping her hands, the Princess drew a long sobbing breath, and he turned and his eyes grew hard as blue steel.

"Go, slave," he cried. "What place have you in Kings' gardens? Go. Let me see you no more."

(The man lying at the feet of the Dweller in the Heights, raised a heavy arm and flung it above his head, despairing, and it fell again on the cross of his torment. And the voice went on.)

And as he said this, her heart broke; and she went and her feet were weary. So she took the wise book she loved and unrolled it until she came to a certain passage, and this she read twice; "If the heart of a slave be broken it may be mended with jewels and soft words, but the heart of a Princess can be healed only by the King who broke it, or in Yamapura, the City under the Sunset where they make all things new. Now, Yama, the Lord of this City, is the Lord of Death." And having thus read the Princess rolled the book and put it from her.

And next day, the King said to his women; "Send for her," for his heart smote him and he desired to atone royally for the shame of his speech. And they sought and came back saying;

"Maharaj, she is gone. We cannot find her."

Fear grew in the heart of the King - a nameless dread, and he said, "Search." And again they sought and returned and the King was striding up and down the great hall and none dared cross his path. But, trembling, they told him, and he replied; "Search again. I will not lose her, and, slave though be, she shall be my Queen."

So they ran, dispersing to the Four Quarters, and King strode up and down the hall, and Loneliness kept step with him and clasped his hand and looked his eyes.

Then the youngest of the women entered with a tale to tell. Majesty, we have found her. She lies beside the lake. When the birds fled this morning she fled with them, but upon a longer journey. Even to Yamapura, the City under the Sunset."

And the King said; "Let none follow." And he strode forth swiftly, white with thoughts he dared not think.

The Princess lay among the gold of the fallen leaves. All was gold, for her bright hair was out-spread in shining waves and in it shone the glory of the hidden crown. On her face was no smile - only at last was revealed the patience she had covered with laughter so long that even the voice of the King could not now break it into joy. The hands that had clung, the swift feet that had run beside his, the tender body, mighty to serve and to love, lay within touch but farther away than the uttermost star was the Far Away Princess, known and loved too late.

And he said; "My Princess - 0 my Princess!" and laid his head on her cold bosom.

"Too late!" a harsh Voice croaked beside him, and it was the voice of the Jester who mocks at all things. "Too late! 0 madness, to despise the blood royal because it humbled itself to service and so was doubly royal. The Far Away Princess came laden with great gifts, and to her the King's gift was the wage of a slave and a broken heart. Cast your crown and sceptre in the dust, 0 King - 0 King of Fools."

(The man at the feet of the Dweller in the Heights moved. Some dim word shaped upon his locked lips. She listened in a divine calm. It seemed that the very Gods drew nearer. Again the man essayed speech, the body dead, life only in the words that none could hear. The voice went on.)

But the Princess flying wearily because of the sore wound in her heart, came at last to the City under the Sunset, where the Lord of Death rules in the House of Quiet, and was there received with royal honours for in that land are no disguises. And she knelt before the Secret One and in a voice broken with agony entreated him to heal her. And with veiled and pitying eyes he looked upon her, for many and grievous as are the wounds he has healed this was more grievous still. And he said;

"Princess, I cannot, But this I can do - I can give a new heart in a new birth - happy and careless as the heart of a child. Take this escape from the anguish you endure and be at peace."

But the Princess, white with pain, asked only;

"In this new heart and birth, is there room for the King?"

And the Lord of Peace replied;

"None. He too will be forgotten."

Then she rose to her feet.

"I will endure and when he comes I will serve him once more. If he will he shall heal me, and if not I will endure for ever."

And He who is veiled replied;

"In this sacred City no pain may disturb the air, therefore you must wait outside in the chill and the dark. Think better, Princess! Also, he must pass through many rebirths, because he beheld the face of Beauty unveiled and knew her not. And when he comes he will be weary and weak as a new-born child, and no more a great King." And the Princess smiled;

"Then he will need me the more," she said; "I will wait and kiss the feet of my King."

And the Lord of Death was silent. So she went outside into the darkness of the spaces, and the souls free passed her like homing doves, and she sat with her hands clasped over the sore wound in her heart, watching the earthward way. And the Princess is keeping still the day of her long patience."

The voice ceased. And there was a great silence, and the listening faces drew nearer.

Then the Dweller in the Heights spoke in a voice soft as the falling of snow in the quiet of frost and moon. I could have wept myself blind with joy to hear that music. More I dare not say.

"He is in the Lower State of Perception. He sorrows for his loss. Let him have one instant's light that still he may hope."

She bowed above the man, gazing upon him as a mother might upon her sleeping child. The dead eyelids stirred, lifted, a faint gleam showed beneath them, an unspeakable weariness. I thought they would fall unsatisfied. Suddenly he saw

What looked upon him, and a terror of joy no tongue can tell flashed over the dark mirror of his face. He stretched a faint hand to touch her feet, a sobbing sigh died upon his lips, and once more the swooning sleep took him. He lay as a dead man before the Assembly.

"The night is far spent," a voice said, from I know not where. And I knew it was said not only for the sleeper but for all, for though the flying feet of Beauty seem for a moment to outspeed us she will one day wait our coming and gather us to her bosom.

As before, the vision spread outward like rings in a broken reflection in water. I saw the girl beside me, but her hand grew light in mine. I felt it no longer. I heard the roaring wind in the trees, or was it a great voice thundering in my ears? Sleep took me. I waked in my little room.

Strange and sad - I saw her next day and did not remember her whom of all things I desired to know. I remembered the vision and knew that whether in dream or waking I had heard an eternal truth. I longed with a great longing to meet my beautiful companion, and she stood at my side and I was blind.

Now that I have climbed a little higher on the Mount of Vision it seems even to myself that this could not be. Yet it was, and it is true of not this only but of how much else!

She knew me. I learnt that later, but she made no sign. Her simplicities had carried her far beyond and above me, to places where only the winged things attain- "as a bird among the bird-droves of God."

I have since known that this power of direct simplicity in her was why among the great mountains we beheld the Divine as the emanation of the terrible beauty about us. We cannot see it as it is - only in some shadowing forth, gathering sufficient strength for manifestation from the spiritual atoms that haunt the region where that form has been for ages the accepted vehicle of adoration. But I was now to set forth to find another knowledge - to seek the Beauty that blinds us to all other. Next day the man who was directing my preparations for travel sent me word from Simla that all was ready and I could start two days later. I told my friends the time of parting was near.

"But it was no surprise to me," I added, "for I had heard already that in a very few days I should be on my way.

Mrs. Ingmar was more than kind. She laid a frail hand on mine.

"We shall miss you indeed. If it is possible to send us word of your adventures in those wild solitudes I hope you will do it. Of course aviation will soon lay bare their secrets and leave them no mysteries, so you don't go too soon. One may worship science and yet feel it injures the beauty of the world. But what is beauty compared with knowledge?"

"Do you never regret it?" I asked.

"Never, dear Mr. Ormond. I am a worshipper of hard facts and however hideous they may be I prefer them to the prismatic colours of romance."

Brynhild, smiling, quoted;

"Their science roamed from star to star   And than itself found nothing greater.   What wonder? In a Leyden jar   They bottled the Creator?"

"There is nothing greater than science," said Mrs. Ingmar with soft reverence. "The mind of man is the foot-rule of the universe."

She meditated for a moment and then added that my kind interests in their plans decided her to tell me that she would be returning to Europe and then to Canada in a few months with a favourite niece as her companion while Brynhild would remain in India with friends in Mooltan for a time. I looked eagerly at her but she was lost in her own thoughts and it was evidently not the time to say more.

If I had hoped for a vision before I left the neighbourhood of that strange House of Beauty where a spirit imprisoned appeared to await the day of enlightenment I was disappointed. These things do not happen as one expects or would choose. The wind bloweth where it listeth until the laws which govern the inner life are understood, and then we would not choose if we could for we know that all is better than well. In this world, either in the blinded sight of daily life or in the clarity of the true sight I have not since seen it, but that has mattered little, for having heard an authentic word within its walls I have passed on my way elsewhere.

Next day a letter from Olesen reached me.

"Dear Ormond, I hope you have had a good time at the House in the Woods. I saw Rup Singh a few days ago and he wrote the odd message I enclose. You know what these natives are, even the most sensible of them, and you will humour the old fellow for he ages very fast and I think is breaking up. But this was not what I wanted to say. I had a letter from a man I had not seen for years - a fellow called

Stephen Clifden, who lives in Kashmir. As a matter of fact I had forgotten his existence but evidently he has not repaid the compliment for he writes as follows - No, I had better send you the note and you can do as you please. I am rushed off my legs with work and the heat is hell with the lid off. And-"

But the rest was of no interest except to a friend of years' standing. I read Rup Singh's message first. It was written in his own tongue.

"To the Honoured One who has attained to the favour of the Favourable.

"You have with open eyes seen what this humble one has dreamed but has not known. If the thing be possible, write me this word that I may depart in peace. 'With that one who in a former birth you loved all is well. Fear nothing for him. The way is long but at the end the lamps of love are lit and the Unstruck music is sounded. He lies at the feet of Mercy and there awaits his hour.' And if it be not possible to write these words, write nothing, 0 Honoured, for though it be in the hells my soul shall find my King, and again I shall serve him as once I served."

I understood, and wrote those words as he had written them. Strange mystery of life - that I who had not known should see, and that this man whose fidelity had not deserted his broken King in his utter downfall should have sought with passion for one sight of the beloved face across the waters of death and sought in vain. I thought of those Buddhist words of Seneca - "The soul may be and is in the mass of men drugged and silenced by the seductions of sense and the deceptions of the world. But if, in some moment of detachment and elation, when its captors and jailors relax their guard, it can escape their clutches, it will seek at once the region of its birth and its true home."

Well - the shell must break before the bird can fly, and the time drew near for the faithful servant to seek his lord. My message reached him in time and gladdened him.

I turned then to Clifden's letter.

"Dear Olesen, you will have forgotten me, and feeling sure of this I should scarcely have intruded a letter into your busy life were it not that I remember your good-nature as a thing unforgettable though so many years have gone by. I hear of you sometimes when Sleigh comes up the Sind valley, for I often camp at Sonamarg and above the Zoji La and farther. I want you to give a message to a man you know who should be expecting to hear from me. Tell him I shall be at the Tashigong Monastery when he reaches Gyumur beyond the Shipki. Tell him I have the information he wants and I will willingly go on with him to Yarkhand and his destination. He need not arrange for men beyond Gyumur. All is fixed. So sorry to bother you, old man, but I don't know Ormond's address, except that he was with you and has gone up Simla way. And of course he will be keen to hear the thing is settled."

Amazing. I remembered the message I had heard and this man's words rang true and kindly, but what could it mean? I really did not question farther than this for now I could not doubt that I was guided. Stronger hands than mine had me in charge, and it only remained for me to set forth in confidence and joy to an end that as yet I could not discern. I turned my face gladly to the wonder of the mountains.

Gladly - but with a reservation. I was leaving a friend and one whom I dimly felt might one day be more than a friend - Brynhild Ingmar. That problem must be met before I could take my way. I thought much of what might be said at parting. True, she had the deepest attraction for me, but true also that I now beheld a quest stretching out into the unknown which I must accept in the spirit of the knight errant. Dare I then bind my heart to any allegiance which would pledge me to a future inconsistent with what lay before me? How could I tell what she might think of the things which to me were now real and external - the revelation of the only reality that underlies all the seeming. Life can never be the same for the man who has penetrated to this, and though it may seem a hard saying there can be but a maimed understanding between him and those who still walk amid the phantoms of death and decay.

Her sympathy with nature was deep and wonderful but might it not be that though the earth was eloquent to her the skies were silent? I was but a beginner myself - I knew little indeed. Dare I risk that little in a sweet companionship which would sink me into the contentment of the life lived by the happily deluded between the cradle and the grave and perhaps close to me for ever that still sphere where my highest hope abides? I had much to ponder, for how could I lose her out of my life - though I knew not at all whether she who had so much to make her happiness would give me a single thought when I was gone.

If all this seem the very uttermost of selfish vanity, forgive a man who grasped in his hand a treasure so new, so wonderful that he walked in fear and doubt lest it should slip away and leave him in a world darkened for ever by the torment of the knowledge that it might have been his and he had bartered it for the mess of pottage that has bought so many birthrights since Jacob bargained with his weary brother in the tents of Lahai-roi. I thought I would come back later with my prize gained and throwing it at her feet ask her wisdom in return, for whatever I might not know I knew well she was wiser than I except in that one shining of the light from Eleusis. I walked alone in the woods thinking of these things and no answer satisfied me.

I did not see her alone until the day I left, for I was compelled by the arrangements I was making to go down to Simla for a night. And now the last morning had come with golden sun - shot mists rolling upward to disclose the far white billows of the sea of eternity, the mountains awaking to their enormous joys. The trees were dripping glory to the steaming earth; it flowed like rivers into their most secret recesses, moss and flower, fern and leaf floated upon the waves of light revealing their inmost soul in triumphant gladness. Far off across the valleys a cuckoo was calling - the very voice of spring, and in the green world above my head a bird sang, a feathered joy, so clear, so passionate that I thought the great summer morning listened in silence to his rapture ringing through the woods. I waited until the Jubilate was ended and then went in to bid good-bye to my friends.

Mrs. Ingmar bid me the kindest farewell and I left her serene in the negation of all beauty, all hope save that of a world run on the lines of a model municipality, disease a memory, sewerage, light and air systems perfected, the charted brain sending its costless messages to the outer parts of the habitable globe, and at least a hundred years of life with a decent cremation at the end of it assured to every eugenically born citizen. No more. But I have long ceased to regret that others use their own eyes whether clear or dim. Better the merest glimmer of light perceived thus than the hearsay of the revelations of others. And by the broken fragments of a bewildered hope a man shall eventually reach the goal and rejoice in that dawn where the morning stars sing together and the sons of God shout for joy. It must come, for it is already here.

Brynhild walked with me through the long glades in the fresh thin air to the bridle road where my men and ponies waited, eager to be off. We stood at last in the fringe of trees on a small height which commanded the way; - a high uplifted path cut along the shoulders of the hills and on the left the sheer drop of the valleys. Perhaps seven or eight feet in width and dignified by the name of the Great Hindustan and Tibet Road it ran winding far away into Wonderland. Looking down into the valleys, so far beneath that the solitudes seem to wall them in I thought of all the strange caravans which have taken this way with tinkle of bells and laughter now so long silenced, and as I looked I saw a lost little monastery in a giant crevice, solitary as a planet on the outermost ring of the system, and remembrance flashed into my mind and I said;

"I have marching orders that have countermanded my own plans. I am to journey to the Buddhist Monastery of Tashigong, and there meet a friend who will tell me what is necessary that I may travel to Yarkhand and beyond. It will be long before I see Kashmir."

In those crystal clear eyes I saw a something new to me - a faint smile, half pitying, half sad;

"Who told you, and where?"

"A girl in a strange place. A woman who has twice guided me -"

I broke off. Her smile perplexed me. I could not tell what to say. She repeated in a soft undertone;

"Great Lady, be pitiful to the blind eyes and give them light."

And instantly I knew. 0 blind - blind! Was the unhappy King of the story duller of heart than I? And shame possessed me. Here was the chrysoberyl that all day hides its secret in deeps of lucid green but when the night comes flames with its fiery ecstasy of crimson to the moon, and I - I had been complacently considering whether I might not blunt my own spiritual instinct by companionship with her, while she had been my guide, as infinitely beyond me in insight as she was in all things beautiful. I could have kissed her feet in my deep repentance. True it is that the gateway of the high places is reverence and he who cannot bow his head shall receive no crown. I saw that my long travel in search of knowledge would have been utterly vain if I had not learnt that lesson there and then. In those moments of silence I learnt it once and for ever.

She stood by me breathing the liquid morning air, her face turned upon the eternal snows. I caught her hand in a recognition that might have ended years of parting, and its warm youth vibrated in mine, the foretaste of all understanding, all unions, of love that asks nothing, that fears nothing, that has no petition to make.

She raised her eyes to mine and her tears were a rainbow of hope. So we stood in silence that was more than any words, and the golden moments went by. I knew her now for what she was, one of whom it might have been written;

"I come from where night falls clearer   Than your morning sun can rise; From an earth that to heaven draws nearer   Than your visions of Paradise,-   For the dreams that your dreamers dream   We behold them with open eyes."

With open eyes! Later I asked the nature of the strange bond that had called her to my side.

"I do not understand that fully myself," she said - "That is part of the knowledge we must wait for. But you have the eyes that see, and that is a tie nothing can break. I had waited long in the House of Beauty for you. I guided you there. But between you and me there is also love."

I stretched an eager hand but she repelled it gently, drawing back a little. "Not love of each other though we are friends and in the future may be infinitely more. But - have you ever seen a drawing of Blake's - a young man stretching his arms to a white swan which flies from him on wings he cannot stay? That is the story of both our lives. We long to be joined in this life, here and now, to an unspeakable beauty and power whose true believers we are because we have seen and known. There is no love so binding as the same purpose. Perhaps that is the only true love. And so we shall never be apart though we may never in this world be together again in what is called companionship."

"We shall meet," I said confidently. She smiled and was silent.

"Do we follow a will-o'-the wisp in parting? Do we give up the substance for the shadow? Shall I stay?"

She laughed joyously;

"We give a single rose for a rose-tree that bears seven times seven. Daily I see more, and you are going where you will be instructed. As you know my mother prefers for a time to have my cousin with her to help her with the book she means to write. So I shall have time to myself. What do you think I shall do?"

"Blow away on a great wind. Ride on the crests of tossing waves. Catch a star to light the fireflies!"

She laughed like a bird's song.

"Wrong - wrong! I shall be a student. All I know as yet has come to me by intuition, but there is Law as well as Love and I will learn. I have drifted like a happy cloud before the wind. Now I will learn to be the wind that blows the clouds."

I looked at her in astonishment. If a flower had desired the same thing it could scarcely have seemed more incredible, for I had thought her whole life and nature instinctive not intellective. She smiled as one who has a beloved secret to keep.

"When you have gained what in this country they call The Knowledge of Regeneration, come back and ask me what I have learnt."

She would say no more of that and turned to another matter, speaking with earnestness;

"Before you came here I had a message for you, and Stephen Clifden will tell you the same thing when you meet. Believe it for it is true. Remember always that the psychical is not the mystical and that what we seek is not marvel but vision. These two things are very far apart, so let the first with all its dangers pass you by, for our way lies to the heights, and for us there is only one danger - that of turning back and losing what the whole world cannot give in exchange. I have never seen Stephen Clifden but I know much of him. He is a safe guide - a man who has had much and strange sorrow which has brought him joy that cannot be told. He will take you to those who know the things that you desire. I wish I might have gone too."

Something in the sweetness of her voice, its high passion, the strong beauty of her presence woke a poignant longing in my heart. I said;

"I cannot leave you. You are the only guide I can follow. Let us search together - you always on before."

"Your way lies there," she pointed to the high mountains. "And mine to the plains, and if we chose our own we should wander. But we shall meet again in the way and time that will be best and with knowledge so enlarged that what we have seen already will be like an empty dream compared to daylight truth. If you knew what waits for you you would not delay one moment."

She stood radiant beneath the deodars, a figure of Hope, pointing steadily to the heights. I knew her words were true though as yet I could not tell how. I knew that whereas we had seen the Wonderful in beautiful though local forms there is a plane where the Formless may be apprehended in clear dream and solemn vision-the meeting of spirit with Spirit. What that revelation would mean I could not guess - how should I? - but I knew the illusion we call death and decay would wither before it. There is a music above and beyond the Ninth Vibration though I must love those words for ever for what their hidden meaning gave me.

I took her hand and held it. Strange - beyond all strangeness that that story of an ancient sorrow should have made us what we were to each other - should have opened to me the gates of that Country where she wandered content. For the first time I had realized in its fulness the loveliness of this crystal nature, clear as flowing water to receive and transmit the light - itself a prophecy and fulfilment of some higher race which will one day inhabit our world when it has learnt the true values. She drew a flower from her breast and gave it to me. It lies before me white and living as I write these words.

I sprang down the road and mounted, giving the word to march. The men shouted and strode on - our faces to the Shipki Pass and what lay beyond.

We had parted.

Once, twice, I looked back, and standing in full sunlight, she waved her hand.

We turned the angle of the rocks.

What I found - what she found is a story strange and beautiful which I may tell one day to those who care to hear. That for me there were pauses, hesitancies, dreads, on the way I am not concerned to deny, for so it must always be with the roots of the old beliefs of fear and ignorance buried in the soil of our hearts and ready to throw out their poisonous fibres. But there was never doubt. For myself I have long forgotten the meaning of that word in anything that is of real value.

Do not let it be thought that the treasure is reserved for the few or those of special gifts. And it is as free to the West as to the East though I own it lies nearer to the surface in the Orient where the spiritual genius of the people makes it possible and the greater and more faithful teachers are found. It is not without meaning that all the faiths of the world have dawned in those sunrise skies. Yet it is within reach of all and asks only recognition, for the universe has been the mine of its jewels-

"Median gold it holds, and silver from Atropatene, Ruby and emerald from Hindustan, and Bactrian agate, Bright with beryl and pearl, sardonyx and sapphire."-

-and more that cannot be uttered - the Lights and Perfections.

So for all seekers I pray this prayer - beautiful in its sonorous Latin, but noble in all the tongues;

"Supplico tibi, Pater et Dux - I pray Thee, Guide of our vision, that we may remember the nobleness with which Thou hast endowed us, and that Thou wouldest be always on our right and on our left in the motion of our wills, that we may be purged from the contagion of the body and the affections of the brute and overcome and rule them. And I pray also that Thou wouldest drive away the blinding darkness from the eyes of our souls that we may know well what is to be held for divine and what for mortal."

"The nobleness with which Thou hast endowed us-" this, and not the cry of the miserable sinner whose very repentance is no virtue but the consequence of failure and weakness is the strong music to which we must march.

And the way is open to the mountains.

THE INTERPRETER
A ROMANCE OF THE EAST

I

There are strange things in this story, but, so far as I understand them, I tell the truth. If you measure the East with a Western foot-rule you will say, "Impossible." I should have said it myself.

Of myself I will say as little as I can, for this story is of Vanna Loring. I am an incident only, though I did not know that at first.

My name is Stephen Clifden, and I was eight-and-thirty; plenty of money, sound in wind and limb. I had been by way of being a writer before the war, the hobby of a rich man; but if I picked up anything in the welter in France, it was that real work is the only salvation this mad world has to offer; so I meant to begin at the beginning, and learn my trade like a journeyman labourer. I had come to the right place. A very wonderful city is Peshawar - rather let us say, two cities - the compounds, the fortifications where Europeans dwell in such peace as their strong right arms can secure them; and the native city and bazaar humming and buzzing like a hive of angry bees with the rumours that come up from Lower India or down the Khyber Pass with the camel caravans loaded with merchandise from Afghanistan, Bokhara, and farther. And it is because of this that Peshawar is the Key of India, and a city of Romance that stands at every corner, and cries aloud in the market - place. For at Peshawar every able-bodied man sleeps with his revolver under his pillow, and the old Fort is always ready in case it should be necessary at brief and sharp notice to hurry the women and children into it, and possibly, to die in their defense. So enlivening is the neighbourhood of the frontier tribes that haunt the famous

Khyber Pass and the menacing hills where danger is always lurking.

But there was society here, and I was swept into it - there was chatter, and it galled me.

I was beginning to feel that I had missed my mark, and must go farther afield, perhaps up into Central Asia, when I met Vanna Loring. If I say that her hair was soft and dark; that she had the deepest hazel eyes I have ever seen, and a sensitive, tender mouth; that she moved with a flowing grace like "a wave of the sea - it sounds like the portrait of a beauty, and she was never that. Also, incidentally, it gives none of her charm. I never heard any one get any further than that she was "oddly attractive" - let us leave it at that. She was certainly attractive to me.

She was the governess of little Winifred Meryon, whose father held the august position of General Commanding the Frontier Forces, and her mother the more commanding position of the reigning beauty of Northern India, generally speaking. No one disputed that. She was as pretty as a picture, and her charming photograph had graced as many illustrated papers as there were illustrated papers to grace.

But Vanna - I gleaned her story by bits when I came across her with the child in the gardens. I was beginning to piece it together now.

Her love of the strange and beautiful she had inherited from a young Italian mother, daughter of a political refugee; her childhood had been spent in a remote little village in the West of England; half reluctantly she told me how she had brought herself up after her mother's death and her father's second marriage. Little was said of that, but I gathered that it had been a grief to her, a factor in her flight to the East.

We were walking in the Circular Road then with Winifred in front leading her Pekingese by its blue ribbon, and we had it almost to ourselves except for a few natives passing slow and dignified on their own occasions, for fashionable Peshawar was finishing its last rubber of bridge, before separating to dress for dinner, and had no time to spare for trivialities and sunsets.

"So when I came to three-and-twenty," she said slowly, "I felt I must break away from our narrow life. I had a call to India stronger than anything on earth. You would not understand but that was so, and I had spent every spare moment in teaching myself India - its history, legends, religions, everything! And I was not wanted at home, and I had grown afraid."

I could divine years of patience and repression under this plain tale, but also a power that would be dynamic when the authentic voice called. That was her charm - gentleness in strength - a sweet serenity.

"What were you afraid of?"

"Of growing old and missing what was waiting for me out here. But I could not get away like other people. No money, you see. So I thought I would come out here and teach. Dare I? Would they let me? I knew I was fighting life and chances and risks if I did it; but it was death if I stayed there. And then- Do you really care to hear?"

"Of course. Tell me how you broke your chain."

"I spare you the family quarrels. I can never go back. But I was spurred - spurred to take some wild leap; and I took it. Six years ago I came out. First I went to a doctor and his wife at Cawnpore. They had a wonderful knowledge of the Indian peoples, and there I learned Hindustani and much else. Then he died. But an aunt had left me two hundred pounds, and I could wait a little and choose; and so I came here."

It interested me. The courage that pale elastic type of woman has!

"Have you ever regretted it? Would they take you back if you failed?"

"Never, to both questions," she said, smiling. "Life is glorious. I've drunk of a cup I never thought to taste; and if I died tomorrow I should know I had done right. I rejoice in every moment I live - even when Winifred and I are wrestling with arithmetic."

"I shouldn't have thought life was very easy with Lady Meryon."

"Oh, she is kind enough in an indifferent sort of way. I am not the persecuted Jane Eyre sort of governess at all. But that is all on the surface and does not matter. It is India I care for -the people, the sun, the infinite beauty. It was coming home. You would laugh if I told you I knew Peshawar long before I came here. Knew it - walked here, lived. Before there were English in India at all." She broke off. "You won't understand."

"Oh, I have had that feeling, too," I said patronizingly. "If one has read very much about a place-"

"That was not quite what I meant. Never mind. The people, the place - that is the real thing to me. All this is the dream." The sweep of her hand took in not only Winifred and myself, but the general's stately residence, which to blaspheme in

Peshawar is rank infidelity.

"By George, I would give thousands to feel that! I can't get out of Europe here. I want to write, Miss Loring," I found myself saying. "I'd done a bit, and then the war came and blew my life to pieces. Now I want to get inside the skin of the East, and I can't do it. I see it from outside, with a pane of glass between. No life in it. If you feel as you say, for God's sake be my interpreter!"

I really meant what I said. I knew she was a harp that any breeze would sweep into music. I divined that temperament in her and proposed to use it for my own ends. She had and I had not, the power to be a part of all she saw, to feel kindred blood running in her own veins. To the average European the native life of India is scarcely interesting, so far is it removed from all comprehension. To me it was interesting, but I could not tell why. I stood outside and had not the fairy gold to pay for my entrance. Here at all events she could buy her way where I could not. Without cruelty, which honestly was not my besetting sin - especially where women were concerned, the egoist in me felt I would use her, would extract the last drop of the enchantment of her knowledge before I went on my way. What more natural than that Vanna or any other woman should minister to my thirst for information? Men are like that. I pretend to be no better than the rest. She pleased my fastidiousness - that fastidiousness which is the only austerity in men not otherwise austere.

"Interpret?" she said, looking at me with clear hazel eyes; "how could I? You were in the native city yesterday. What did you miss?"

"Everything! I saw masses of colour, light, movement. Brilliantly picturesque people. Children like Asiatic angels. Magnificently scowling ruffians in sheepskin coats. In fact, a movie staged for my benefit. I was afraid they would ring down the curtain before I had had enough. It had no meaning. When I got back to my diggings I tried to put down what I had just seen, and I swear there's more inspiration in the guide-book."

"Did you go alone?"

"Yes, I certainly would not go sight-seeing with the Meryon crowd. Tell me what you felt when you saw it first."

"I went with Sir John's uncle. He was a great traveler. The colour struck me dumb. It flames - it sings. Think of the grey pinched life in the West! I saw a grave dark potter turning his wheel, while his little girl stood by, glad at our pleasure, her head veiled like a miniature woman, tiny baggy trousers, and a silver nose-stud, like a star, in one delicate nostril. In her thin arms she held a heavy baby in a gilt cap, like a monkey. And the wheel turned and whirled until it seemed to be spinning dreams, thick as motes in the sun. The clay rose in smooth spirals under his hand, and the wheel sang, 'Shall the vessel reprove him who made one to honour and one to dishonour?' And I saw the potter thumping his wet clay, and the clay, plastic as dream-stuff, shaped swift as light, and the three Fates stood at his shoul- der. Dreams, dreams, and all in the spinning of the wheel, and the rich shadows of the old broken courtyard where he sat. And the wheel stopped and the thread broke, and the little new shapes he had made stood all about him, and he was only a potter in Peshawar."

Her voice was like a song. She had utterly forgotten my existence. I did not dislike it at the moment, for I wanted to hear more, and the impersonal is the rarest gift a woman can give a man.

"Did you buy anything?"

"He gave me a gift - a flawed jar of turquoise blue, faint turquoise green round the lip. He saw I understood. And then I bought a little gold cap and a wooden box of jade-green Kabul grapes. About a rupee, all told. But it was Eastern merchandise, and I was trading from Balsora and Baghdad, and Eleazar's camels were swaying down from Damascus along the Khyber Pass, and coming in at the great Darwazah, and friends' eyes met me everywhere. I am profoundly happy here."

The sinking sun lit an almost ecstatic face.

I envied her more deeply than I had ever envied any one. She had the secret of immortal youth, and I felt old as I looked at her. One might be eighty and share that passionate impersonal joy. Age could not wither nor custom stale the infinite variety of her world's joys. She had a child's dewy youth in her eyes.

There are great sunsets at Peshawar, flaming over the plain, dying in melan- choly splendour over the dangerous hills. They too were hers, in a sense in which they could never be mine. But what a companion! To my astonishment a wild thought of marriage flashed across me, to be instantly rebuffed with a shrug. Mar- riage - that one's wife might talk poetry to one about the East! Absurd! But what was it these people felt and I could not feel? Almost, shut up in the prison of self, I knew what Vanna had felt in her village - a maddening desire to escape, to be a part of the loveliness that lay beyond me. So might a man love a king's daughter in her hopeless heights.

"It may be very beautiful on the surface," I said morosely; "but there's a lot of misery below - hateful, they tell me."

"Of course. We shall get to work one day. But look at the sunset. It opens like a mysterious flower. I must take Winifred home now."

"One moment," I pleaded; "I can only see it through your eyes. I feel it while you speak, and then the good minute goes."

She laughed.

"And so must I. Come, Winifred. Look, there's an owl; not like the owls in the summer dark in England-

"Lovely are the curves of the white owl sweeping, Wavy in the dark, lit by one low star."

Suddenly she turned again and looked at me half wistfully.

"It is good to talk to you. You want to know. You are so near it all. I wish I could help you; I am so exquisitely happy myself."

My writing was at a standstill. It seemed the groping of a blind man in a radiant world. Once perhaps I had felt that life was good in itself - when the guns came thundering toward the Vimy Ridge in a mad gallop of horses, and men shouting and swearing and frantically urging them on. Then, riding for more than life, I had tasted life for an instant. Not before or since. But this woman had the secret.

Lady Meryon, with her escort of girls and subalterns, came daintily past the hotel compound, and startled me from my brooding with her pretty silvery voice.

"Dreaming, Mr. Clifden? It isn't at all wholesome to dream in the East. Come and dine with us tomorrow. A tiny dance afterwards, you know; or bridge for those who like it."

I had not the faintest notion whether governesses dined with the family or came in afterward with the coffee; but it was a sporting chance, and I took it.

Then Sir John came up and joined us.

"You can't well dance tomorrow, Kitty," he said to his wife. "There's been an outpost affair in the Swat Hills, and young Fitzgerald has been shot. Come to dinner of course, Clifden. Glad to see you. But no dancing, I think."

Kitty Meryon's mouth drooped like a pouting child's. Was it for the lost dance, or the lost soldier lying out on the hills in the dying sunset. Who could tell? In either case it was pretty enough for the illustrated papers.

"How sad! Such a dear boy. We shall miss him at tennis." Then brightly; "Well, we'll have to put the dance off for a week, but come tomorrow anyhow."

II

Next evening I went into Lady Meryon's flower-scented drawing-room. The electric fans were fluttering and the evening air was cool. Five or six pretty girls and as many men made up the party - Kitty Meryon the prettiest of them all, fashionably undressed in faint pink and crystal, with a charming smile in readiness, all her gay little flags flying in the rich man's honour. I am no vainer than other men, but I saw that. Whatever her charm might be it was none for me. What could I say to interest her who lived in her foolish little world as one shut in a bright bubble? And she had said the wrong word about young Fitzgerald - I wanted Vanna, with her deep seeing eyes, to say the right one and adjust those cruel values.

Governesses dine, it appeared, only to fill an unexpected place, or make a decorous entry afterward, to play accompaniments. Fortunately Kitty Meryon sang, in a pinched little soprano, not nearly so pretty as her silver ripple of talk.

It was when the party had settled down to bridge and I was standing out, that I ventured to go up to her as she sat knitting by a window - not unwatched by the quick flash of Lady Meryon's eyes as I did it.

"I think you hypnotize me, Miss Loring. When I hear anything I straightway want to know what you will say. Have you heard of Fitzgerald's death?"

"That is why we are not dancing tonight. Tomorrow the cable will reach his home in England. He was an only child, and they are the great people of the village where we are the little people. I knew his mother as one knows a great lady who is kind to all the village folk. It may kill her. It is travelling tonight like a bullet to her heart, and she does not know."

"His father?"

"A brave man - a soldier himself. He will know it was a good death and that Harry would not fail. He did not at Ypres. He would not here. But all joy and hope will be dead in that house tomorrow."

"And what do you think?"

"I am not sorry for Harry, if you mean that. He knew - we all know - that he was on guard here holding the outposts against blood and treachery and terrible things - playing the Great Game. One never loses at that game if one plays it straight, and I am sure that at the last it was joy he felt and not fear. He has not lost. Did you notice in the church a niche before every soldier's seat to hold his loaded gun? And the tablets on the walls; "Killed at Kabul River, aged 22." - "Killed on outpost duty." - "Murdered by an Afghan fanatic." This will be one memory more. Why be sorry."

Presently:-

"I am going up to the hills tomorrow, to the Malakhand Fort, with Mrs. Delany, Lady Meryon's aunt, and we shall see the wonderful Tahkt-i-Bahi Monastery on the way. You should do that run before you go. The fort is the last but one on the way to Chitral, and beyond that the road is so beset that only soldiers may go farther, and indeed the regiments escort each other up and down. But it is an early start, for we must be back in Peshawar at six for fear of raiding natives."

"I know; they hauled me up in the dusk the other day, and told me I should be swept off to the hills if I fooled about after dusk. But I say - is it safe for you to go? You ought to have a man. Could I go too?"

I thought she did not look enthusiastic at the proposal.

"Ask. You know I settle nothing. I go where I am sent." She said it with the happiest smile. I knew they could send her nowhere that she would not find joy. I thought her mere presence must send the vibrations of happiness through the household. Yet again - why? For where there is no receiver the current speaks in vain; and for an instant I seemed to see the air full of messages - of speech striving to utter its passionate truths to deaf ears stopped for ever against the breaking waves of sound. But Vanna heard.

She left the room; and when the bridge was over, I made my request. Lady Meryon shrugged her shoulders and declared it would be a terribly dull run - the scenery nothing, "and only" (she whispered) "Aunt Selina and poor Miss Loring?"

Of course I saw at once that she did not like it; but Sir John was all for my going, and that saved the situation.

I certainly could have dispensed with Aunt Selina when the automobile drew up in the golden river of the sunrise at the hotel. There were only the driver, a personal servant, and the two ladies; Mrs. Delany, comely, pleasant, talkative, and Vanna-

Her face in its dark motoring veil, fine and delicate as a young moon in a cloud drift - the sensitive sweet mouth that had quivered a little when she spoke of Fitzgerald - the pure glance that radiated such kindness to all the world. She sat there with the Key of Dreams pressed against her slight bosom - her eyes dreaming above it. Already the strange airs of her unknown world were breathing about me, and as yet I knew not the things that belonged unto my peace.

We glided along the straight military road from Peshawar to Nowshera, the gold-bright sun dazzling in its whiteness - a strange drive through the flat, burned country, with the ominous Kabul River flowing through it. Military preparations everywhere, and the hills looking watchfully down - alive, as it were, with keen, hostile eyes. War was at present about us as behind the lines in France; and when we crossed the Kabul River on a bridge of boats, and I saw its haunted waters, I began to feel the atmosphere of the place closing down upon me. It had a sinister beauty; it breathed suspense; and I wished, as I was sure Vanna did, for silence that was not at our command.

For Mrs. Delany felt nothing of it. A bright shallow ripple of talk was her contribution to the joys of the day; though it was, fortunately, enough for her happiness if we listened and agreed. I knew Vanna listened only in show. Her intent eyes were fixed on the Tahkt-i-Bahi hills after we had swept out of Nowshera; and when the car drew up at the rough track, she had a strange look of suspense and pallor. I remember I wondered at the time if she were nervous in the wild open country.

"Now pray don't be shocked," said Mrs. Delany comfortably; "but you two young people may go up to the monastery, and I shall stay here. I am dreadfully ashamed of myself, but the sight of that hill is enough for me. Don't hurry. I may have a little doze, and be all the better company when you get back. No, don't try to persuade me, Mr. Clifden. It isn't the part of a friend."

I cannot say I was sorry, though I had a moment of panic when Vanna offered to stay with her - very much, too, as if she really meant it. So we set out perforce, Vanna leading steadily, as if she knew the way. She never looked up, and her wish for silence was so evident, that I followed, lending my hand mutely when the difficulties obliged it, she accepting absently, and as if her thoughts were far away.

Suddenly she quickened her pace. We had climbed about nine hundred feet, and now the narrow track twisted through the rocks - a track that looked as age-worn as no doubt it was. We threaded it, and struggled over the ridge, and looked down victorious on the other side.

There she stopped. A very wonderful sight, of which I had never seen the like, lay below us. Rock and waste and towering crags, and the mighty ruin of the monastery set in the fangs of the mountain like a robber baron's castle, looking far away to the blue mountains of the Debatable Land - the land of mystery and danger. It stood there - the great ruin of a vast habitation of men. Building after building, mysterious and broken, corridors, halls, refectories, cells; the dwelling of a faith so alien that I could not reconstruct the life that gave it being. And all sinking gently into ruin that in a century more would confound it with the roots of the mountains.

Grey and wonderful, it clung to the heights and looked with eyeless windows at the past. Somehow I found it infinitely pathetic; the very faith it expressed is dead in India, and none left so poor to do it reverence.

But Vanna knew her way. Unerringly she led me from point to point, and she was visibly at home in the intricacies. Such knowledge in a young woman bewildered me. Could she have studied the plans in the Museum? How else should she know where the abbot lived, or where the refractory brothers were punished?

Once I missed her, while I stooped to examine some scroll-work, and following, found her before one of the few images of the Buddha that the rapacious Museum had spared - a singularly beautiful bas-relief, the hand raised to enforce the truth the calm lips were speaking, the drapery falling in stately folds to the bare feet. As I came up, she had an air as if she had just ceased from movement, and I had a distinct feeling that she had knelt before it - I saw the look of worship! The thing troubled me like a dream, haunting, impossible, but real.

"How beautiful!" I said in spite of myself, as she pointed to the image. "In this utter solitude it seems the very spirit of the place."

"He was. He is," said Vanna.

"Explain to me. I don't understand. I know so little of him. What is the subject?"

She hesitated; then chose her words as if for a beginner;- "It is the Blessed One preaching to the Tree-Spirits. See how eagerly they lean from the boughs to listen. This other relief represents him in the state of mystic vision. Here he is drowned in peace. See how it overflows from the closed eyes; the closed lips. The air is filled with his quiet."

"What is he dreaming?"

"Not dreaming - seeing. Peace. He sits at the point where time and infinity meet. To attain that vision was the aim of the monks who lived here."

"Did they attain?" I found myself speaking as if she could certainly answer.

"A few. There was one, Vasettha, the Brahman, a young man who had renounced all his possessions and riches, and seated here before this image of the Blessed One, he fell often into the mystic state. He had a strange vision at one time of the future of India, which will surely be fulfilled. He did not forget it in his rebirths. He remembers-"

She broke off suddenly and said with forced indifference, - "He would sit here often looking out over the mountains; the monks sat at his feet to hear. He became abbot while still young. But his story is a sad one."

"I entreat you to tell me."

She looked away over the mountains. "While he was abbot here,- still a young man,- a famous Chinese Pilgrim came down through Kashmir to visit the Holy Places in India. The abbot went forward with him to Peshawar, that he might make him welcome. And there came a dancer to Peshawar, named Lilavanti, most beautiful! I dare not tell you her beauty. I tremble now to think-"

Again she paused, and again the faint creeping sense of mystery invaded me. She resumed;-

"The abbot saw her and he loved her. He was young still, you remember. She was a woman of the Hindu faith and hated Buddhism. It swept him down into the lower worlds of storm and desire. He fled with Lilavanti and never returned here. So in his rebirth he fell-"

She stopped dead; her face pale as death.

"How do you know? Where have you read it? If I could only find what you find and know what you know! The East is like an open book to you. Tell me the rest."

"How should I know any more?" she said hurriedly. "We must be going back.

You should study the plans of this place at Peshawar. They were very learned monks who lived here. It is famous for learning."

The life had gone out of her words-out of the ruins. There was no more to be said.

We clambered down the hill in the hot sunshine, speaking only of the view, the strange shrubs and flowers, and, once, the swift gliding of a snake, and found Mrs. Delany blissfully asleep in the most padded corner of the car. The spirit of the East vanished in her comfortable presence, and luncheon seemed the only matter of moment.

"I wonder, my dears," she said, "if you would be very disappointed and think me very dense if I proposed our giving up the Malakhand Fort? The driver has been giving me in very poor English such an account of the dangers of that awful road up the hill that I feel no Fort would repay me for its terrors. Do say what you feel, Miss Loring. Mr. Clifden can lunch with the officers at Nowshera and come any time. I know I am an atrocity."

There could be only one answer, though Vanna and I knew perfectly well the crafty design of the driver to spare himself work. Mrs. Delany remained brightly awake for the run home, and favored us with many remarkable views on India and its shortcomings, Vanna, who had a sincere liking for her, laughing with delight at her description of a visit of condolence with Lady Meryon to the five widows of one of the hill Rajas.

But I own I was pre-occupied. I knew those moments at the monastery had given me a glimpse into the wonderland of her soul that made me long for more. It was rapidly becoming clear to me that unless my intentions developed on very different lines I must flee Peshawar. For love is born of sympathy, and sympathy was strengthening daily, but for love I had no courage yet.

I feared it as men fear the unknown. I despised myself - but I feared. I will confess my egregious folly and vanity - I had no doubt as to her reception of my offer if I should make it, but possessed by a colossal selfishness, I thought only of myself, and from that point of view could not decide how I stood to lose or gain. In my wildest accesses of vanity I did not suppose Vanna loved me, but I felt she liked me, and I believe the advantages I had to offer would be overwhelming to a woman in her position. So, tossed on the waves of indecision, I inclined to flight.

That night I resolutely began my packing, and wrote a note of farewell to Lady Meryon. The next morning I furiously undid it, and destroyed the note. And that afternoon I took the shortest way to the sun-set road to lounge about and wait for Vanna and Winifred. She never came, and I was as unreasonably angry as if I had deserved the blessing of her presence.

Next day I could see that she tried gently hut clearly to discourage our meeting and for three days I never saw her at all. Yet I knew that in her solitary life our talks counted for a pleasure, and when we met again I thought I saw a new softness in the lovely hazel deeps of her eyes.

III

On the day when things became clear to me, I was walking towards the Meryons' gates when I met her coming alone along the sunset road, in the late gold of the afternoon. She looked pale and a little wearied, and I remembered I wished I did not know every change of her face as I did. It was a symptom that alarmed my selfishness - it galled me with the sense that I was no longer my own despot.

"So you have been up the Khyber Pass," she said as I fell into step at her side. "Tell me - was it as wonderful as you expected?"

"No, no, -you tell me! It will give me what I missed. Begin at the beginning. Tell me what I saw."

I could not miss the delight of her words, and she laughed, knowing my whim.

"Oh, that Pass! -the wonder of those old roads that have borne the traffic and romance of the world for ages. Do you think there is anything in the world so fascinating as they are? But did you go on Tuesday or Friday?"

For these are the only days in the week when the Khyber can be safely entered. The British then turn out the Khyber Rifles and man every crag, and the loaded caravans move like a tide, and go up and down the narrow road on their occasions.

Naturally mere sightseers are not welcomed, for much business must be got through in that urgent forty eight hours in which life is not risked in entering.

"Tuesday. But make a picture for me."

"Well, you gave your word not to photograph or sketch - as if one wanted to when every bit of it is stamped on one's brain! And you went up to Jumrood Fort at the entrance. Did they tell you it is an old Sikh Fort and has been on duty in that turbulent place for five hundred years And did you see the machine guns in the court? And every one armed - even the boys with belts of cartridges? Then you went up the narrow winding track between the mountains, and you said to your-self, 'This is the road of pure romance. It goes up to silken Samarkhand, and I can ride to Bokhara of the beautiful women and to all the dreams. Am I alive and is it real?' You felt that?"

"All. Every bit. Go on!"

She smiled with pleasure.

"And you saw the little forts on the crags and the men on guard all along the bills, rifles ready! You could hear the guns rattle as they saluted. Do you know that up there men plough with rifles loaded beside them? They have to be men indeed."

"Do you mean to imply that we are not men?"

"Different men at least. This is life in a Border ballad. Such a life as you knew in France but beautiful in a wild - hawk sort of way. Don't the Khyber Rifles bewilder you? They are drawn from these very Hill tribes, and will shoot their own fathers and brothers in the way of duty as comfortably as if they were jackals. Once there was a scrap here and one of the tribesmen sniped our men unbearably. What do you suppose happened? A Khyber Rifle came to the Colonel and said, 'Let me put an end to him, Colonel Sahib. I know exactly where he sits. He is my grandfather.' And he did it!"

"The bond of bread and salt?"

"Yes, and discipline. I'm sometimes half frightened of discipline. It moulds a man like wax. Even God doesn't do that. Well - then you had the traders - wild shaggy men in sheepskin and women in massive jewelry of silver and turquoise,- great earrings, heavy bracelets loading their arms, wild, fierce, handsome. And the camels - thousands of them, some going up, some coming down, a mass of human and animal life. Above you, moving figures against the keen blue sky, or deep below you in the ravines.

"The camels were swaying along with huge bales of goods, and dark beautiful women in wicker cages perched on them. Silks and carpets from Bokhara, and blue - eyed Persian cats, and bluer Persian turquoises. Wonderful! And the dust, gilded by the sunshine, makes a vaporous golden atmosphere for it all."

"What was the most wonderful thing you saw there?"

"The most beautiful, I think, was a man - a splendid dark ruffian lounging along. He wanted to show off, and his swagger was perfect. Long black onyx eyes and a tumble of black curls, and teeth like almonds. But what do you think he carried on his wrist - a hawk with fierce yellow eyes, ringed and chained. Hawking is a favourite sport in the hills. Oh, why doesn't some great painter come and paint it all before they take to trains and cars? I long to see it all again, but I never shall."

"Why not," said I. "Surely Sir John can get you up there any day?"

"Not now. The fighting makes it difficult. But it isn't that. I am leaving."

"Leaving?" My heart gave a leap. "Why? Where?"

"Leaving Lady Meryon."

"Why - for Heaven's sake?"

"I had rather not tell you."

"But I must know."

"You cannot."

"I shall ask Lady Meryon."

"I forbid you."

And then the unexpected happened, and an unbearable impulse swept me into folly - or was it wisdom?

"Listen to me. I would not have said it yet, but this settles it. I want you to marry me. I want it atrociously!"

It was a strange word. What I felt for her at that moment was difficult to describe. I endured it like a pain that could only be assuaged by her presence, but I endured it angrily. We were walking on the sunset road - very deserted and quiet at the time. The place was propitious if nothing else was.

She looked at me in transparent astonishment;

"Mr. Clifden, are you dreaming? You can't mean what you say."

"Why can't I? I do. I want you. You have the key of all I care for. I think of the world without you and find it tasteless."

"Surely you have all the world can give? What do you want more?"

"The power to enjoy it - to understand it. You have got that - I haven't. I want you always with me to interpret, like a guide to a blind fellow. I am no better."

"Say like a dog, at once!" she interrupted. "At least you are frank enough to put it on that ground. You have not said you love me. You could not say it."

"I don't know whether I do or not. I know nothing about love. I want you. Indescribably. Perhaps that is love - is it? I never wanted any one before. I have tried to get away and I can't."

I was brutally frank, you see. She compelled my very thoughts.

"Why have you tried?"

"Because every man likes freedom. But I like you better." "I can tell you the reason," she said in her gentle unwavering voice. "I am Lady Meryon's governess, and an undesirable. You have felt that?"

"Don't make me out such a snob. No - yes. You force me into honesty. I did feel it at first like the miserable fool I am, but I could kick myself when I think of that now. It is utterly forgotten. Take me and make me what you will, and forgive me. Only tell me your secret of joy. How is it you understand everything alive or dead? I want to live - to see, to know."

It was a rhapsody like a boy's. Yet at the moment I was not even ashamed of it, so sharp was my need.

"I think," she said, slowly, looking straight before her, "that I had better be quite frank. I don't love you. I don't know what love means in the Western sense. It has a very different meaning for me. Your voice comes to me from an immense distance when you speak in that way. You want me - but never with a thought of what I might want. Is that love? I like you very deeply as a friend, but we are of different races. There is a gulf."

"A gulf? You are English."

"By birth, yes. In mind, no. And there are things that go deeper, that you could not understand. So I refuse quite definitely, and our ways part here, for in a few days I go. I shall not see you again, but I wish to say good-bye."

The bitterest chagrin was working in my soul. I felt as if all were deserting me-a sickening feeling of loneliness. I did not know the man who was in me, and was a stranger to myself.

"I entreat you to tell me why, and where."

"Since you have made me this offer, I will tell you why. Lady Meryon objected to my friendship with you, and objected in a way which–"

She stopped, flushing palely. I caught her hand.

"That settles it!–that she should have dared! I'll go up this minute and tell her we are engaged. Vanna–Vanna !"

For she disengaged her hand, quietly but firmly.

"On no account. How can I make it more plain to you? I should have gone soon in any case. My place is in the native city - that is the life I want. I have work there, I knew it before I came out. My sympathies are all with them. They know what life is - why even the beggars, poorer than poor, are perfectly happy, basking in the great generous sun. Oh, the splendour and riot of life and colour! That's my life - I sicken of this."

"But I'll give it to you. Marry me, and we will travel till you're tired of it."

"Yes, and look on as at a play - sitting in the stalls, and applauding when we are pleased. No, I'm going to work there." "For God's sake, how? Let me come too."

"You can't. You're not in it. I am going to attach myself to the medical mission at Lahore and learn nursing, and then I shall go to my own people."

"Missionaries? You've nothing in common with them?"

"Nothing. But they teach what I want. Mr. Clifden, I shall not come this way again. If I remember - I'll write to you, and tell you what the real world is like."

She smiled, the absorbed little smile I knew and feared. I saw pleading was useless then. I would wait, and never lose sight of her and of hope.

"Vanna, before you go, give me your gift of sight. Interpret for me. Stay with me a little and make me see."

"What do you mean exactly?" she asked in her gentlest voice, half turning to me.

"Make one journey with me, as my sister, if you will do no more. Though I warn you that all the time I shall be trying to win my wife. But come with me once, and after that - if you will go, you must. Say yes."

Madness! But she hesitated - a hesitation full of hope, and looked at me with intent eyes.

"I will tell you frankly," she said at last, "that I know my knowledge of the East and kinship with it goes far beyond mere words. In my case the doors were not shut. I believe - I know that long ago this was my life. If I spoke for ever I could not make you understand how much I know and why. So I shall quite certainly go back to it. Nothing - you least of all, can hold me. But you are my friend - that is a true bond. And if you would wish me to give you two months before I go, I might do that if it would in any way help you. As your friend only - you clearly understand. You would not reproach me afterwards when I left you, as I should most certainly do?"

"I swear I would not. I swear I would protect you even from myself. I want you for ever, but if you will only give me two months - come! But have you thought that people will talk. It may injure you.

I'm not worth that, God knows. And you will take nothing I could give you in return."

She spoke very quietly.

"That does not trouble me. - It would only trouble me if you asked what I have not to give. For two months I would travel with you as a friend, if, like a friend, I paid my own expenses-"

I would have interrupted, but she brushed that firmly aside. "No, I must do as I say, and I am quite able to or I should not suggest it. I would go on no other terms. It would be hard if because we are man and woman I might not do one act of friend-ship for you before we part. For though I refuse your offer utterly, I appreciate it, and I would make what little return I can. It would be a sharp pain to me to distress you."

Her gentleness and calm, the magnitude of the offer she was making stunned me so that I could scarcely speak. There was such an extraordinary simplicity and generosity in her manner that it appeared to me more enthralling and bewildering than the most finished coquetry I had ever known. She gave me opportunities that the most ardent lover could in his wildest dream desire, and with the remoteness in her eyes and her still voice she deprived them of all hope. It kindled in me a flame that made my throat dry when I tried to speak.

"Vanna, is it a promise? You mean it?"

"If you wish it, yes. But I warn you I think it will not make it easier for you when the time is over.

"Why two months?"

"Partly because I can afford no more. No! I know what you would say. Partly because I can spare no more time. But I will give you that, if you wish, though, honestly, I had very much rather not. I think it unwise for you. I would protect you if I could - indeed I would!"

It was my turn to hesitate now. Every moment revealed to me some new sweetness, some charm that I saw would weave itself into the very fibre of my I had been! Was I not now a fool? Would it not being if the opportunity were given. Oh, fool that be better to let her go before she had become a part of my daily experience? I began to fear I was courting my own shipwreck. She read my thoughts clearly.

"Indeed you would be wise to decide against it. Release me from my promise. It was a mad scheme."

The superiority - or so I felt it - of her gentleness maddened me. It might have been I who needed protection, who was running the risk of misjudgment - not she, a lonely woman. She looked at me, waiting - trying to be wise for me, never for one instant thinking of herself. I felt utterly exiled from the real purpose of her life.

"I will never release you. I claim your promise. I hold to it."

"Very well then - I will write, and tell you where I shall be. Good-bye, and if you change your mind, as I hope you will, tell me."

She extended her hand cool as a snowflake, and was gone, walking swiftly up the road. Ah, let a man beware when his wishes fulfilled, rain down upon him!

To what had I committed myself? She knew her strength and had no fears. I could scarcely realize that she had liking enough for me to make the offer. That it meant no shade more than she had said I knew well. She was safe, but what was to be the result for me? I knew nothing - she was a beloved mystery.

"Strange she is and secret, Strange her eyes; her cheeks are cold as cold seashells."

Yet I would risk it, for I knew there was no hope if I let her go now, and if I saw her again, some glimmer might fall upon my dark.

Next day this reached me:- Dear Mr. Clifden,-

I am going to some Indian friends for a time. On the 15th of June I shall he at Srinagar in Kashmir. A friend has allowed me to take her little houseboat, the "Kedarnath." If you like this plan we will share the cost for two months. I warn you it is not luxurious, but I think you will like it. I shall do this whether you come or no, for I want a quiet time before I take up my nursing in Lahore. In thinking of all this will you remember that I am not a girl but a woman. I shall he twenty-nine my next birthday. Sincerely yours, VANNA LORING.

P.S. But I still think you would be wiser not to come. I hope to hear you will not.

I replied only this :- Dear Miss Loring,- I think I understand the position fully. I will be there. I thank you with all my heart. Gratefully yours, STEPHEN CLIFDEN.

IV

Three days later I met Lady Meryon, and was swept in to tea. Her manner was distinctly more cordial as she mentioned casually that Vanna had left - she understood to take up missionary work - "which is odd," she added with a woman's acrimony, "for she had no more in common with missionaries than I have, and that is saying a good deal. Of course she speaks Hindustani perfectly, and could be useful, but I haven't grasped the point of it yet" I saw she counted on my knowing nothing of the real reason of Vanna's going and left it, of course, at that. The talk drifted away under my guidance. Vanna evidently puzzled her. She half feared, and wholly misunderstood her.

No message came to me, as time went by, and for the time she had vanished completely, but I held fast to her promise and lived on that only.

I take up my life where it ceased to be a mere suspense and became life once more.

On the 15th of June, I found myself riding into Srinagar in Kashmir, through the pure tremulous green of the mighty poplars that hedge the road into the city. The beauty of the country had half stunned me when I entered the mountain barrier of Baramula and saw the snowy peaks that guard the Happy Valley, with the Jhelum flowing through its tranquil loveliness. The flush of the almond blossom was over, but the iris, like a blue sea of peace had overflowed the world - the azure meadows smiled back at the radiant sky. Such blossom! the blue shading into clear violet, like a shoaling sea. The earth, like a cup held in the hand of a god, brimmed with the draught of youth and summer and - love? But no, for me the very word was sinister. Vanna's face, immutably calm, confronted it.

That night I slept in a boat at Sopor, and I remember that, waking at midnight, I looked out and saw a mountain with a gloriole of hazy silver about it, misty and faint as a cobweb threaded with dew. The river, there spreading into a lake, was dark under it, flowing in a deep smooth blackness of shadow, and everything await-ed - what? And even while I looked, the moon floated serenely above the peak, and all was bathed in pure light, the water rippling and shining in broken silver and pearl. So had Vanna floated into my sky, luminous, sweet, remote. I did not ques-tion my heart any more. I knew I loved her.

Two days later I rode into Srinagar, and could scarcely see the wild beauty of that strange Venice. of the East, my heart was so beating in my eyes. I rode past the lovely wooden bridges where the balconied houses totter to each other across the canals in dim splendour of carving and age; where the many-coloured native life crowds down to the river steps and cleanses its flower-bright robes, its gold-bright brass vessels in the shining stream, and my heart said only - Vanna, Vanna!

One day, one thought, of her absence had taught me what she was to me, and if humility and patient endeavor could raise me to her feet, I was resolved that I would spend my life in labor and think it well spent.

My servant dismounted and led his horse, asking from every one where the "Kedarnath" could be found, and eager black eyes sparkled and two little bronze images detached themselves from the crowd of boys, and ran, fleet as fauns, before us.

Above the last bridge the Jhelum broadens out into a stately river, controlled at one side by the banked walk known as the Bund, with the Club House upon it and the line of houseboats beneath. Here the visitors flutter up and down and exchange the gossip, the bridge appointments, the little dinners that sit so incongruously on the pure Orient that is Kashmir.

She would not be here. My heart told me that, and sure enough the boys were leading across the bridge and by a quiet shady way to one of the many backwaters that the great river makes in the enchanting city. There is one waterway stretching on afar to the Dal Lake. It looks like a river - it is the very haunt of peace. Under those mighty chenar, or plane trees, that are the glory of Kashmir, clouding the water with deep green shadows, the sun can scarcely pierce, save in a dipping sparkle here and there to intensify the green gloom. The murmur of the city, the chatter of the club, are hundreds of miles away. We rode downward under the towering trees, and dismounting, saw a little houseboat tethered to the bank. It was not of the richer sort that haunts the Bund, where the native servants follow in a separate boat, and even the electric light is turned on as part of the luxury. This was a long low craft, very broad, thatched like a country cottage afloat. In the forepart lived the native owner, and his family, their crew, our cooks and servants; for they played many parts in our service. And in the afterpart, room for a life, a dream, the joy or curse & many days to be.

But then, I saw only one thing - Vanna sat under the trees, reading, or looking at the cool dim watery vista, with a single boat, loaded to the river's edge with melons and scarlet tomatoes, punting lazily down to Srinagar in the sleepy afternoon.

She was dressed in white with a shady hat, and her delicate dark face seemed to glow in the shadow like the heart of a pale rose. For the first time I knew she was beautiful. Beauty shone in her like the flame in an alabaster lamp, serene, diffused in the very air about her, so that to me she moved in a mild radiance. She rose to meet me with both hands outstretched - the kindest, most cordial welcome. Not an eyelash flickered, not a trace of self- consciousness. If I could have seen her flush or tremble - but no - her eyes were clear and calm as a forest pool. So I remembered her. So I saw her once more.

I tried, with a hopeless pretence, to follow her example and hide what I felt, where she had nothing to hide.

"What a place you have found. Why, it's like the deep heart of a wood!"

"Yes, I saw it once when I was here with the Meryons. But we lay at the Bund then - just under the Club. This is better. Did you like the ride up?"

I threw myself on the grass beside her with a feeling of perfect rest.

"It was like a new heaven and a new earth. What a country!"

The very spirit of Quiet seemed to be drowsing in those branches towering up into the blue, dipping their green fingers into the crystal of the water. What a heaven!

"Now you shall have your tea and then I will show you your rooms," she said, smiling at my delight. "We shall stay here a few days more that you may see Srinagar, and then they tow us up into the Dal Lake opposite the Gardens of the Mogul Emperors. And if you think this beautiful what will you say then?"

I shut my eyes and see still that first meal of my new life. The little table that Pir Baksh, breathing full East in his jade-green turban, set before her, with its cloth worked in a pattern of the chenar leaves that are the symbol of Kashmir; the brown cakes made by Ahmad Khan in a miraculous kitchen of his own invention - a few holes burrowed in the river bank, a smoldering fire beneath them, and a width of canvas for a roof. But it served, and no more need be asked of luxury. And Vanna, making it mysteriously the first home I ever had known, the central joy of it all. Oh, wonderful days of life that breathe the spirit of immortality and pass so quickly - surely they must be treasured somewhere in Eternity that we may look upon their beloved light once more.

"Now you must see the boat. The Kedarnath is not a Dreadnought, but she is broad and very comfortable. And we have many chaperons. They all live in the bows, and exist simply to protect the Sahiblog from all discomfort, and very well they do it. That is Ahmad Khan by the kitchen. He cooks for us. Salama owns the boat, and steers her and engages the men to tow us when we move. And when I arrived he aired a little English and said piously; The Lord help me to give you no trouble, and the Lord help you!" That is his wife sitting on the bank. She speaks little but Kashmiri, but I know a little of that. Look at the hundred rat-tail plaits of her hair, lengthened with wool, and see her silver and turquoise jewelry. She wears much of the family fortune and is quite a walking bank. Salama, Ahmad Khan and I talk by the hour. Ahmad comes from Fyzabad. Look at Salama's boy - I call him the Orange Imp. Did you ever see anything so beautiful?"

I looked in sheer delight, and grasped my camera. Sitting near us was a lovely little Kashmiri boy of about eight, in a faded orange coat, and a turban exactly like his father's. His curled black eyelashes were so long that they made a soft gloom over the upper part of the little golden face. The perfect bow of the scarlet lips, the long eyes, the shy smile, suggested an Indian Eros. He sat dipping his feet in the water with little pigeon-like cries of content.

"He paddles at the bow of our little shikara boat with a paddle exactly like a water-lily leaf. Do you like our friends? I love them already, and know all their affairs. And now for the boat."

"One moment - If we are friends on a great adventure, I must call you Vanna, and you me Stephen."

"Yes, I suppose that is part of it," she said, smiling. "Come, Stephen."

It was like music, but a cold music that chilled me. She should have hesitated, should have flushed - it was I who trembled. So I followed her across the broad plank into our new home.

"This is our sitting-room. Look, how charming!"

It was better than charming; it was home indeed. Windows at each side opening down almost to the water, a little table for meals that lived mostly on the bank, with a grey pot of iris in the middle. Another table for writing, photography, and all the little pursuits of travel. A bookshelf with some well - worn friends. Two long cushioned chairs. Two for meals, and a Bokhara rug, soft and pleasant for the feet. The interior was plain unpainted wood, but set so that the grain showed like satin in the rippling lights from the water.

That is the inventory of the place I have loved best in the world, but what eloquence can describe what it gave me, what its memory gives me to this day? And I have no eloquence - what I felt leaves me dumb.

"It is perfect," was all I said as she waved her hand proudly. "It is home."

"And if you had come alone to Kashmir you would have had a great rich boat with electric light and a butler. You would never have seen the people except at meal - times. I think you will like this better. Well, this is your tiny bedroom, and your bathroom, and beyond the sitting - room are mine. Do you like it all?"

But I could say no more. The charm of her own personality had touched everything and left its fragrance like a flower - breath in the air. I was beggared of thanks, but my whole soul was gratitude. We dined on the bank that evening, the lamp burning steadily in the still air and throwing broken reflections in the water, while the moon looked in upon them through the leaves. I felt extraordinarily young and happy.

The quiet of her voice was soft as the little lap of water against the bows of the boat, and Kahdra, the Orange Imp, was singing a little wordless song to himself as he washed the plates beside us. It was a simple meal, and Vanna, abstemious as a hermit never ate anything but rice and fruit, but I could remember no meal in all my days of luxury where I had eaten with such zest.

"It looks very grand to have so many to wait upon us, doesn't it? But this is one of the cheapest countries in the world though the old timers mourn over present expenses. You will laugh when I show you your share of the cost."

"The wealth of the world could not buy this," I said, and was silent.

"But you must listen to my plans. We must do a little camping the last three weeks before we part. Up in the mountains. Are they not marvellous? They stand like a rampart round us, but not cold and terrible, but "Like as the hills stand round about Jerusalem" - they are guardian presences. And running up into them, high -very high, are the valleys and hills where we shall camp. Tomorrow we shall row through Srinagar, by the old Maharaja's palace."

V

And so began a life of sheer enchantment. We knew no one. The visitors in Kashmir change nearly every season, and no one cared-no one asked anything of us, and as for our shipmates, a willing affectionate service was their gift, and no more. Looking back, I know in what a wonder-world I was privileged to live. Vanna could talk with them all. She did not move apart, a condescending or indifferent foreigner. Kahdra would come to her knee and prattle to her of the great snake that lived up on Mahadeo to devour erring boys who omitted their prayers at proper Moslem intervals. She would sit with the baby in her lap while the mother busied herself in the sunny bows with the mysterious dishes that smelt so savory to a hungry man. The cuts, the bruises of the neighbourhood all came to Vanna for treatment.

"I am graduating as a nurse," she would say laughing as she bent over the lean arm of some weirdly wrinkled old lady, bandaging and soothing at the same moment. Her reward would be some bit of folk-lore, some quaintness of gratitude that I noted down in the little book I kept for remembrance - that I do not need, for every word is in my heart.

We rowed down through the city next day - Salama rowing, and little Kahdra lazily paddling at the bow - a wonderful city, with its narrow ways begrimed with the dirt of ages, and its balconied houses looking as if disease and sin had soaked into them and given them a vicious tottering beauty, horrible and yet lovely too.

We saw the swarming life of the bazaar, the white turbans coming and going, diversified by the rose and yellow Hindu turbans, and the caste-marks, orange and red, on the dark brows.

I saw two women - girls - painted and tired like Jezebel, looking out of one window carved and old, and the grey burnished doves flying about it. They leaned indolently, like all the old, old wickedness of the East that yet is ever young - "Flowers of Delight," with smooth black hair braided with gold and blossoms, and covered with pale rose veils, and gold embossed disks swinging like lamps beside the olive cheeks, the great eyes artificially lengthened and darkened with soorma, and the curves of the full lips emphasized with vermilion. They looked down on us with apathy, a dull weariness that held all the old evil of the wicked humming city.

It had taken shape in those indolent bodies and heavy eyes that could flash into life as a snake wakes into fierce darting energy when the time comes to spring - direct inheritrixes from Lilith, in the fittest setting in the world - the almost exhausted vice of an Oriental city as old as time.

"And look-below here," said Vanna, pointing to one of the ghauts - long rugged steps running down to the river.

"When I came yesterday, a great broken crowd was collected here, almost shouldering each other into the water where a boat lay rocking. In it lay the body of a man brutally murdered for the sake of a few rupees and flung into the river. I could see the poor brown body stark in the boat with a friend weeping beside it. On the lovely deodar bridge people leaned over, watching with a grim open-mouthed curiosity, and business went on gaily where the jewelers make the silver bangles for slender wrists, and the rows of silver chains that make the necks like 'the Tower of Damascus builded for an armory.' It was all very wild and cruel. I went down to them-"

"Vanna - you went down? Horrible!"

"No, you see I heard them say the wife was almost a child and needs help. So I went. Once long ago at Peshawar I saw the same thing happen, and they came and took the child for the service of the gods, for she was most lovely, and she clung to the feet of a man in terror, and the priest stabbed her to the heart. She died in my arms.

"Good God!" I said, shuddering; "what a sight for you! Did they never hang him?"

"He was not punished. I told you it was a very long time ago. Her expression had a brooding quiet as she looked down into the running river, almost it might be as if she saw the picture of that past misery in the deep water. She said no more. But in her words and the terrible crowding of its life, Srinagar seemed to me more of a nightmare than anything I had seen, excepting only Benares; for the holy Benares is a memory of horror, with a sense of blood hidden under its frantic crazy devotion, and not far hidden either.

Our own green shade, when we pulled back to it in the evening cool, was a refuge of unspeakable quiet. She read aloud to me that evening by the small light of our lamp beneath the trees, and, singularly, she read of joy.

"I have drunk of the Cup of the Ineffable, I have found the key of the Mystery, Travelling by no track I have come to the Sorrowless Land; very easily has the mercy of the great Lord come upon me. Wonderful is that Land of rest to which no merit can win. There have I seen joy filled to the brim, perfection of joy. He dances in rapture and waves of form arise from His dance. He holds all within his bliss."

"What is that?"

"It is from the songs of the great Indian mystic - Kabir. Let me read you more. It is like the singing of a lark, lost in the infinite of light and heaven."

So in the soft darkness I heard for the first time those immortal words; and hearing, a faint glimmer of understanding broke upon me as to the source of the peace that surrounded her. I had accepted it as an emanation of her own heart when it was the pulsing of the tide of the Divine. She read, choosing a verse here and there, and I listened with absorption.

Suppose I had been wrong in believing that sorrow is the keynote of life; that pain is the road of ascent, if road there be; that an implacable Nature and that only, presides over all our pitiful struggles and seekings and writes a black "Finis" to the holograph of our existence?

What then? What was she teaching me? Was she the Interpreter of a Beauty eternal in the heavens, and reflected like a broken prism in the beauty that walked visible beside me? So I listened like a child to an unknown language, yet ventured my protest.

"In India, in this wonderful country where men have time and will for speculation such thoughts may be natural. Can they be found in the West?"

"This is from the West - might not Kabir himself have said it? Certainly he would have felt it. 'Happy is he who seeks not to understand the Mystery of God, but who, merging his spirit into Thine, sings to Thy face, 0 Lord, like a harp, understanding how difficult it is to know - how easy to love Thee.' We debate and argue and the Vision passes us by. We try to prove it, and kill it in the laboratory of our minds, when on the altar of our souls it will dwell for ever."

Silence - and I pondered. Finally she laid the book aside, and repeated from memory and in a tone of perfect music; "Kabir says, 'I shall go to the House of my Lord with my Love at my side; then shall I sound the trumpet of triumph.'"

And when she left me alone in the moonlight silence the old doubts came back to me - the fear that I saw only through her eyes, and began to believe in joy only because I loved her. I remember I wrote in the little book I kept for my stray thoughts, these words which are not mine but reflect my thought of her; "Thine is the skill of the Fairy Woman, and the virtue of St. Bride, and the faith of Mary the Mild, and the gracious way of the Greek woman, and the beauty of lovely Emer, and the tenderness of heart-sweet Deirdre, and the courage of Maev the great Queen, and the charm of Mouth-of-Music."

Yes, all that and more, but I feared lest I should see the heaven of joy through her eyes only and find it mirage as I had found so much else.

SECOND PART Early in the pure dawn the men came and our boat was towed up into the Dal Lake through crystal waterways and flowery banks, the men on the path keeping step and straining at the rope until the bronze muscles stood out on their legs and backs, shouting strong rhythmic phrases to mark the pull.

"They shout the Wondrous Names of God - as they are called," said Vanna when I asked. "They always do that for a timid effort. Bad shah! The Lord, the Compassionate, and so on. I don't think there is any religion about it but it is as natural to them as One, Two, Three, to us. It gives a tremendous lift. Watch and see."

It was part of the delightful strangeness that we should move to that strong music. We sat on the upper deck and watched the dream - like beauty drift slowly by until we emerged beneath a little bridge into the fairy land of the lake which the Mogul Emperors loved so well that they made their noble pleasance gardens on the banks, and thought it little to travel up yearly from far - off Delhi over the snowy

Pir Panjal with their Queens and courts for the perfect summer of Kashmir.

We moored by a low bank under a great wood of chenar trees, and saw the little table in the wilderness set in the greenest shade with our chairs beside it, and my pipe laid reverently upon it by Kahdra.

Across the glittering water lay on one side the Shalimar Garden known to all readers of "Lalla Ruhk" - a paradise of roses; and beyond it again the lovelier gardens of Nour-Mahal, the Light of the Palace, that imperial woman who ruled India under the weak Emperor's name - she whose name he set thus upon his coins:

"By order of King Jehangir. Gold has a hundred splendours added to it by receiving the name of Nour-Jahan the Queen."

Has any woman ever had a more royal homage than this most royal lady - known first as Mihr-u- nissa - Sun of Women, and later, Nour-Mahal, Light of the Palace, and latest, Nour-Jahan- Begam, Queen, Light of the World?

Here in these gardens she had lived - had seen the snow mountains change from the silver of dawn to the illimitable rose of sunset. The life, the colour beat insistently upon my brain. They built a world of magic where every moment was pure gold. Surely - surely to Vanna it must be the same. I believed in my very soul that she who gave and shared such joy could not be utterly apart from me? Could I then feel certain that I had gained any ground in these days we had been together? Could she still define the cruel limits she had laid down, or were her eyes kinder, her tones a more broken music? I did not know. Whenever I could hazard a guess the next minute baffled me.

Just then, in the sunset, she was sitting on deck, singing under her breath and looking absently away to the Gardens across the Lake. I could catch the words here and there, and knew them.

"Pale hands I loved beside the Shalimar,
Where are you now - who lies beneath your spell?
Whom do you lead on Rapture's roadway far,
Before you agonize them in farewell?"

"Don't!" I said abruptly. It stung me.
"What?" she asked in surprise. "That is the song every one remembers here.

Poor Laurence Hope! How she knew and loved this India! What are you grumbling at?"

Her smile stung me.

"Never mind," I said morosely. "You don't understand. You never will."

And yet I believed sometimes that she would - that time was on my side.

When Kahdra and I pulled her across to Nour-Mahal's garden next day, how could I not believe it - her face was so full of joy as she looked at me for sympathy?

"I don't think so much beauty is crowded into any other few miles in the world - beauty of association, history, nature, everything!" she said with shining eyes. "The lotus flowers are not out yet but when they come that is the last touch of perfection. Do you remember Homer - 'But whoso ate of the honey-sweet fruit of the lotus, was neither willing to bring me word again, nor to depart. Nay, their desire was to remain there for ever, feeding on the lotus with the Lotus Eaters, forgetful of all return.' You know the people here eat the roots and seeds? I ate them last year and perhaps that is why I cannot stay away. But look at Nour- Mahal's garden!"

We were pulling in among the reeds and the huge carven leaves of the water plants, and the snake-headed buds lolling upon them with the slippery half-sinister look that water-flowers have, as though their cold secret life belonged to the hidden water world and not to ours. But now the boat was touching the little wooden steps.

O beautiful - most beautiful the green lawns, shaded with huge pyramids of the chenar trees, the terraced gardens where the marble steps climbed from one to the other, and the mountain streams flashed singing and shining down the carved marble slopes that cunning hands had made to delight the Empress of Beauty, between the wildernesses of roses. Her pavilion stands still among the flowers, and the waters ripple through it to join the lake - and she is - where? Even in the glory of sunshine the passing of all fair things was present with me as I saw the empty shell that had held the Pearl of Empire, and her roses that still bloom, her waters that still sing for others.

The spray of a hundred fountains was misty diamond dust in the warm air laden with the scent of myriad flowers. Kahdra followed us everywhere, singing his little tuneless happy song. The world brimmed with beauty and joy. And we were together. Words broke from me.

"Vanna, let it be for ever! Let us live here. I'll give up all the world for this and you."

"But you see," she said delicately, "it would be 'giving up.' You use the right word. It is not your life. It is a lovely holiday, no more. You would weary of it. You would want the city life and your own kind."

I protested with all my soul.

"No. Indeed I will say frankly that it would be lowering yourself to live a lotus-eating life among my people. It is a life with which you have no tie. A Westerner who lives like that steps down; he loses his birthright just as an Oriental does who Europeanizes himself. He cannot live your life nor you his. If you had work here it would be different. No - six or eight weeks more; then go away and forget it."

I turned from her. The serpent was in Paradise. When is he absent?

On one of the terraces a man was beating a tom-tom, and veiled women listened, grouped about him in brilliant colours.

"Isn't that all India?" she said; "that dull reiterated sound? It half stupefies, half maddens. Once at Darjiling I saw the Lamas' Devil Dance - the soul, a white-faced child with eyes unnaturally enlarged, fleeing among a rabble of devils - the evil passions. It fled wildly here and there and every way was blocked. The child fell on its knees, screaming dumbly - you could see the despair in the staring eyes, but all was drowned in the thunder of Tibetan drums. No mercy - no escape. Horrible!"

"Even in Europe the drum is awful," I said. "Do you remember in the French Revolution how they Drowned the victims' voices in a thunder roll of drums?"

"I shall always see the face of the child, hunted down to hell, falling on its knees, and screaming without a sound, when I hear the drum. But listen - a flute! Now if that were the Flute of Krishna you would have to follow. Let us come!"

I could hear nothing of it, but she insisted and we followed the music, inaudible to me, up the slopes of the garden that is the foot-hill of the mighty mountain of Mahadeo, and still I could hear nothing. And Vanna told me strange stories of the Apollo of India whom all hearts must adore, even as the herd-girls adored him in his golden youth by Jumna river and in the pastures of Brindaban.

Next day we were climbing the hill to the ruins where the evil magician brought the King's daughter nightly to his will, flying low under a golden moon.

Vanna took my arm and I pulled her laughing up the steepest flowery slopes until we reached the height, and lo! the arched windows were eyeless and a lonely breeze blowing through the cloisters, and the beautiful yellowish stone arches supported nothing and were but frames for the blue of far lake and mountain and the divine sky. We climbed the broken stairs where the lizards went by like flashes, and had I the tongue of men and angels I could not tell the wonder that lay before us, - the whole wide valley of Kashmir in summer glory, with its scented breeze singing, singing above it.

We sat on the crushed aromatic herbs and among the wild roses and looked down.

"To think," she said, "that we might have died and never seen it!"

There followed a long silence. I thought she was tired, and would not break it. Suddenly she spoke in a strange voice, low and toneless;

"The story of this place. She was the Princess Padmavati, and her home was in Ayodhya. When she woke and found herself here by the lake she was so terrified that she flung herself in and was drowned. They held her back, but she died."

"How do you know?"

"Because a wandering monk came to the abbey of Tahkt-i-Bahi near Peshawar and told Vasettha the Abbot."

I had nearly spoilt all by an exclamation, but I held myself back. I saw she was dreaming awake and was unconscious of what she said.

"The Abbot said, 'Do not describe her. What talk is this for holy men? The young monks must not hear. Some of them have never seen a woman. Should a monk speak of such toys?' But the wanderer disobeyed and spoke, and there was a great tumult, and the monks threw him out at the command of the young Abbot, and he wandered down to Peshawar, and it was he later - the evil one! - that brought his sister, Lilavanti the Dancer, to Peshawar, and the Abbot fell into her snare. That was his revenge!"

Her face was fixed and strange, for a moment her cheek looked hollow, her eyes dim and grief- worn. What was she seeing? - what remembering? Was it a story - a memory? What was it?

"She was beautiful?" I prompted.

"Men have said so, but for it he surrendered the Peace. Do not speak of her accursed beauty."

Her voice died away to a drowsy murmur; her head dropped on my shoulder and for the mere de- light of contact I sat still and scarcely breathed, praying that she might speak again, but the good minute was gone. She drew one or two deep breaths, and sat up with a bewildered look that quickly passed.

"I was quite sleepy for a minute. The climb was so strenuous. Hark - I hear the Flute of Krishna again."

And again I could hear nothing, but she said it was sounding from the trees at the base of the hill. Later when we climbed down I found she was right - that a peasant lad, dark and amazingly beautiful as these Kashmiris often are, was playing on the flute to a girl at his feet - looking up at him with rapt eyes. He flung Vanna a flower as we passed. She caught it and put it in her bosom. A singular blossom, three petals of purest white, set against three leaves of purest green, and lower down the stem the three green leaves were repeated. It was still in her bosom after dinner, and I looked at it more closely.

"That is a curious flower," I said. "Three and three and three. Nine. That makes the mystic number. I never saw a purer white. What is it?"

"Of course it is mystic," she said seriously. "It is the Ninefold Flower. You saw who gave it?"

"That peasant lad."

She smiled.

"You will see more some day. Some might not even have seen that."

"Does it grow here?"

"This is the first I have seen. It is said to grow only where the gods walk. Do you know that throughout all India Kashmir is said to be holy ground? It was called long ago the land of the gods, and of strange, but not evil, sorceries. Great marvels were seen here."

I felt the labyrinthine enchantments of that enchanted land were closing about me - a slender web, grey, almost impalpable, finer than fairy silk, was winding it-self about my feet. My eyes were opening to things I had not dreamed. She saw my thought.

"Yes, you could not have seen even that much of him in Peshawar. You did not know then."

"He was not there," I answered, falling half unconsciously into her tone.

"He is always there - everywhere, and when he plays, all who hear must follow. He was the Pied Piper in Hamelin, he was Pan in Hellas. You will hear his wild fluting in many strange places when you know how to listen. When one has seen him the rest comes soon. And then you will follow."

"Not away from you, Vanna."

"From the marriage feast, from the Table of the Lord," she said, smiling strangely. "The man who wrote that spoke of another call, but it is the same - Krishna or Christ. When we hear the music we follow. And we may lose or gain heaven."

It might have been her compelling personality - it might have been the marvels of beauty about me, but I knew well I had entered at some mystic gate. A pass word had been spoken for me - I was vouched for and might go in. Only a little way as yet. Enchanted forests lay beyond, and perilous seas, but there were hints, breaths like the wafting of the garments of unspeakable Presences. My talk with Vanna grew less personal, and more introspective. I felt the touch of her finger-tips leading me along the ways of Quiet - my feet brushed a shining dew. Once, in the twilight under the chenar trees, I saw a white gleaming and thought it a swiftly passing Being, but when in haste I gained the tree I found there only a Ninefold flower, white as a spirit in the evening calm. I would not gather it but told Vanna what I had seen.

"You nearly saw;' she said. "She passed so quickly. It was the Snowy One, Uma, Parvati, the Daughter of the Himalaya. That mountain is the mountain of her lord - Shiva. It is natural she should be here. I saw her last night lean over the height - her face pillowed on her folded arms, with a low star in the mists of her hair. Her eyes were like lakes of blue darkness. Vast and wonderful. She is the Mystic Mother of India. You will see soon. You could not have seen the flower until now."

"Do you know," she added, "that in the mountains there are poppies of clear blue - blue as turquoise. We will go up into the heights and find them."

And next moment she was planning the camping details, the men, the ponies, with a practical zest that seemed to relegate the occult to the absurd. Yet the very next day came a wonderful moment.

The sun was just setting and, as it were, suddenly the purple glooms banked up heavy with thunder. The sky was black with fury, the earth passive with dread.

I never saw such lightning - it was continuous and tore in zigzag flashes down the mountains like rents in the substance of the world's fabric. And the thunder roared up in the mountain gorges with shattering echoes. Then fell the rain, and the whole lake seemed to rise to meet it, and the noise was like the rattle of musketry. We were standing by the cabin window and she suddenly caught my hand, and I saw in a light of their own two dancing figures on the tormented water before us. Wild in the tumult, embodied delight, with arms tossed violently above their heads, and feet flung up behind them, skimming the waves like seagulls, they passed. Their sex I could not tell - I think they had none, but were bubble emanations of the rejoicing rush of the rain and the wild retreating laughter of the thunder. I saw the fierce aerial faces and their inhuman glee as they fled by, and she dropped my hand and they were gone. Slowly the storm lessened, and in the west the clouds tore raggedly asunder and a flood of livid yellow light poured down upon the lake - an awful light that struck it into an abyss of fire. Then, as if at a word of command, two glorious rainbows sprang across the water with the mountains for their piers, each with its proper colours chorded. They made a Bridge of Dread that stood out radiant against the background of storm - the Twilight of the Gods, and the doomed gods marching forth to the last fight. And the thunder growled sullenly away into the recesses of the hill and the terrible rainbows faded until the stars came quietly out and it was a still night.

But I had seen that what is our dread is the joy of the spirits of the Mighty Mother, and though the vision faded and I doubted what I had seen, it prepared the way for what I was yet to see. A few days later we started on what was to be the most exquisite memory of my life. A train of ponies carried our tents and camping necessaries and there was a pony for each of us. And so, in the cool grey of a divine morning, with little rosy clouds flecking the eastern sky, we set out from Islamabad for Vernag. And this was the order of our going. She and I led the way, attended by a sais (groom) and a coolie carrying the luncheon basket. Half way we would stop in some green dell, or by some rushing stream, and there rest and eat our little meal while the rest of the cavalcade passed on to the appointed camping place, and in the late afternoon we would follow, riding slowly, and find the tents pitched and the kitchen department in full swing. If the place pleased us we lingered for some days; - if not, the camp was struck next morning, and again we wandered in search of beauty.

The people were no inconsiderable part of my joy. I cannot see what they have to gain from such civilization as ours - a kindly people and happy. Courtesy and friendliness met us everywhere, and if their labor was hard, their harvest of beauty and laughter seemed to be its reward. The little villages with their groves of walnut and fruit trees spoke of no unfulfilled want, the mulberries which fatten the sleek bears in their season fattened the children too. I compared their lot with that of the toilers in our cities and knew which I would choose. We rode by shimmering fields of barley, with red poppies floating in the clear transparent green as in deep sea water, through fields of millet like the sky fallen on the earth, so innocently blue were its blossoms, and the trees above us were trellised with the wild roses, golden and crimson, and the ways tapestried with the scented stars of the large white jasmine.

It was strange that later much of what she said, escaped me. Some I noted down at the time, but there were hints, shadows of lovelier things beyond that eluded all but the fringes of memory when I tried to piece them together and make a coherence of a living wonder. For that reason, the best things cannot be told in this history. It is only the cruder, grosser matters that words will hold. The half-touchings -vanishing looks, breaths - O God, I know them, but cannot tell.

In the smaller villages, the head man came often to greet us and make us welcome, bearing on a flat dish a little offering of cakes and fruit, the produce of the place. One evening a man so approached, stately in white robes and turban, attended by a little lad who carried the patriarchal gift beside him. Our tents were pitched under a glorious walnut tree with a run- ning stream at our feet.

Vanna of course, was the interpreter, and I called her from her tent as the man stood salaaming before me. It was strange that when she came, dressed in white, he stopped in his salutation, and gazed at her in what, I thought, was silent wonder.

She spoke earnestly to him, standing before him with clasped hands, almost, I could think, in the attitude of a suppliant. The man listened gravely, with only an interjection, now and again, and once he turned and looked curiously at me. Then he spoke, evidently making some announcement which she received with bowed head - and when he turned to go with a grave salute, she performed a very singular ceremony, moving slowly round him three times with clasped hands; keeping him always on the right. He repaid it with the usual salaam and greeting of peace, which he bestowed also on me, and then departed in deep meditation, his eyes fixed on the ground. I ventured to ask what it all meant, and she looked thoughtfully at me before replying.

"It was a strange thing. I fear you will not altogether understand, but I will tell you what I can. That man though living here among Mahomedans, is a Brahman from Benares, and, what is very rare in India, a Buddhist. And when he saw me he believed he remembered me in a former birth. The ceremony you saw me perform is one of honour in India. It was his due."

"Did you remember him?" I knew my voice was incredulous.

"Very well. He has changed little but is further on the upward path. I saw him with dread for he holds the memory of a great wrong I did. Yet he told me a thing that has filled my heart with joy."

"Vanna-what is it?"

She had a clear uplifted look which startled me. There was suddenly a chill air blowing between us.

"I must not tell you yet but you will know soon. He was a good man. I am glad we have met."

She buried herself in writing in a small book I had noticed and longed to look into, and no more was said.

We struck camp next day and trekked on towards Vernag - a rough march, but one of great beauty, beneath the shade of forest trees, garlanded with pale roses that climbed from bough to bough and tossed triumphant wreaths into the uppermost blue.

In the afternoon thunder was flapping its wings far off in the mountains and a little rain fell while we were lunching under a big tree. I was considering anxiously how to shelter Vanna, when a farmer invited us to his house - a scene of Biblical hospitality that delighted us both. He led us up some break-neck little stairs to a large bare room, open to the clean air all round the roof, and with a kind of rough enclosure on the wooden floor where the family slept at night. There he opened our basket, and then, with anxious care, hung clothes and rough draperies about us that our meal might be unwatched by one or two friends who had followed us in with breathless interest. Still further to entertain us a great rarity was brought out and laid at Vanna's feet as something we might like to watch - a curious bird in a cage, with brightly barred wings and a singular cry. She fed it with fruit, and it fluttered to her hand. Just so Abraham might have welcomed his guests, and when we left with words of deepest gratitude, our host made the beautiful obeisance of touching his forehead with joined hands as he bowed. To me the whole incident had an extraordinary grace, and ennobled both host and guest. But we met an ascending scale of loveliness so varied in its aspects that I passed from one emotion to another and knew no sameness.

That afternoon the camp was pitched at the foot of a mighty hill, under the waving pyramids of the chenars, sweeping their green like the robes of a goddess. Near by was a half circle of low arches falling into ruin, and as we went in among them I beheld a wondrous sight - the huge octagonal tank or basin made by the Mogul Emperor Jehangir to receive the waters of a mighty Spring which wells from the hill and has been held sacred by Hindu and Moslem. And if loveliness can sanctify surely it is sacred indeed.

The tank was more than a hundred feet in diameter and circled by a roughly paved pathway where the little arched cells open that the devotees may sit and contemplate the lustral waters. There on a black stone, is sculptured the Imperial inscription comparing this spring to the holier wells of Paradise, and I thought no less of it, for it rushes straight from the rock with no aiding stream, and its waters are fifty feet deep, and sweep away from this great basin through beautiful low arches in a wild foaming river - the crystal life-blood of the mountains for ever welling away. The colour and perfect purity of this living jewel were most marvellous -clear blue-green like a chalcedony, but changing as the lights in an opal - a wonderful quivering brilliance, flickering with the silver of shoals of sacred fish.

But the Mogul Empire is with the snows of yesteryear and the wonder has passed from the Moslems into the keeping of the Hindus once more, and the Lingam of Shiva, crowned with flowers, is the symbol in the little shrine by the entrance. Surely in India, the gods are one and have no jealousies among them - so swiftly do their glories merge the one into the other.

"How all the Mogul Emperors loved running water," said Vanna. "I can see them leaning over it in their carved pavilions with delicate dark faces and pensive eyes beneath their turbans, lost in the endless reverie of the East while liquid melody passes into their dream. It was the music they best loved."

She was leading me into the royal garden below, where the young river flows beneath the pavilion set above and across the rush of the water.

"I remember before I came to India," she went on, "there were certain words and phrases that meant the whole East to me. It was an enchantment. The. first flash picture I had was Milton's-

'Dark faces with white silken turbans wreathed.'

and it still is. I have thought ever since that every man should wear a turban. It dignifies the un-comeliest and it is quite curious to see how many inches a man descends in the scale of beauty the moment he takes it off and you see only the skull-cap about which they wind it. They wind it with wonderful skill too. I have seen a man take eighteen yards of muslin and throw it round his head with a few turns, and in five or six minutes the beautiful folds were all in order and he looked like a king. Some of the Gujars here wear black ones and they are very effective and worth painting - the black folds and the sullen tempestuous black brows underneath."

We sat in the pavilion for awhile looking down on the rushing water, and she spoke of Akbar, the greatest of the Moguls, and spoke with a curious personal touch, as I thought.

"I wish you would try to write a story of him - one on more human lines than has been done yet. No one has accounted for the passionate quest of truth that was the real secret of his life. Strange in an Oriental despot if you think of it! It really can only be understood from the Buddhist belief, which curiously seems to have been the only one he neglected, that a mysterious Karma influenced all his thoughts. If I tell you as a key-note for your story, that in a past life he had been a Buddhist priest - one who had fallen away, would that in any way account to you for attempts to recover the lost way? Try to think that out, and to write the story, not as a Western mind sees it, but pure East."

"That would be a great book to write if one could catch the voices of the past. But how to do it?"

"I will give you one day a little book that may help you. The other story I wish you would write is the story of a Dancer of Peshawar. There is a connection between the two - a story of ruin and repentance."

"Will you tell it to me?"

"A part. In this same book you will find much more, hut not all. All cannot be told. You must imagine much. But I think your imagination will be true."

"Why do you think so?"

"Because in these few days you have learnt so much. You have seen the Nine-fold Flower, and the rain spirits. You will soon hear the Flute of Krishna which none can hear who cannot dream true."

That night I heard it. I waked, suddenly, to music, and standing in the door of my tent, in the dead silence of the night, lit only by a few low stars, I heard the poignant notes of a flute. If it had called my name it could not have summoned me more clearly, and I followed without a thought of delay, forgetting even Vanna in the strange urgency that filled me. The music was elusive, seeming to come first from one side, then from the other, but finally I tracked it as a bee does a flower by the scent, to the gate of the royal garden - the pleasure place of the dead Emperors.

The gate stood ajar - strange! for I had seen the custodian close it that evening. Now it stood wide and I went in, walking noiselessly over the dewy grass. I knew and could not tell how, that I must be noiseless. Passing as if I were guided, down the course of the strong young river, I came to the pavilion that spanned it - the place where we had stood that afternoon - and there to my profound amazement, I saw Vanna, leaning against a slight wooden pillar. As if she had expected me, she laid one finger on her lip, and stretching out her hand, took mine and drew me beside her as a mother might a child. And instantly I saw!

On the further bank a young man in a strange diadem or miter of jewels, bare-breasted and beautiful, stood among the flowering oleanders, one foot lightly crossed over the other as he stood. He was like an image of pale radiant gold, and I could have sworn that the light came from within rather than fell upon him, for the night was very dark. He held the flute to his lips, and as I looked, I became aware that the noise of the rushing water was tapering off into a murmur scarcely louder than that of a summer bee in the heart of a rose. Therefore the music rose like a fountain of crystal drops, cold, clear, and of an entrancing sweetness, and the face above it was such that I had no power to turn my eyes away. How shall I say what it was? All I had ever desired, dreamed, hoped, prayed, looked at me from the remote beauty of the eyes and with the most persuasive gentleness entreated me, rather than commanded to follow fearlessly and win. But these are words, and words shaped in the rough mould of thought cannot convey the deep desire that would have hurled me to his feet if Vanna had not held me with a firm restraining hand. Looking up in adoring love to the dark face was a ring of woodland creatures. I thought I could distinguish the white clouded robe of a snow- leopard, the soft clumsiness of a young bear, and many more, but these shifted and blurred like dream creatures - I could not be sure of them nor define their numbers. The eyes of the Player looked down upon their passionate delight with careless kindness.

Dim images passed through my mind. Orpheus - No, this was no Greek. Pan- yet again, No. Where were the pipes, the goat hoofs? The young Dionysos - No, there were strange jewels instead of his vines. And then Vanna's voice said as if from a great distance;

"Krishna - the Beloved." And I said aloud, "I see!" And even as I said it the whole picture blurred together like a dream, and I was alone in the pavilion and the water was foaming past me. Had I walked in my sleep, I thought, as I made my way hack? As I gained the garden gate, before me, like a snowflake, I saw the Ninefold Flower.

When I told her next day, speaking of it as a dream, she said simply; "They have opened the door to you. You will not need me soon.

"I shall always need you. You have taught me everything. I could see nothing last night until you took my hand."

"I was not there," she said smiling. "It was only the thought of me, and you can have that when I am very far away. I was sleeping in my tent. What you called in me then you can always call, even if I am - dead."

"That is a word which is beginning to have no meaning for me. You have said things to me - no, thought them, that have made me doubt if there is room in the universe for the thing we have called death."

She smiled her sweet wise smile.

"Where we are death is not. Where death is we are not. But you will understand better soon."

Our march curving took us by the Mogul gardens of Achibal, and the glorious ruins of the great Temple at Martund, and so down to Bawan with its crystal waters and that loveliest camping ground beside them. A mighty grove of chenar trees, so huge that I felt as if we were in a great sea cave where the air is dyed with the deep shadowy green of the inmost ocean, and the murmuring of the myriad leaves was like a sea at rest. I looked up into the noble height and my memory of Westminster dwindled, for this led on and up to the infinite blue, and at night the stars hung like fruit upon the branches. The water ran with a great joyous rush of release from the mountain behind, but was first received in a broad basin full of sacred fish and reflecting a little temple of Maheshwara and one of Surya the Sun. Here in this basin the water lay pure and still as an ecstasy, and beside it was musing the young Brahman priest who served the temple. Since I had joined Vanna I had begun with her help to study a little Hindustani, and with an aptitude for language could understand here and there. I caught a word or two as she spoke with him that startled me, when the high-bred ascetic face turned serenely upon her, and he addressed her as "My sister," adding a sentence beyond my learning, but which she willingly translated later. - "May He who sits above the Mysteries, have mercy upon thy rebirth."

She said afterwards;

"How beautiful some of these men are. It seems a different type of beauty from ours, nearer to nature and the old gods. Look at that priest - the tall figure, the clear olive skin, the dark level brows, the long lashes that make a soft gloom about the eyes - eyes that have the fathomless depth of a deer's, the proud arch of the lip. I think there is no country where aristocracy is more clearly marked than in India. The Brahmans are aristocrats of the world. You see it is a religious aristocracy as well. It has everything that can foster pride and exclusiveness. They spring from the Mouth of Deity. They are His word incarnate. Not many kings are of the Brahman caste, and the Brahmans look down upon them from Sovereign heights. I have known men who would not eat with their own rulers who would have drunk the water that washed the Brahmans' feet."

She took me that day, the Brahman with us, to see a cave in the mountain. We climbed up the face of the cliff to where a little tree grew on a ledge, and the black mouth yawned. We went in and often it was so low we had to stoop, leaving the sunlight behind until it was like a dim eye glimmering in the velvet blackness. The air was dank and cold and presently obscene with the smell of bats, and alive with their wings, as they came sweeping about us, gibbering and squeaking. I thought of the rush of the ghosts, blown like dead leaves in the Odyssey. And then a small rock chamber branched off, and in this, lit by a bit of burning wood, we saw the bones of a holy man who lived and died there four hundred years ago. Think of it! He lived there always, with the slow dropping of water from the dead weight of the mountain above his head, drop by drop tolling the minutes away: the little groping feet through the cave that would bring him food and drink, hurrying into the warmth and sunlight again, and his only companion the sacred Lingam which means the Creative Energy that sets the worlds dancing for joy round the sun - that, and the black solitude to sit down beside him. Surely his bones can hardly be dryer and colder now than they were then! There must be strange ecstasies in such a life - wild visions in the dark, or it could never be endured.

And so, in marches of about ten miles a day, we came to Pahlgam on the banks of the dancing Lidar. There was now only three weeks left of the time she had promised. After a few days at Pahlgam the march would turn and bend its way back to Srinagar, and to - what? I could not believe it was to separation - in her lovely kindness she had grown so close to me that, even for the sake of friendship, I believed our paths must run together to the end, and there were moments when I could still half convince myself that I had grown as necessary to her as she was to me. No - not as necessary, for she was life and soul to me, but a part of her daily experience that she valued and would not easily part with. That evening we were sitting outside the tents, near the camp fire, of pine logs and cones, the leaping flames making the night beautiful with gold and leaping sparks, in an attempt to reach the mellow splendours of the moon. The men, in various attitudes of rest, were lying about, and one had been telling a story which had just ended in excitement and loud applause.

"These are Mahomedans," said Vanna, "and it is only a story of love and fighting like the Arabian Nights. If they had been Hindus, it might well have been of Krishna or of Rama and Sita. Their faith comes from an earlier time and they still see visions. The Moslem is a hard practical faith for men - men of the world too. It is not visionary now, though it once had its great mysteries."

"I wish you would tell me what you think of the visions or apparitions of the gods that are seen here. Is it all illusion? Tell me your thought."

"How difficult that is to answer. I suppose if love and faith are strong enough they will always create the vibrations to which the greater vibrations respond, and so make God in their own image at any time or place. But that they call up what is the truest reality I have never doubted. There is no shadow without a substance. The substance is beyond us but under certain conditions the shadow is projected and we see it.

"Have I seen or has it been dream?"

"I cannot tell. It may have been the impress of my mind on yours, for I see such things always. You say I took your hand?"

"Take it now."

She obeyed, and instantly, as I felt the firm cool clasp, I heard the rain of music through the pines - the Flute Player was passing. She dropped it smiling and the sweet sound ceased.

"You see! How can I tell what you have seen? You will know better when I am gone. You will stand alone then."

"You will not go - you cannot. I have seen how you have loved all this wonderful time. I believe it has been as dear to you as to me. And every day I have loved you more. I depend upon you for everything that makes life worth living. You could not - you who are so gentle - you could not commit the senseless cruelty of leaving me when you have taught me to love you with every beat of my heart. I have been patient - I have held myself in, but I must speak now. Marry me, and teach me. I know nothing. You know all I need to know. For pity's sake be my wife."

I had not meant to say it; it broke from me in the firelight moonlight with a power that I could not stay. She looked at me with a disarming gentleness.

"Is this fair? Do you remember how at Peshawar I told you I thought it was a dangerous experiment, and that it would make things harder for you. But you took the risk like a brave man because you felt there were things to be gained - knowledge, insight, beauty. Have you not gained them?"

"Yes. Absolutely."

"Then, is it all loss if I go?"

"Not all. But loss I dare not face."

"I will tell you this. I could not stay if I would. Do you remember the old man on the way to Vernag? He told me that I must very soon take up an entirely new life. I have no choice, though if I had I would still do it."

There was silence and down a long arcade, without any touch of her hand I heard the music, receding with exquisite modulations to a very great distance, and between the pillared stems, I saw a faint light.

"Do you wish to go?"

"Entirely. But I shall not forget you, Stephen. I will tell you something. For me, since I came to India, the gate that shuts us out at birth has opened. How shall I explain? Do you remember Kipling's 'Finest Story in the World'?"

"Yes. Fiction!"

"Not fiction - true, whether he knew it or no. But for me the door has opened wide. First, I remembered piecemeal, with wide gaps, then more connectedly. Then, at the end of the first year, I met one day at Cawnpore, an ascetic, an old man of great beauty and wisdom, and he was able by his own knowledge to enlighten mine. Not wholly - much has come since then. Has come, some of it in ways you could not understand now, but much by direct sight and hearing. Long, long ago I lived in Peshawar, and my story was a sorrowful one. I will tell you a little before I go."

"I hold you to your promise. What is there I cannot believe when you tell me? But does that life put you altogether away from me? Was there no place for me in any of your memories that has drawn us together now? Give me a little hope that in the eternal pilgrimage there is some bond between us and some rebirth where we may met again."

"I will tell you that also before we part. I have grown to believe that you do love me - and therefore love something which is infinitely above me."

"And do you love me at all? Am I nothing, Vanna - Vanna?"

"My friend," she said, and laid her hand on mine.

A silence, and then she spoke, very low.

"You must be prepared for very great change, Stephen, and yet believe that it does not really change things at all. See how even the gods pass and do not change! The early gods of India are gone and Shiva, Vishnu, Krishna have taken their places and are one and the same. The old Buddhist stories say that in heaven "The flowers of the garland the God wore are withered, his robes of majesty are waxed old and faded; he falls from his high estate, and is re-born into a new life." But he lives still in the young God who is born among men. The gods cannot die, nor can we nor anything that has life. Now I must go in.

I sat long in the moonlight thinking. The whole camp was sunk in sleep and the young dawn was waking upon the peaks when I turned in.

The days that were left we spent in wandering up the Lidar River to the hills that are the first ramp of the ascent to the great heights. We found the damp corners where the mushrooms grow like pearls - the mushrooms of which she said - "To me they have always been fairy things. To see them in the silver-grey dew of the early mornings - mysteriously there like the manna in the desert - they are elfin plunder, and as a child I was half afraid of them. No wonder they are the darlings of folklore, especially in Celtic countries where the Little People move in the starlight. Strange to think they are here too among strange gods!"

We climbed to where the wild peonies bloom in glory that few eyes see, and the rosy beds of wild sweet strawberries ripen. Every hour brought with it some new delight, some exquisiteness of sight or of words that I shall remember for ever. She sat one day on a rock, holding the sculptured leaves and massive seed-vessels of some glorious plant that the Kashmiris believe has magic virtues hidden in the seeds of pure rose embedded in the white down.

"If you fast for three days and eat nine of these in the Night of No Moon, you can rise on the air light as thistledown and stand on the peak of Haramoukh. And on Haramoukh, as you know it is believed, the gods dwell. There was a man here who tried this enchantment. He was a changed man for ever after, wandering and muttering to himself and avoiding all human intercourse as far as he could. He was no Kashmiri - A Jat from the Punjab, and they showed him to me when I was here with the Meryons, and told me he would speak to none. But I knew he would speak to me, and he did."

"Did he tell you anything of what he had seen in the high world up yonder?"

"He said he had seen the Dream of the God. I could not get more than that. But there are many people here who believe that the Universe as we know it is but an image in the dream of Ishvara, the Universal Spirit - in whom are all the gods - and that when He ceases to dream we pass again into the Night of Brahm, and all is darkness until the Spirit of God moves again on the face of the waters. There are few temples to Brahm. He is above and beyond all direct worship."

"Do you think he had seen anything?"

"What do I know? Will you eat the seeds? The Night of No Moon will soon be here."

She held out the seed-vessels, laughing. I write that down but how record the lovely light of kindliness in her eyes - the almost submissive gentleness that yet was a defense stronger than steel. I never knew - how should I? - whether she was sitting by my side or heavens away from me in her own strange world. But always she was a sweetness that I could not reach, a cup of nectar that I might not drink, unalterably her own and never mine, and yet - my friend.

She showed me the wild track up into the mountains where the Pilgrims go to pay their devotions at the Great God's shrine in the awful heights, regretting that we were too early for that most wonderful sight. Above where we were sitting the river fell in a tormented white cascade, crashing and feathering into spray-dust of diamonds. An eagle was flying above it with a mighty spread of wings that seemed almost double-jointed in the middle - they curved and flapped so wide and free. The fierce head was outstretched with the rake of a plundering galley as he swept down the wind, seeking his meat from God, and passed majestic from our sight. The valley beneath us was littered with enormous boulders spilt from the ancient hollows of the hills. It must have been a great sight when the giants set them trundling down in work or play! - I said this to Vanna, who was looking down upon it with meditative eyes. She roused herself.

"Yes, this really is Giant-Land up here - everything is so huge. And when they quarrel up in the heights - in Jotunheim - and the black storms come down the valleys it is like colossal laughter or clumsy boisterous anger. And the Frost giants are still at work up there with their great axes of frost and rain. They fling down the side of a mountain or make fresh ways for the rivers. About sixty years ago - far above here - they tore down a mountain side and damned up the mighty Indus, so that for months he was a lake, shut back in the hills. But the river giants are no less strong up here in the heights of the world, and lie lay brooding and hiding his time. And then one awful day he tore the barrier down and roared down the valley carrying death and ruin with him, and swept away a whole Sikh army among other unconsidered trifles. That must have been a soul-shaking sight."

She spoke on, and as she spoke I saw. What are her words as I record them? Stray dead leaves pressed in a book - the life and grace dead. Yet I record, for she taught me what I believe the world should learn, that the Buddhist philosophers are right when they teach that all forms of what we call matter are really but aggregates of spiritual units, and that life itself is a curtain hiding reality as the vast veil of day conceals from our sight the countless orbs of space. So that the purified mind even while prisoned in the body, may enter into union with the Real and, according to attainment, see it as it is.

She was an interpreter because she believed this truth profoundly. She saw the spiritual essence beneath the lovely illusion of matter, and the air about her was radiant with the motion of strange forces for which the dull world has many names aiming indeed at the truth, but falling - O how far short of her calm perception! She was indeed of a Household higher than the Household of Faith. She had received enlightenment. She beheld with open eyes.

Next day our camp was struck and we turned our faces again to Srinagar and to the day of parting. I set down but one strange incident of our journey, of which I did not speak even to her.

We were camping at Bijbehara, awaiting our house boat, and the site was by the Maharaja's lodge above the little town. It was midnight and I was sleepless - the shadow of the near future was upon me. I wandered down to the lovely old wooded bridge across the Jhelum, where the strong young trees grow up from the piles. Beyond it the moon was shining on the ancient Hindu remains close to the new temple, and as I stood on the bridge I could see the figure of a man in deepest meditation by the ruins. He was no European. I saw the straight dignified folds of the robes. But it was not surprising he should be there and I should have thought no more of it, had I not heard at that instant from the further side of the river the music of the Flute. I cannot hope to describe that music to any who have not heard it. Suffice it to say that where it calls he who hears must follow whether in the body or the spirit. Nor can I now tell in which I followed. One day it will call me across the River of Death, and I shall ford it or sink in the immeasurable depths and either will be well.

But immediately I was at the other side of the river, standing by the stone Bull of Shiva where he kneels before the Symbol, and looking steadfastly upon me a few paces away was a man in the dress of a Buddhist monk. He wore the yellow robe that leaves one shoulder bare; his head was bare also and he held in one hand a small bowl like a stemless chalice. I knew I was seeing a very strange inexplicable sight - one that in Kashmir should be incredible, but I put wonder aside for I knew now that I was moving in the sphere where the incredible may well be the actual. His expression was of the most unbroken calm. If I compare it to the passionless gaze of the Sphinx I misrepresent, for the Riddle of the Sphinx still awaits solution, but in this face was a noble acquiescence and a content that had it vibrated must have passed into joy.

Words or their equivalent passed between us. I felt his voice.

"You have heard the music of the Flute?"

"I have heard."

"What has it given?"

"A consuming longing."

"It is the music of the Eternal. The creeds and the faiths are the words that men have set to that melody. Listening, it will lead you to Wisdom. Day by day you will interpret more surely."

"I cannot stand alone."

"You will not need. What has led you will lead you still. Through many births it has led you. How should it fail?"

"What should I do?"

"Go forward."

"What should I shun?"

"Sorrow and fear."

"What should I seek?"

"Joy."

"And the end?"

"Joy. Wisdom. They are the Light and Dark of the Divine." A cold breeze passed and touched my forehead. I was still standing in the middle of the bridge above the water gliding to the Ocean, and there was no figure by the Bull of Shiva. I was alone. I passed back to the tents with the shudder that is not fear but akin to death upon me. I knew I had been profoundly withdrawn from what we call actual life, and the return is dread.

The days passed as we floated down the river to Srinagar. On board the Kedarnath, now lying in our first berth beneath the chenars near and yet far from the city, the last night had come. Next morning I should begin the long ride to Baramula and beyond that barrier of the Happy Valley down to Murree and the Punjab. Where afterwards? I neither knew nor cared. My lesson was before me to be learned. I must try to detach myself from all I had prized - to say to my heart it was but a loan and no gift, and to cling only to the imperishable. And did I as yet certainly know more than the A B C of the hard doctrine by which I must live? "Que vivre est difficile, 0 mon cocur fatigue!" - an immense weariness possessed me - a passive grief.

Vanna would follow later with the wife of an Indian doctor. I believed she was bound for Lahore but on that point she had not spoken certainly and I felt we should not meet again.

And now my packing was finished, and, as far as my possessions went, the little cabin had the soulless emptiness that comes with departure. I was enduring as best I could. If she had held loyally to her pact, could I do less. Was she to blame for my wild hope that in the end she would relent and step down to the household levels of love?

She sat by the window - the last time I should see the moonlit banks and her clear face against them. I made and won my fight for the courage of words.

"And now I've finished everything - thank goodness! and we can talk. Vanna - you will write to me?"

"Once. I promise that."

"Only once? Why? I counted on your words."

"I want to speak to you of something else now. I want to tell you a memory. But look first at the pale light behind the Takht-i-Suliman."

So I had seen it with her. So I should not see it again. We watched until a line of silver sparkled on the black water, and then she spoke again.

"Stephen, do you remember in the ruined monastery near Peshawar, how I told you of the young Abbot, who came down to Peshawar with a Chinese pilgrim? And he never returned."

"I remember. There was a Dancer."

"There was a Dancer. She was Lilavanti, and she was brought there to trap him but when she saw him she loved him, and that was his ruin and hers. Trickery he would have known and escaped. Love caught him in an unbreakable net, and they fled down the Punjab and no one knew any more. But I know. For two years they lived together and she saw the agony in his heart - the anguish of his broken vows, the face of the Blessed One receding into an infinite distance. She knew that every day added a link to the heavy Karma that was bound about the feet she loved, and her soul said "Set him free," and her heart refused the torture. But her soul was the stronger. She set him free."

"How?"

"She took poison. He became an ascetic in the hills and died in peace but with a long expiation upon him."

"And she?"

"I am she."

"You!" I heard my voice as if it were another man's. Was it possible that I - a man of the twentieth century, believed this impossible thing? Impossible, and yet - what had I learnt if not the unity of Time, the illusion of matter? What is the twentieth century, what the first? Do they not lie before the Supreme as one, and clean from our petty divisions? And I myself had seen what, if I could trust it, asserted the marvels that are no marvels to those who know.

"You loved him?"

"I love him."

"Then there is nothing at all for me."

She resumed as if she had heard nothing.

"I have lost him for many lives. He stepped above me at once, for he was clean gold though he fell, and though I have followed I have not found. But that Buddhist beyond Islamabad - you shall hear now what he said. It was this. 'The shut door opens, and this time he awaits.' I cannot yet say all it means, but there is no Lahore for me. I shall meet him soon."

"Vanna, you would not harm yourself again?"

"Never. I should not meet him. But you will see. Now I can talk no more. I will be there tomorrow when you go, and I will ride with you to the poplar road."

She passed like a shadow into her little dark cabin, and I was left alone. I will not dwell on that black loneliness of the spirit, for it has passed - it was the darkness of hell, a madness of jealousy, and could have no enduring life in any heart that had known her. But it was death while it lasted. I had moments of horrible belief, of horrible disbelief, but however it might be I knew that she was out of reach for ever. Near me - yes! but only as the silver image of the moon floated in the water by the boat, with the moon herself cold myriads of miles away. I will say no more of that last eclipse of what she had wrought in me.

The bright morning came, sunny as if my joys were beginning instead of ending. Vanna mounted her horse and led the way from the boat. I cast one long look at the little Kedarnath, the home of those perfect weeks, of such joy and sorrow as would have seemed impossible to me in the chrysalis of my former existence. Little Kahdra stood crying bitterly on the bank - the kindly folk who had served us were gathered saddened and quiet. I set my teeth and followed her.

How dear she looked, how kind, how gentle her appealing eyes, as I drew up beside her. She knew what I felt. She knew that the sight of little Kahdra crying as he said good - bye was the last pull at my sore heart. Still she rode steadily on, and still I followed. Once she spoke.

"Stephen, there was a man in Peshawar, kind and true, who loved that Lilavanti who had no heart for him. And when she died, it was in his arms, as a sister might cling to a brother, for the man she loved had left her. It seems that will not be in this life, but do not think I have been so blind that I did not know my friend."

I could not answer - it was the realization of the utmost I could hope and it came like healing to my spirit. Better that bond between us, slight as most men might think it, than the dearest and closest with a woman not Vanna. It was the first thrill of a new joy in my heart - the first, I thank the Infinite, of many and steadily growing joys and hopes that cannot be uttered here.

I bent to take the hand she stretched to me, but even as they touched, I saw, passing behind the trees by the road, the young man I had seen in the garden at Vernag - most beautiful, in the strange miter of his jewelled diadem. His flute was at his lips and the music rang out sudden and crystal clear as though a woodland god were passing to awaken all the joys of the dawn.

The horses heard too. In an instant hers had swerved wildly, and she lay on the ground at my feet. The music had ceased.

Days had gone before I could recall what had happened then. I lifted her in my arms and carried her into the rest-house near at hand, and the doctor came and looked grave, and a nurse was sent from the Mission Hospital. No doubt all was done that was possible, hut I knew from the first what it meant and how it would be. She lay in a white stillness, and the room was quiet as death. I remembered with unspeakable gratitude later that the nurse had been merciful and had not sent me away.

So Vanna lay all day and through the night, and when the dawn came again she stirred and motioned with her hand, although her eyes were closed. I understood, and kneeling, I put my hand under her head, and rested it against my shoulder. Her faint voice murmured at my ear.

"I dreamed - I was in the pine wood at Pahlgam and it was the Night of No Moon, and I was afraid for it was dark, but suddenly all the trees were covered with little lights like stars, and the greater light was beyond. Nothing to be afraid of."

"Nothing, Beloved."

"And I looked beyond Peshawar, further than eyes could see, and in the ruins of the monastery where we stood, you and I - I saw him, and he lay with his head at the feet of the Blessed One. That is well, is it not?"

"Well, Beloved."

"And it is well I go? Is it not?"

"It is well."

A long silence. The first sun ray touched the floor. Again the whisper.

"Believe what I have told you. For we shall meet again." I repeated-

"We shall meet again."

In my arms she died.

Later, when all was over I asked myself if I believed this and answered with full assurance - Yes.

If the story thus told sounds incredible it was not incredible to me. I had had a profound experience. What is a miracle? It is simply the vision of the Divine behind nature. It will come in different forms according to the eyes that see, but the soul will know that its perception is authentic.

I could not leave Kashmir, nor was there any need. On the contrary I saw that there was work for me here among the people she had loved, and my first aim was to fit myself for that and for the writing I now felt was to be my career in life. After much thought I bought the little Kedarnath and made it my home, very greatly to the satisfaction of little Kahdra and all the friendly people to whom I owed so much.

Vanna's cabin I made my sleeping room, and it is the simple truth that the first night I slept in the place that was a Temple of Peace in my thoughts, I had a dream of wordless bliss, and starting awake for sheer joy I saw her face in the night, human and dear, looking down upon me with that poignant sweetness which would seem to be the utmost revelation of love and pity. And as I stretched my hands, another face dawned solemnly from the shadow beside her with grave brows bent on mine - one I had known and seen in the ruins at Bijbehara. Outside and very near I could hear the silver weaving of the Flute that in India is the symbol of the call of the Divine. A dream - yes, but it taught me to live. At first, in my days of grief and loss, I did but dream - the days were hard to endure. I will not dwell on that illusion of sorrow, now long dead. I lived only for the night.

"When sleep comes to close each difficult day,   When night gives pause to the long watch I keep,   And all my bonds I needs must loose apart,   Must doff my will as raiment laid away-   With the first dream that comes with the first sleep, I run - I run! I am gathered to thy heart!"

To the heart of her pity. Thus for awhile I lived. Slowly I became conscious of her abiding presence about me, day or night It grew clearer, closer.

Like the austere Hippolytus to his unseen Goddess, I could say;

"Who am more to thee than other mortals are,   Whose is the holy lot,   As friend with friend to walk and talk with thee,   Hearing thy sweet mouth's music in mine ear,   But thee beholding not."

That was much, but later, the sunshine was no bar, the bond strengthened and there have been days in the heights of the hills, in the depths of the woods, when I saw her as in life, passing at a distance, but real and lovely. Life? She had never lived as she did now - a spirit, freed and rejoicing. For me the door she had opened would never shut. The Presences were about me, and I entered upon my heritage of joy, knowing that in Kashmir, the holy land of Beauty, they walk very near, and lift up the folds of the Dark that the initiate may see the light behind.

So I began my solitary life of gladness. I wrote, aided by the little book she had left me, full of strangest stories, stranger by far than my own brain could conceive. Some to be revealed - some to be hidden. And thus the world will one day receive the story of the Dancer of Peshawar in her upward lives, that it may know, if it will, that death is nothing - for Life and Love are all.

THE INCOMPARABLE LADY
A STORY OF CHINA WITH A MORAL

It is recorded that when the Pearl Empress (his mother) asked of the philosophic Yellow Emperor which he considered the most beautiful of the Imperial concubines, he replied instantly: "The Lady A-Kuei": and when the Royal Parent in profound astonishment demanded bow this could be, having regard to the exquisite beauties in question, the Emperor replied;

"I have never seen her. It was dark when I entered the Dragon Chamber and dusk of dawn when I rose and left her."

Then said the Pearl Princess;

"Possibly the harmony of her voice solaced the Son of Heaven?"

But he replied;

"She spoke not."

And the Pearl Empress rejoined:

"Her limbs then are doubtless softer than the kingfisher's plumage?"

But the Yellow Emperor replied;

"Doubtless. Yet I have not touched them. I was that night immersed in speculations on the Yin and the Yang. How then should I touch a woman?"

And the Pearl Empress was silent from very great amazement, not daring to question further but marveling how the thing might be. And seeing this, the Yellow Emperor recited a poem to the following effect:

"It is said that Power rules the world   And who shall gainsay it?   But Loveliness is the head-jewel upon the brow of Power."

And when the Empress had listened with reverence to the Imperial Poet, she quitted the August Presence.

Immediately, having entered her own palace of the Tranquil Motherly Virtues, she caused the Lady A-Kuei to be summoned to her presence, who came, habited in a purple robe and with pins of jade and coral in her hair. And the Pearl Empress considered her attentively, recalling the perfect features of the White Jade Concubine, the ambrosial smile of the Princess of Feminine Propriety, and the willow-leaf eyebrows of the Lady of Chen, and her astonishment was excessive, because the Lady A-Kuei could not in beauty approach any one of these ladies. Reflecting further she then placed her behind the screen, and summoned the court artist, Lo Cheng, who had been formerly commissioned to paint the heavenly features of the Emperor's Ladies, mirrored in still water, though he had naturally not been permitted to view the beauties themselves. Of him the Empress demanded:

"Who is the most beautiful - which the most priceless jewel of the dwellers in the Dragon Palace?"

And, with humility, Lo Cheng replied:

"What mortal man shall decide between the white Crane and the Swan, or between the paeony flower and the lotus?" And having thus said he remained silent, and in him was no help. Finally and after exhortation the Pearl Empress condescended to threaten him with the loss of a head so useless to himself and to her majesty. Then, in great fear and haste he replied:

"Of all the flowers that adorn the garden of the Sun of Heaven, the Lady A-Kuei is the fittest to be gathered by the Imperial Hand, and this is my deliberate opinion."

Now, hearing this statement, the Pearl Empress was submerged in bewilderment, knowing that the Lady A-Kuei had modestly retired when the artist had depicted the reflection of the assembled loveliness of the Inner Chambers, as not counting herself worthy of portraiture, and her features were therefore unknown to him. Nor could the Empress further question the artist, for when she had done so, he replied only:

"This is the secret of the Son of Heaven," and, having gained permission, he swiftly departed.

Nor could the Lady A-Kuei herself aid her Imperial Majesty, for on being questioned she was overwhelmed with modesty and confusion, and with stammering lips could only repeat:

"This is the secret of his Divine Majesty," imploring with the utmost humility, forgiveness from the Imperial Mother.

The Pearl Empress was unable to eat her supper. In vain were spread before her the delicacies of the Empire. She could but trifle with a shark's fin and a "Silver Ear" fungus and a dish of slugs entrapped upon roses, with the dew-like pearls upon them. Her burning curiosity had wholly deprived her of appetite, nor could the amusing exertions of the Palace mimes, or a lantern fete upon the lake restore her to any composure. "This circumstance will cause my flight on the Dragon (death)," she said to herself, "unless I succeed in unveiling the mystery. What therefore should be my next proceeding?"

And so, deeply reflecting, she caused the Chief of the Eunuchs to summon the Princess of Feminine Propriety, the White Jade Concubine and all the other exalted beauties of the Heavenly Palace.

In due course of time these ladies arrived, paying suitable respect and obeisance to the Mother of his Divine Majesty. They were resplendent in king-fisher ornaments, in jewels of jade, crystal and coral, in robes of silk and gauze, and still more resplendent in charms that not the Celestial Empire itself could equal, setting aside entirely all countries of the foreign barbarians. And in grace and elegance of manners, in skill in the arts of poetry and the lute, what could surpass them?

Like a parterre of flowers they surrounded her Majesty, and awaited her pleasure with perfect decorum, when, having saluted them with affability she thus addressed them - "Lovely ones - ladies distinguished by the particular attention of your sovereign and mine, I have sent for you to resolve a doubt and a difficulty. On questioning our sovereign as to whom he regarded as the loveliest of his garden of beauty he benignantly replied: "The Lady A-Kuei is incomparable," and though this may well be, he further graciously added that he had never seen her. Nor, on pursuing the subject, could I learn the Imperial reason. The artist Lo Cheng follows in his Master's footsteps, he also never having seen the favored lady, and he and she reply to me that this is an Imperial secret. Declare to me therefore if your perspicacity and the feminine interest which every lady property takes in the other can unravel this mystery, for my liver is tormented with anxiety beyond measure."

As soon as the Pearl Empress had spoken she realized that she had committed a great indiscretion. A babel of voices, of cries, questions and contradictions instantly arose. Decorum was abandoned. The Lady of Chen swooned, nor could she be revived for an hour, and the Princess of Feminine Propriety and the White Jade Concubine could be dragged apart only by the united efforts of six of the Palace matrons, so great was their fury the one with the other, each accusing each of encouragement to the Lady A-Kuei's pretensions. So also with the remaining ladies. Shrieks resounded through the Hall of Virtuous Tranquillity, and when the Pearl Empress attempted to pour oil on the troubled waters by speaking soothing and comfortable words, the august Voice was entirely inaudible in the tumult.

All sought at length in united indignation for the Lady A-Kuei, but she had modestly withdrawn to the Pearl Pavilion in the Imperial Garden and, foreseeing anxieties, had there secured herself on hearing the opening of the Royal Speech.

Finally the ladies were led away by their attendants, weeping, lamenting, raging, according to their several dispositions, and the Pearl Empress, left with her own maidens, beheld the floor strewn with jade pins, kingfisher and coral jewels, and even with fragments of silk and gauze. Nor was she any nearer the solution of the desired secret.

That night she tossed upon a bed sleepless though heaped with down, and her mind raged like a fire up and down all possible answers to the riddle, but none would serve. Then, at the dawn, raising herself on one august elbow she called to her venerable nurse and foster mother, the Lady Ma, wise and resourceful in the affairs and difficulties of women, and, repeating the circumstances, demanded her counsel.

The Lady Ma considering the matter long and deeply, slowly replied:

"This is a great riddle and dangerous, for to intermeddle with the divine secrets is the high road to the Yellow Springs (death). But the child of my breasts and my exalted Mistress shall never ask in vain, for a thwarted curiosity is dangerous as a suppressed fever. I will conceal myself nightly in the Dragon Bedchamber and this will certainly unveil the truth. And if I perish I perish."

It is impossible to describe how the Empress heaped Lady Ma with costly jewels and silken brocades and taels of silver beyond measuring - how she placed on her breast the amulet of jade that had guarded herself from all evil influences, how she called the ancestral spirits to witness that she would provide for the Lady Ma's remotest descendants if she lost her life in this sublime devotion to duty.

That night Lady Ma concealed herself behind the Imperial couch in the Dragon

Chamber, to await the coming of the Son of Heaven. Slowly dripped the water-clock as the minutes fled away; sorely ached the venerable limbs of the Lady Ma as she crouched in the shadows and saw the rising moon scattering silver through the elegant traceries of carved ebony and ivory; wildly beat her heart as delicately tripping footsteps approached the Dragon Chamber, and the Princess of Feminine Propriety, attended by her maidens, ascended the Imperial Couch and hastily dismissed them. Yet no sweet repose awaited this favored lady. The Lady Ma could hear her smothered sobs, her muttered exclamations - nay could even feel the couch itself tremble as the Princess uttered the hated name of the Lady A-Kuei, the poison of jealousy running in every vein. It was impossible for Lady Ma to decide which was the most virulent, this, or the poison of curiosity in the heart of the Pearl Empress. Though she loved not the Princess she was compelled to pity such suffering. But all thought was banished by the approach of the Yellow Emperor, prepared for repose and unattended, in simple but divine grandeur.

It cannot indeed be supposed that a Celestial Emperor is human, yet there was mortality in the start which his Augustness gave when the Princess of Feminine Propriety flinging herself from the Dragon couch, threw herself at his feet and with tears that flowed like that river known as "The Sorrow of China," demanded to know what she had done that another should be preferred before her; reciting in frantic haste such imperfections of the Lady A-Kuei's appearance as she could recall (or invent) in the haste of that agitating moment.

"That one of her eyes is larger than the other - no human being can doubt" sobbed the lady -" and surely your Divine Majesty cannot be aware that her hair reaches but to her waist, and that there is a brown mole on the nape of her neck? When she sings it resembles the croak of the crow. It is true that most of the Palace ladies are chosen for anything but beauty, yet she is the most ill-favored. And is it this - this bat-faced lady who is preferred to me! Would I had never been born: Yet even your Majesty's own lips have told me I am fair!"

The Yellow Emperor supported the form of the Princess in his arms. There are moments when even a Son of Heaven is but human. "Fair as the rainbow," he murmured, and the Princess faintly smiled; then gathering the resolution of the Philosopher he added manfully - "But the Lady A-Kuei is incomparable. And the reason is -"

The Lady Ma eagerly stretched her head forward with a hand to either ear. But the Princess of Feminine Propriety with one shriek had swooned and in the hurry of summoning attendants and causing her to be conveyed to her own apartments that precious sentence was never completed.

Still the Lady Ma groveled behind the Dragon Couch as the Son of Heaven, left alone, approached the veranda and apostrophizing the moon, murmured -

"O loveliest pale watcher of the destinies of men, illuminate the beauty of the Lady A-Kuei, and grant that I who have never seen that beauty may never see it, but remain its constant admirer!" So saying, he sought his solitary couch and slept, while the Lady Ma, in a torment of bewilderment, glided from the room.

The matter remained in suspense for several days. The White Jade Concubine was the next lady commanded to the Dragon Chamber, and again the Lady Ma was in her post of observation. Much she heard, much she saw that was not to the point, but the scene ended as before by the dismissal of the lady in tears, and the departure of the Lady Ma in ignorance of the secret.

The Emperor's peace was ended.

The singular circumstance was that the Lady A-Kuei was never summoned by the Yellow Emperor. Eagerly as the Empress watched, no token of affection for her was ever visible. Nothing could be detected. It was inexplicable. Finally, devoured by curiosity that gave her no respite, she resolved on a stratagem that should dispel the mystery, though it carried with it a risk on which she trembled to reflect. It was the afternoon of a languid summer day, and the Yellow Emperor, almost unattended, had come to pay a visit of filial respect to the Pearl Empress. She received him with the ceremony due to her sovereign in the porcelain pavilion of the Eastern Gardens, with the lotos fish ponds before them, and a faint breeze occasionally tinkling the crystal wind-bells that decorated the shrubs on the cloud and dragon-wrought slopes of the marble approach. A bird of brilliant plumage uttered a cry of reverence from its gold cage as the Son of Heaven entered. As was his occasional custom, and after suitable inquiries as to his parent's health, the attendants were all dismissed out of earshot and the Emperor leaned on his cushions and gazed reflectively into the sunshine outside. So had the Court Artist represented him as "The Incarnation of Philosophic Calm."

"These gardens are fair," said the Empress after a respectful silence, moving her fan illustrated with the emblem of Immortality - the Ho Bird.

"Fair indeed," returned the Emperor. - "It might be supposed that all sorrow and disturbance would be shut without the Forbidden Precincts. Yet it is not so. And though the figures of my ladies moving among the flowers appear at this distance instinct with joy, yet -"

He was silent.

"They know not," said the Empress with solemnity "that death entered the Forbidden Precincts but last night. A disembodied spirit has returned to its place and doubtless exists in bliss." "Indeed?" returned the Yellow Emperor with indifference - "yet if the spirit is absorbed into the Source whence it came, and the bones have crumbled into nothingness, where does the Ego exist? The dead are venerable, but no longer of interest."

"Not even when they were loved in life?" said the Empress, caressing the bird in the cage with one jewelled finger, but attentively observing her son from the corner of her august eye. "They were; they are not," he remarked sententiously and stifling a yawn; it was a drowsy afternoon. "But who is it that has abandoned us? Surely not the Lady Ma - your Majesty's faithful foster-mother?"

"A younger, a lovelier spirit has sought the Yellow Springs" replied the trembling Empress. "I regret to inform your Majesty that a sudden convulsion last night deprived the Lady A-Kuei of life. I would not permit the news to reach you lest it should break your august night's rest."

There was a silence, then the Emperor turned his eyes serenely upon his Imperial Mother. "That the statement of my august Parent is merely - let us say - allegoric - does not detract from its interest. But had the Lady A-Kuei in truth departed to the Yellow Springs I should none the less have received the news without uneasiness. What though the sun set - is not the memory of his light all surpassing?"

No longer could the Pearl Empress endure the excess of her curiosity. Deeply kowtowing, imploring pardon, with raised hands and tears which no son dare neglect, she besought the Emperor to enlighten her as to this mystery, recounting his praises of the lady and his admission that he had never beheld her, and all the circumstances connected with this remark- able episode. She omitted only, (from considerations of delicacy and others,) the vigils of the Lady Ma in the Dragon Chamber. The Emperor, sighing, looked upon the ground, and for a time was silent.

Then he replied as follows:

"Willingly would I have kept silence, but what child dare withstand the plea of a parent? Is it necessary to inform the Heavenly Empress that beauty seen is beauty made familiar and that familiarity is the foe of admiration? How is it possible that I should see the Princess of Feminine Propriety, for instance, by night and day without becoming aware of her imperfections as well as her graces? How awake in the night without hearing the snoring of the White Jade Concubine and considering the mouth from which it issues as the less lovely. How partake of the society of any woman without finding her chattering as the crane, avid of admiration, jealous, destructive of philosophy, fatal to composure, fevered with curiosity; a creature, in short, a little above the gibbon, but infinitely below the notice of the sage, save as a temporary measure of amusement in itself unworthy the philosopher. The faces of all my ladies are known to me. All are fair and all alike. But one night, as I lay in the Dragon Couch, lost in speculation, absorbed in contemplation of the Yin and the Yang, the night passed for the solitary dreamer as a dream. In the darkness of the dawn I rose still dreaming, and departed to the Pearl Pavilion in the garden, and there remained an hour viewing the sunrise and experiencing ineffable opinions on the destiny of man. Returning then to a couch which I believed to have been that of the solitary philosopher I observed a depression where another form had lain, and in it a jade hairpin such as is worn by my junior beauties. Petrified with amazement at the display of such reserve, such continence, such august self-restraint, I perceived that, lost in my thoughts, I had had an unimagined companion and that this gentle reminder was from her gentle hand. But whom? I knew not. I then observed Lo Cheng the Court Artist in attendance and immediately despatched him to make secret enquiry and ascertain the name and circumstances of that beauty who, unknown, had shared my vigil. I learnt on his return that it was the Lady A-Kuei. I had entered the Dragon Chamber in a low moonlight, and guessed not her presence. She spoke no word. Finding her Imperial Master thus absorbed, she invited no attention, nor in any way obtruded her beauties upon my notice. Scarcely did she draw breath. Yet reflect upon what she might have done! The night passed and I remained entirely unconscious of her presence, and out of respect she would not sleep but remained reverently and modestly awake, assisting, if it may so be expressed, at a humble distance, in the speculations which held me prisoner. What a pearl was here! On learning these details by Lo Cheng from her own roseate lips, and remembering the unexampled temptation she had resisted (for well she knew that had she touched the Emperor the Philosopher had vanished) I despatched an august rescript to this favored Lady, conferring on her the degree of Incomparable Beauty of the First Rank. On condition of secrecy."

The Pearl Empress, still in deepest bewilderment, besought his majesty to proceed. He did so, with his usual dignity.

"Though my mind could not wholly restrain its admiration, yet secrecy was necessary, for had the facts been known, every lady, from the Princess of Feminine Propriety to the Junior Beauty of the Bed Chamber would henceforward have observed only silence and a frigid decorum in the Dragon Bed Chamber. And though the Emperor be a philosopher, yet a philosopher is still a man, and there are moments when decorum -"

The Emperor paused discreetly; then resumed.

"The world should not be composed entirely of A-Kueis, yet in my mind I behold the Incomparable Lady fair beyond expression. Like the moon she sails glorious in the heavens to be adored only in vision as the one woman who could respect the absorption of the Emperor, and of whose beauty as she lay beside him the philosopher could remain unconscious and therefore untroubled in body. To see her, to find her earthly, would be an experience for which the Emperor might have courage, but the philosopher never. And attached to all this is a moral:"

The Pearl Empress urgently inquired its nature.

"Let the wisdom of my august parent discern it," said the Emperor sententiously.

"And the future?" she inquired.

"The - let us call it parable -" said the Emperor politely -"with which your Majesty was good enough to entertain me, has suggested a precaution to my mind. I see now a lovely form moving among the flowers. It is possible that it may be the Incomparable Lady, or that at any moment I may come upon her and my ideal be shattered. This must be safeguarded. I might command her retirement to her native province, but who shall insure me against the weakness of my own heart demanding her return? No. Let Your Majesty's words spoken - well - in parable, be fulfilled in truth. I shall give orders to the Chief Eunuch that the Incomparable Lady tonight shall drink the Draught of Crushed Pearls, and be thus restored to the sphere that alone is worthy of her. Thus are all anxieties soothed, and the honours offered to her virtuous spirit shall be a glorious repayment of the ideal that will ever illuminate my soul."

The Empress was speechless. She had borne the Emperor in her womb, but the philosopher outsoared her comprehension. She retired, leaving his Majesty in a reverie, endeavoring herself to grasp the moral of which he had spoken, for the guidance of herself and the ladies concerned. But whether it inculcated reserve or the reverse in the Dragon Chamber, and what the Imperial ladies should follow as an example she was, to the end of her life, totally unable to say. Philosophy indeed walks on the heights. We cannot all expect to follow it.

That night the Incomparable Lady drank the Draught of Crushed Pearls.

The Princess of Feminine Propriety and the White Jade Concubine, learning these circumstances, redoubled their charms, their coquetries and their efforts to occupy what may be described as the inner sanctuary of the Emperor's esteem. Both lived to a green old age, wealthy and honored, alike firm in the conviction that if the Incomparable Lady had not shown herself so superior to temptation the Emperor might have been on the whole better pleased, whatever the sufferings of the philosopher. Both lived to be the tyrants of many generations of beauties at the Celestial Court. Both were assiduous in their devotions before the spirit tablet of the departed lady, and in recommending her example of reserve and humility to every damsel whom it might concern.

It will probably occur to the reader of this unique but veracious story that there is more in it than meets the eye, and more than the one moral alluded to by the Emperor according to the point of view of the different actors.

To the discernment of the reader it must accordingly be left.

THE HATRED OF THE QUEEN
A Story of Burma

Most wonderful is the Irawadi, the mighty river of Burma. In all the world elsewhere is no such river, bearing the melted snows from its mysterious sources in the high places of the mountains. The dawn rises upon its league. wide flood; the moon walks upon it with silver feet. It is the pulsing heart of the land, living still though so many rules and rulers have risen and fallen beside it, their pomps and glories drifting like flotsam dawn the river to the eternal ocean that is the end of all - and the beginning. Dead civilizations strew its banks, dreaming in the torrid sunshine of glories that were - of blood-stained gold, jewels wept from woeful crowns, nightmare dreams of murder and terror; dreaming also of heavenly beauty, for the Lord Buddha looks down in moonlight peace upon the land that leaped to kiss His footprints, that has laid its heart in the hand of the Blessed One, and shares therefore in His bliss and content. The Land of the Lord Buddha, where the myriad pagodas lift their golden flames of worship everywhere, and no idlest wind can pass but it ruffles the bells below the htees until they send forth their silver ripple of music to swell the hymn of praise!

There is a little bay on the bank of the flooding river - a silent, deserted place of sand- dunes and small bills. When a ship is in sight, some poor folk come and spread out the red lacquer that helps their scanty subsistence, and the people from the passing ship land and barter and in a few minutes are gone on their busy way and silence settles down once more. They neither know nor care that, near by, a mighty city spread its splendour for miles along the river bank, that the king known as Lord of the Golden Palace, The Golden Foot, Lord of the White Elephant, held his state there with balls of magnificence, obsequious women, fawning courtiers and all the riot and colour of an Eastern tyranny. How should they care? Now there are ruins - ruins, and the cobras slip in and out through the deserted holy places. They breed their writhing young in the sleeping-chambers of queens, the tigers mew in the moonlight, and the giant spider, more terrible than the cobra, strikes with its black poison- claw and, paralyzing the life of the victim, sucks its brain with slow, lascivious pleasure.

Are these foul creatures more dreadful than some of the men, the women, who dwelt in these palaces - the more evil because of the human brain that plotted and foresaw? That is known only to the mysterious Law that in silence watches and decrees.

But this is a story of the dead days of Pagan, by the Irawadi, and it will be shown that, as the Lotus of the Lord Buddha grows up a white splendour from the black mud of the depths, so also may the soul of a woman.

In the days of the Lord of the White Elephant, the King Pagan Men, was a boy named Mindon, son of second Queen and the King. So, at least, it was said in the Golden Palace, but those who knew the secrets of such matters whispered that, when the King had taken her by the hand she came to him no maid, and that the boy was the son of an Indian trader. Furthermore it was said that she herself was woman of the Rajputs, knowledgeable in spells, incantations and elemental spirits such as the Beloos that terribly haunt waste places, and all Powers that move in the dark, and that thus she had won the King. Certainly she had been captured by the King's war-boats off the coast from a trading-ship bound for Ceylon, and it was her story that, because of her beauty, she was sent thither to serve as concubine to the King, Tissa of Ceylon. Being captured, she was brought to the Lord of the Golden Palace. The tongue she spoke was strange to all the fighting men, but it was wondrous to see how swiftly she learnt theirs and spoke it with a sweet ripple such as is in the throat of a bird.

She was beautiful exceedingly, with a colour of pale gold upon her and lengths of silk-spun hair, and eyes like those of a jungle-deer, and water might run beneath the arch of her foot without wetting it, and her breasts were like the cloudy pillows where the sun couches at setting. Now, at Pagan, the name they called her was Dwaymenau, but her true name, known only to herself, was Sundari, and she knew not the Law of the Blessed Buddha but was a heathen accursed. In the strong hollow of her hand she held the heart of the King, so that on the birth of her son she had risen from a mere concubine to be the second Queen and a power to whom all bowed. The First Queen, Maya, languished in her palace, her pale beauty wasting daily, deserted and lonely, for she had been the light of the King's eyes until the coming of the Indian woman, and she loved her lord with a great love and was a noble woman brought up in honour and all things becoming a queen. But sigh as she would, the King came never. All night he lay in the arms of Dwaymenau, all day he sat beside her, whether at the great water pageants or at the festival when the dancing-girls swayed and postured before him in her gilded chambers. Even when be went forth to hunt the tiger, she went with him as far as a woman may go, and then stood back only because he would not risk his jewel, her life. So all that was evil in the man she fostered and all that was good she cherished not at all, fearing lest he should return to the Queen. At her will he had consulted the Hlwot Daw, the Council of the Woon-gyees or Ministers, concerning a divorce of the Queen, but this they told him could not be since she had kept all the laws of Manu, being faithful, noble and beautiful and having borne him a son.

For, before the Indian woman had come to the King, the Queen had borne a son, Ananda, and he was pale and slender and the King despised him because of the wiles of Dwaymenau, saying he was fit only to sit among the women, having the soul of a slave, and he laughed bitterly as the pale child crouched in the corner to see him pass. If his eyes had been clear, he would have known that here was no slave, but a heart as much greater than his own as the spirit is stronger than the body. But this he did not know and he strode past with Dwaymenau's boy on his shoulder, laughing with cruel glee.

And this boy, Mindon, was beautiful and strong as his mother, pale olive of face, with the dark and crafty eyes of the cunning Indian traders, with black hair and a body straight, strong and long in the leg for his years - apt at the beginnings of bow, sword and spear - full of promise, if the promise was only words and looks.

And so matters rested in the palace until Ananda had ten years and Mindon nine.

It was the warm and sunny winter and the days were pleasant, and on a certain day the Queen, Maya, went with her ladies to worship the Blessed One at the Thapinyu Temple, looking down upon the swiftly flowing river. The temple was exceedingly rich and magnificent, so gilded with pure gold-leaf that it appeared of solid gold. And about the upper part were golden bells beneath the jewelled htee, which wafted very sweetly in the wind and gave forth a crystal-clear music. The ladies bore in their hands more gold-leaf, that they might acquire merit by offering this for the service of the Master of the Law, and indeed this temple was the offering of the Queen herself, who, because she bore the name of the Mother of the Lord, excelled in good works and was the Moon of this lower world in charity and piety.

Though wan with grief and anxiety, this Queen was beautiful. Her eyes, like mournful lakes of darkness, were lovely in the pale ivory of her face. Her lips were nobly cut and calm, and by the favour of the Guardian Nats, she was shaped with grace and health, a worthy mother of kings. Also she wore her jewels like a mighty princess, a magnificence to which all the people shikoed as she passed, folding their hands and touching the forehead while they bowed down, kneeling.

Before the colossal image of the Holy One she made her offering and, attended by her women, she sat in meditation, drawing consolation from the Tranquillity above her and the silence of the shrine. This ended, the Queen rose and did obeisance to the Lord and, retiring, paced back beneath the White Canopy and entered the courtyard where the palace stood - a palace of noble teakwood, brown and golden and carved like lace into strange fantasies of spires and pinnacles and branches where Nats and Tree Spirits and Beloos and swaying river maidens mingled and met amid fruits and leaves and flowers in a wild and joyous confusion. The faces, the blowing garments, whirled into points with the swiftness of the dance, were touched with gold, and so glad was the building that it seemed as if a very light wind might whirl it to the sky, and even the sad Queen stopped to rejoice in its beauty as it blossomed in the sunlight.

And even as she paused, her little son Ananda rushed to meet her, pale and panting, and flung himself into her arms with dry sobs like those of an overrun man. She soothed him until he could speak, and then the grief made way in a rain of tears.

"Mindon has killed my deer. He bared his knife, slit his throat and cast him in the ditch and there he lies."

"There will he not lie long!" shouted Mindon, breaking from the palace to the group where all were silent now. "For the worms will eat him and the dogs pick clean his bones, and he will show his horns at his lords no more. If you loved him, White-liver, you should have taught him better manners to his betters.

With a stifled shriek Ananda caught the slender knife from his girdle and flew at Mindon like a cat of the woods. Such things were done daily by young and old, and this was a long sorrow come to a head between the boys.

Suddenly, lifting the hangings of the palace gateway, before them stood the mother of Mindon, the Lady Dwaymenau, pale as wool, having heard the shout of her boy, so that the two Queens faced each other, each holding the shoulders of her son, and the ladies watched, mute as fishes, for it was years since these two had met.

"What have you done to my son?" breathed Maya the Queen, dry in the throat and all but speechless with passion. For indeed his face, for a child, was ghastly.

"Look at his knife! What would he do to my son?" Dwaymenau was stiff with hate and spoke as to a slave.

"He has killed my deer and mocks me because I loved him, He is the devil in this place. Look at the devils in his eyes. Look quick before he smiles, my mother."

And indeed, young as the boy was, an evil thing sat in either eye and glittered upon them. Dwaymenau passed her hand across his brow, and he smiled and they were gone.

"The beast ran at me and would have flung me with his horns," he said, looking up brightly at his mother. "He had the madness upon him. I struck once and he was dead. My father would have done the same.

"That would he not!" said Queen Maya bitterly. "Your father would have crept up, fawning on the deer, and offered him the fruits he loved, stroking him the while. And in trust the beast would have eaten, and the poison in the fruit would have slain him. For the people of your father meet neither man nor beast in fair fight. With a kiss they stab!"

Horror kept the women staring and silent. No one had dreamed that the scandal had reached the Queen. Never had she spoken or looked her knowledge but endured all in patience. Now it sprang out like a sword among them, and they feared for Maya, whom all loved.

Mindon did not understand. It was beyond him, but he saw he was scorned. Dwaymenau, her face rigid as a mask, looked pitilessly at the shaking Queen, and each word dropped from her mouth, hard and cold as the falling of diamonds. She refused the insult.

"If it is thus you speak of our lord and my love, what wonder he forsakes you? Mother of a craven milk runs in your veins and his for blood. Take your slinking brat away and weep together! My son and I go forth to meet the King as he comes from hunting, and to welcome him kingly!" She caught her boy to her with a magnificent gesture; he flung his little arm about her, and laughing loudly they went off together.

The tension relaxed a little when they were out of sight. The women knew that, since Dwaymenau had refused to take the Queen's meaning, she would certainly not carry her complaint to the King. They guessed at her reason for this forbearance, but, be that as it might, it was Certain that no other person would dare to tell him and risk the fate that waits the messenger of evil.

The eldest lady led away the Queen, now almost tottering in the reaction of fear and pain. Oh, that she had controlled her speech! Not for her own sake - for she had lost all and the beggar can lose no more - but for the boy's sake, the unloved child that stood between the stranger and her hopes. For him she had made a terrible enemy. Weeping, the boy followed her.

"Take comfort, little son," she said, drawing him to her tenderly. "The deer can suffer no more. For the tigers, he does not fear them. He runs in green woods now where there is none to hunt. He is up and away. The Blessed One was once a deer as gentle as yours."

But still the child wept, and the Queen broke down utterly. "Oh, if life be a dream, let us wake, let us wake!" she sobbed. "For evil things walk in it that cannot live in the light. Or let us dream deeper and forget. Go, little son, yet stay - for who can tell what waits us when the King comes. Let us meet him here."

For she believed that Dwaymenau would certainly carry the tale of her speech to the King, and, if so, what hope but death together?

That night, after the feasting, when the girls were dancing the dance of the fairies and spirits, in gold dresses, winged on the legs and shoulders, and high, gold-spired and pinnacled caps, the King missed the little Prince, Ananda, and asked why he was absent.

No one answered, the women looking upon each other, until Dwaymenau, sitting beside him, glimmering with rough pearls and rubies, spoke smoothly: "Lord, worshipped and beloved, the two boys quarreled this day, and Ananda's deer attacked our Mindon. He had a madness upon him and thrust with his horns. But, Mindon, your true son, flew in upon him and in a great fight he slit the beast's throat with the knife you gave him. Did he not well?"

"Well," said the King briefly. "But is there no hurt? Have searched? For he is mine."

There was arrogance in the last sentence and her proud soul rebelled, but smoothly as ever she spoke: "I have searched and there is not the littlest scratch. But Ananda is weeping because the deer is dead, and his mother is angry. What should I do?"

"Nothing. Ananda is worthless and worthless let him be! And for that pale shadow that was once a woman, let her be forgotten. And now, drink, my Queen!"

And Dwaymenau drank but the drink was bitter to her, for a ghost had risen upon her that day. She had never dreamed that such a scandal had been spoken, and it stunned her very soul with fear, that the Queen should know her vileness and the cheat she had put upon the King. As pure maid he had received her, and she knew, none better, what the doom would be if his trust were broken and he knew the child not his. She herself had seen this thing done to a concubine who had a little offended. She was thrust living in a sack and this hung between two earthen jars pierced with small holes, and thus she was set afloat on the terrible river. And not till the slow filling and sinking of the jars was the agony over and the cries for mercy stilled. No, the Queen's speech was safe with her, but was it safe with the Queen? For her silence, Dwaymenau must take measures.

Then she put it all aside and laughed and jested with the King and did indeed for a time forget, for she loved him for his black-browed beauty and his courage and royalty and the childlike trust and the man's passion that mingled in him for her. Daily and nightly such prayers as she made to strange gods were that she might bear a son, true son of his.

Next day, in the noonday stillness when all slept, she led her young son by the hand to her secret chamber, and, holding him upon her knees in that rich and golden place, she lifted his face to hers and stared into his eyes. And so unwavering was her gaze, so mighty the hard, unblinking stare that his own was held against it, and he stared back as the earth stares breathless at the moon. Gradually the terror faded out of his eyes; they glazed as if in a trance; his head fell stupidly against her bosom; his spirit stood on the borderland of being and waited.

Seeing this, she took his palm and, molding it like wax, into the cup of it she dropped clear fluid from a small vessel of pottery with the fylfot upon its side and the disks of the god Shiva. And strange it was to see that lore of India in the palace where the Blessed Law reigned in peace. Then, fixing her eyes with power upon Mindon, she bade him, a pure child, see for her in its clearness.

"Only virgin-pure can see!" she muttered, staring into his eyes. "See! See!"

The eyes of Mindon were closing. He half opened them and looked dully at his palm. His face was pinched and yellow.

"A woman - a child, on a long couch. Dead! I see!"

"See her face. Is her head crowned with the Queen's jewels? See!"

"Jewels. I cannot see her face. It is hidden."

"Why is it hidden?"

"A robe across her face. Oh, let me go!"

"And the child? See!"

"Let me go. Stop - my head - my head! I cannot see. The child is hidden. Her arm holds it. A woman stoops above them."

"A woman? Who? Is it like me? Speak! See!"

"A woman. It is like you, mother - it is like you. I fear very greatly. A knife - a knife! Blood! I cannot see - I cannot speak! I - I sleep."

His face was ghastly white now, his body cold and collapsed. Terrified, she caught him to her breast and relaxed the power of her will upon him. For that moment, she was only the passionate mother and quaked to think she might have hurt him. An hour passed and he slept heavily in her arms, and in agony she watched to see the colour steal back into the olive cheek and white lips. In the second hour he waked and stretched himself indolently, yawning like a cat. Her tears dropped like rain upon him as she clasped him violently to her.

He writhed himself free, petulant and spoilt. "Let me be. I hate kisses and women's tricks. I want to go forth and play. I have had a devil's dream.

"What did you see in your dream, prince of my heart?" She caught frantically at the last chance.

"A deer - a tiger. I have forgotten. Let me go." He ran off and she sat alone with her doubts and fears. Yet triumph coloured them too. She saw a dead woman, a dead child, and herself bending above them. She hid the vessel in her bosom and went out among her women.

Weeks passed, and never a word that she dreaded from Maya the Queen. The women of Dwaymenau, questioning the Queen's women, heard that she seemed to have heavy sorrow upon her. Her eyes were like dying lamps and she faded as they. The King never entered her palace. Drowned in Dwaymenau's wiles and beauty, her slave, her thrall, he forgot all else but his fighting, his hunting and his long war-boats, and whether the Queen lived or died, he cared nothing. Better indeed she should die and her place be emptied for the beloved, without offence to her powerful kindred.

And now he was to sail upon a raid against the Shan Tsaubwa, who had denied him tribute of gold and jewels and slaves. Glorious were the boats prepared for war, of brown teak and gilded until they shone like gold. Seventy men rowed them, sword and lance beside each. Warriors crowded them, flags and banners fluttered about them; the shining water reflected the pomp like a mirror and the air rang with song. Dwaymenau stood beside the water with her women, bidding the King farewell, and so he saw her, radiant in the dawn, with her boy beside her, and waved his hand to the last.

The ships were gone and the days languished a little at Pagan. They missed the laughter and royalty of the King, and few men, and those old and weak, were left in the city. The pulse of life beat slower.

And Dwaymenau took rule in the Golden Palace. Queen Maya sat like one in a dream and questioned nothing, and Dwaymenau ruled with wisdom but none loved her. To all she was the interloper, the witch-woman, the out-land upstart. Only the fear of the King guarded her and her boy, but that was strong. The boys played together sometimes, Mindon tyrannizing and cruel, Ananda fearing and complying, broken in spirit.

Maya the Queen walked daily in the long and empty Golden Hall of Audience, where none came now that the King was gone, pacing up and down, gazing wearily at the carved screens and all their woodland beauty of gods that did not hear, of happy spirits that had no pity. Like a spirit herself she passed between the red pillars, appearing and reappearing with steps that made no sound, consumed with hate of the evil woman that had stolen her joy. Like a slow fire it burned in her soul, and the face of the Blessed One was hidden from her, and she had forgotten His peace. In that atmosphere of hate her life dwindled. Her son's dwindled also, and there was talk among the women of some potion that Dwaymenau had been seen to drop into his noontide drink as she went swiftly by. That might be the gossip of malice, but he pined. His eyes were large like a young bird's; his hands like little claws. They thought the departing year would take him with it. What harm? Very certainly the King would shed no tear.

It was a sweet and silent afternoon and she wandered in the great and lonely hall, sickened with the hate in her soul and her fear for her boy. Suddenly she heard flying footsteps - a boy's, running in mad haste in the outer hall, and, following them, bare feet, soft, thudding.

She stopped dead and every pulse cried - Danger! No time to think or breathe when Mindon burst into sight, wild with terror and following close beside him a man - a madman, a short bright dah in his grasp, his jaws grinding foam, his wild eyes starting - one passion to murder. So sometimes from the Nats comes pitiless fury, and men run mad and kill and none knows why.

Maya the Queen stiffened to meet the danger. Joy swept through her soul; her weariness was gone. A fierce smile showed her teeth - a smile of hate, as she stood there and drew her dagger for defense. For defense - the man would rend the boy and turn on her and she would not die. She would live to triumph that the mongrel was dead, and her son, the Prince again and his father's joy - for his heart would turn to the child most surely. Justice was rushing on its victim. She would see it and live content, the long years of agony wiped out in blood, as was fitting. She would not flee; she would see it and rejoice. And as she stood in gladness - these broken thoughts rushing through her like flashes of lightning - Mindon saw her by the pillar and, screaming in anguish for the first time, fled to her for refuge.

She raised her knife to meet the staring eyes, the chalk white face, and drive him back on the murderer. If the man failed, she would not! And even as she did this a strange thing befell. Something stronger than hate swept her away like a leaf on the river; something primeval that lives in the lonely pangs of childbirth, that hides in the womb and breasts of the mother. It was stronger than she. It was not the hated Mindoin - she saw him no more. Suddenly it was the eternal Child, lifting dying, appealing eyes to the Woman, as he clung to her knees. She did not think this - she felt it, and it dominated her utterly. The Woman answered. As if it had been her own flesh and blood, she swept the panting body behind her and faced the man with uplifted dagger and knew her victory assured, whether in life or death. On came the horrible rush, the flaming eyes, and, if it was chance that set the dagger against his throat, it was cool strength that drove it home and never wavered until the blood welling from the throat quenched the flame in the wild eyes, and she stood triumphing like a war-goddess, with the man at her feet. Then, strong and flushed, Maya the Queen gathered the half-dead boy in her arms, and, both drenched with blood, they moved slowly down the hall and outside met the hurrying crowd, with Dwaymenau, whom the scream had brought to find her son.

"You have killed him! She has killed him!" Scarcely could the Rajput woman speak. She was kneeling beside him - he hideous with blood. "She hated him always. She has murdered him. Seize her!"

"Woman, what matter your hates and mine?" the Queen said slowly. "The boy is stark with fear. Carry him in and send for old Meh Shway Gon. Woman, be silent!"

When a Queen commands, men and women obey, and a Queen commanded then. A huddled group lifted the child and carried him away, Dwaymenau with them, still uttering wild threats, and the Queen was left alone.

She could not realize what she had done and left undone. She could not understand it. She had hated, sickened with loathing, as it seemed for ages, and now, in a moment it had blown away like a whirlwind that is gone. Hate was washed out of her soul and had left it cool and white as the Lotus of the Blessed One. What power had Dwaymenau to hurt her when that other Power walked beside her? She seemed to float above her in high air and look down upon her with compassion. Strength, virtue flowed in her veins; weakness, fear were fantasies. She could not understand, but knew that here was perfect enlightenment. About her echoed the words of the Blessed One: "Never in this world doth hatred cease by hatred, but only by love. This is an old rule."

"Whereas I was blind, now I see," said Maya the Queen slowly to her own heart. She had grasped the hems of the Mighty.

Words cannot speak the still passion of strength and joy that possessed her. Her step was light. As she walked, her soul sang within her, for thus it is with those that have received the Law. About them is the Peace.

In the dawn she was told that the Queen, Dwaymenau, would speak with her, and without a tremor she who had shaken like a leaf at that name commanded that she should enter. It was Dwaymenau that trembled as she came into that unknown place.

With cloudy brows and eyes that would reveal no secret, she stood before the high seat where the Queen sat pale and majestic.

"Is it well with the boy?" the Queen asked earnestly.

"Well," said Dwaymenau, fingering the silver bosses of her girdle.

"Then - is there more to say?" The tone was that of the great lady who courteously ends an audience. "There is more. The men brought in the body and in its throat your dagger was sticking. And my son has told me that your body was a shield to him. You offered your life for his. I did not think to thank you - but I thank you." She ended abruptly and still her eyes had never met the Queen's.

"I accept your thanks. Yet a mother could do no less."

The tone was one of dismissal but still Dwaymenau lingered.

"The dagger," she said and drew it from her bosom. On the clear, pointed blade the blood had curdled and dried. "I never thought to ask a gift of you, but this dagger is a memorial of my son's danger. May I keep it?"

"As you will. Here is the sheath." From her girdle she drew it - rough silver, encrusted with rubies from the mountains.

The hand rejected it.

"Jewels I cannot take, but bare steel is a fitting gift between us two."

"As you will."

The Queen spoke compassionately, and Dwaymenau, still with veiled eyes, was gone without fare well. The empty sheath lay on the seat - a symbol of the sharp-edged hate that had passed out of her life. She touched the sheath to her lips and, smiling, laid it away.

And the days went by and Dwaymenau came no more before her, and her days were fulfilled with peace. And now again the Queen ruled in the palace wisely and like a Queen, and this Dwaymenau did not dispute, but what her thoughts were no man could tell.

Then came the end.

One night the city awakened to a wild alarm. A terrible fleet of war-boats came sweeping along the river thick as locusts - the war fleet of the Lord of Prome. Battle shouts broke tile peace of the night to horror; axes battered on the outer doors; the roofs of the outer buildings were all aflame. It was no wonderful incident, but a common one enough of those turbulent days - reprisal by a powerful ruler with raids and hates to avenge on the Lord of the Golden Palace. It was indeed a right to be gainsaid only by the strong arm, and the strong arm was absent; as for the men of Pagan, if the guard failed and the women's courage sank, they would return to blackened walls, empty chambers and desolation.

At Pagan the guard was small, indeed, for the King's greed of plunder had taken almost every able man with him. Still, those who were left did what they could, and the women, alert and brave, with but few exceptions, gathered the children and handed such weapons as they could muster to the men, and themselves, taking knives and daggers, helped to defend the inner rooms.

In the farthest, the Queen, having given her commands and encouraged all with brave words, like a wise, prudent princess, sat with her son beside her. Her duty was now to him. Loved or unloved, he was still the heir, the root of the House tree. If all failed, she must make ransom and terms for him, and, if they died, it must be together. He, with sparkling eyes, gay in the danger, stood by her. Thus Dway-menau found them.

She entered quietly and without any display of emotion and stood before the high seat.

"Great Queen" - she used that title for the first time - "the leader is Meng Kyinyo of Prome. There is no mercy. The end is near. Our men fall fast, the women are fleeing. I have come to say this thing: Save the Prince."

"And how?" asked the Queen, still seated. "I have no power."

"I have sent to Maung Tin, abbot of the Golden Monastery, and he has said this thing. In the Kyoung across the river he can hide one child among the novices. Cut his hair swiftly and put upon him this yellow robe. The time is measured in minutes."

Then the Queen perceived, standing by the pillar, a monk of a stern, dark presence, the creature of Dwaymenau. For an instant she pondered. Was the woman selling the child to death? Dwaymenau spoke no word. Her face was a mask. A minute that seemed an hour drifted by, and the yelling and shrieks for mercy drew nearer.

"There will be pursuit," said the Queen. "They will slay him on the river. Better here with me."

"There will be no pursuit." Dwaymenau fixed her strange eyes on the Queen for the first time.

What moved in those eyes? The Queen could not tell. But despairing, she rose and went to the silent monk, leading the Prince by the hand. Swiftly he stripped the child of the silk pasoh of royalty, swiftly he cut the long black tresses knotted on the little head, and upon the slender golden body he set the yellow robe worn by the Lord Himself on earth, and in the small hand he placed the begging-bowl of the Lord. And now, remote and holy, in the dress that is of all most sacred, the Prince, standing by the monk, turned to his mother and looked with grave eyes upon her, as the child Buddha looked upon his Mother - also a Queen. But Dwaymenau stood by silent and lent no help as the Queen folded the Prince in her arms and laid his hand in the hand of the monk and saw them pass away among the pillars, she standing still and white.

She turned to her rival. "If you have meant truly, I thank you."

"I have meant truly."

She turned to go, but the Queen caught her by the hand.

"Why have you done this?" she asked, looking into the strange eyes of the strange woman.

Something like tears gathered in them for a moment, but she brushed them away as she said hurriedly:

"I was grateful. You saved my son. Is it not enough?"

"No, not enough!" cried the Queen. "There is more. Tell me, for death is upon us."

"His footsteps are near," said the Indian. "I will speak. I love my lord. In death I will not cheat him. What you have known is true. My child is no child of his. I will not go down to death with a lie upon my lips. Come and see."

Dwaymenau was no more. Sundari, the Indian woman, awful and calm, led the

Queen down the long ball and into her own chamber, where Mindon, the child, slept a drugged sleep. The Queen felt that she had never known her; she herself seemed diminished in stature as she followed the stately figure, with its still, dark face. Into this room the enemy were breaking, shouldering their way at the door - a rabble of terrible faces. Their fury was partly checked when only a sleeping child and two women confronted them, but their leader, a grim and evil- looking man, strode from the huddle.

"Where is the son of the King?" be shouted. "Speak, women! Whose is this boy?"

Sundari laid her hand upon her son's shoulder. Not a muscle of her face flickered.

"This is his son."

"His true son - the son of Maya the Queen?"

"His true son, the son of Maya the Queen."

"Not the younger - the mongrel?"

"The younger - the mongrel died last week of a fever."

Every moment of delay was precious. Her eyes saw only a monk and a boy fleeing across the wide river.

"Which is Maya the Queen?"

"This," said Sundari. "She cannot speak. It is her son - the Prince."

Maya had veiled her face with her hands. Her brain swam, but she understood the noble lie. This woman could love. Their lord would not be left childless. Thought beat like pulses in her - raced along her veins. She held her breath and was dumb.

His doubt was assuaged and the lust of vengeance was on him - a madness seized the man. But even his own wild men shrank back a moment, for to slay a sleeping child in cold blood is no man's work.

"You swear it is the Prince. But why? Why do you not lie to save him if you are the King's woman?"

"Because his mother has trampled me to the earth. I am the Indian woman - the mother of the younger, who is dead and safe. She jeered at me - she mocked me. It is time I should see her suffer. Suffer now as I have suffered, Maya the Queen!"

This was reasonable - this was like the women he bad known. His doubt was gone - he laughed aloud.

"Then feed full of vengeance!" he cried, and drove his knife through the child's heart.

For a moment Sundari wavered where she stood, but she held herself and was rigid as the dead.

"Tha-du! Well done!" she said with an awful smile. "The tree is broken, the roots cut. And now for us women - our fate, 0 master?"

"Wait here," he answered. "Let not a hair of their heads be touched. Both are fair. The two for me. For the rest draw lots when all is done."

The uproar surged away. The two stood by the dead boy. So swift had been his death that he lay as though he still slept - the black lashes pressed upon his cheek.

With the heredity of their different races upon them, neither wept. But silently the Queen opened her arms; wide as a woman that entreats she opened them to the Indian Queen, and speechlessly the two clung together. For a while neither spoke.

"My sister!" said Maya the Queen. And again, "0 great of heart!"

She laid her cheek against Sundari's, and a wave of solemn joy seemed to break in her soul and flood it with life and light.

"Had I known sooner!" she said. "For now the night draws on."

"What is time?" answered the Rajput woman. "We stand before the Lords of Life and Death. The life you gave was yours, and I am unworthy to kiss the feet of the Queen. Our lord will return and his son is saved. The House can be rebuilt. My son and I were waifs washed up from the sea. Another wave washes us back to nothingness. Tell him my story and he will loathe me."

"My lips are shut," said the Queen. "Should I betray my sister's honour? When he speaks of the noble women of old, your name will be among them. What matters which of us he loves and remembers? Your soul and mine have seen the same thing, and we are one. But I - what have I to do with life? The ship and the bed of the conqueror await us. Should we await them, my sister?"

The bright tears glittered in the eyes of Sundari at the tender name and the love in the face of the Queen. At last she accepted it.

"My sister, no," she said, and drew from her bosom the dagger of Maya, with the man's blood rusted upon it. "Here is the way. I have kept this dagger in token of my debt. Nightly have I kissed it, swearing that, when the time came, I would repay my debt to the great Queen. Shall I go first or follow, my sister?"

Her voice lingered on the word. It was precious to her. It was like clear water, laying away the stain of the shameful years.

"Your arm is strong," answered the Queen. "I go first. Because the King's son is safe, I bless you. For your love of the King, I love you. And here, standing on the verge of life, I testify that the words of the Blessed One are truth - that love is All; that hatred is Nothing."

She bared the breast that this woman had made desolate - that, with the love of this woman, was desolate ho longer, and, stooping, laid her hand on the brow of Mindon. Once more they embraced, and then, strong and true, and with the Rajput passion behind the blow, the stroke fell and Sundari had given her sister the crowning mercy of deliverance. She laid the body beside her own son, composing the stately limbs, the quiet eyelids, the black lengths of hair into majesty. So, she thought, in the great temple of the Rajput race, the Mother Goddess shed silence and awe upon her worshippers. The two lay like mother and son - one slight hand of the Queen she laid across the little body as if to guard it.

Her work done, she turned to the entrance and watched the dawn coming glorious over the river. The men shouted and quarreled in the distance, but she heeded them no more than the chattering of apes. Her heart was away over the distance to the King, but with no passion now: so might a mother have thought of her son. He was sleeping, forgetful of even her in his dreams. What matter? She was glad at heart. The Queen was dearer to her than the King - so strange is life; so healing is death. She remembered without surprise that she had asked no forgiveness of the Queen for all the cruel wrongs, for the deadly intent - had made no confession. Again what matter? What is forgiveness when love is all?

She turned from the dawn-light to the light in the face of the Queen. It was well. Led by such a hand, she could present herself without fear before the Lords of Life and Death - she and the child. She smiled. Life is good, but death, which is more life, is better. The son of the King was safe, but her own son safer.

When the conqueror reentered the chamber, he found the dead Queen guarding the dead child, and across her feet, as not worthy to lie beside her, was the body of the Indian woman, most beautiful in death.

FIRE OF BEAUTY

(Salutation to Ganesa the Lord of Wisdom, and to Saraswate the Lady of Sweet Speech!)

This story was composed by the Brahmin Visravas, that dweller on the banks of holy Kashi; and though the events it records are long past, yet it is absolutely and immutably true because, by the power of his yoga, he summoned up every scene before him, and beheld the persons moving and speaking as in life. Thus he had naught to do but to set down what befell.

What follows, that hath he seen.

I

Wide was the plain, the morning sun shining full upon it, drinking up the dew as the Divine drinks up the spirit of man. Far it stretched, resembling the ocean, and riding upon it like a stately ship was the league-long Rock of Chitor. It is certainly by the favour of the Gods that this great fortress of the Rajput Kings thus rises from the plain, leagues in length, noble in height; and very strange it is to see the flat earth fall away from it like waters from the bows of a boat, as it soars into the sky with its burden of palaces and towers.

Here dwelt the Queen Padmini and her husband Bhimsi, the Rana of the Rajputs.

The sight of the holy ascetic Visravas pierced even the secrets of the Rani's bower, where, in the inmost chamber of marble, carved until it appeared like lace of the foam of the sea, she was seated upon cushions of blue Bokhariot silk, like the lotus whose name she bore floating upon the blue depths of the lake. She had just risen from the shallow bath of marble at her feet.

Most beautiful was this Queen, a haughty beauty such as should be a Rajput lady; for the name "Rajput" signifies Son of a King, and this lady was assuredly the daughter of Kings and of no lesser persons. And since that beauty is long since ashes (all things being transitory), it is permitted to describe the mellowed ivory of her body, the smooth curves of her hips, and the defiance of her glimmering bosom, half veiled by the long silken tresses of sandal- scented hair which a maiden on either side, bowing toward her, knotted upon her head. But even he who with his eyes has seen it can scarce tell the beauty of her face - the slender arched nose, the great eyes like lakes of darkness in the reeds of her curled lashes, the mouth of roses, the glance, deer-like but proud, that courted and repelled admiration. This cannot be told, nor could the hand of man paint it. Scarcely could that fair wife of the Pandava Prince, Draupadi the Beautiful (who bore upon her perfect form every auspicious mark) excel this lady.

(Ashes - ashes! May Maheshwara have mercy upon her rebirths!)

Throughout India had run the fame of this beauty. In the bazaar of Kashmir they told of it. It was recorded in the palaces of Travancore, and all the lands that lay between; and in an evil hour - may the Gods curse the mother that bore him! - it reached the ears of Allah-u- Din, the Moslem dog, a very great fighting man who sat in Middle India, looting and spoiling.

(Ahi! for the beauty that is as a burning flame!)

In the gardens beneath the windows of the Queen, the peacocks, those maharajas of the birds, were spreading the bronze and emerald of their tails. The sun shone on them as on heaps of jewels, so that they dazzled the eyes. They stood about the feet of the ancient Brahmin sage, he who had tutored the Queen in her childhood and given her wisdom as the crest-jeweled of her loveliness. He, the Twice-born sat under the shade of a neem tree, hearing the gurgle of the sacred waters from the Cow's Mouth, where the great tank shone under the custard-apple boughs; and, at peace with all the world, he read in the Scripture which affirms the transience of all things drifting across the thought of the Supreme like clouds upon the surface of the Ocean.

(Ahi! that loveliness is also illusion!)

Her women placed about the Queen - that Lotus of Women - a robe of silk of which none could say that it was green or blue, the noble colours so mingled into each other under the latticed gold work of Kashi. They set the jewels on her head, and wide thin rings of gold heavy with great pearls in her ears. Upon the swell of her bosom they clasped the necklace of table emeralds, large, deep, and full of green lights, which is the token of the Chitor queens. Upon her slender ankles they placed the chooris of pure soft gold, set also with grass-green emeralds, and the delicate souls of her feet they reddened with lac. Nor were her arms forgotten, but loaded with bangles so free from alloy that they could be bent between the hands of a child. Then with fine paste they painted the Symbol between her dark brows, and, rising, she shone divine as a nymph of heaven who should cause the righteous to stumble in his austerities and arrest even the glances of Gods.

(Ahi! that the Transient should be so fair!)

II

Now it was the hour that the Rana should visit her; for since the coming of the Lotus Lady, be had forgotten his other women, and in her was all his heart. He came from the Hall of Audience where petitions were heard, and justice done to rich and poor; and as he came, the Queen, hearing his step on the stone, dismissed her women, and smiling to know her loveliness, bowed before him, even as the Goddess Uma bows before Him who is her other half.

Now he was a tall man, with the falcon look of the Hill Rajputs, and moustaches that curled up to his eyes, lion-waisted and lean in the flanks like Arjoon himself, a very ruler of men; and as he came, his hand was on the hilt of the sword that showed beneath his gold coat of khincob. On the high cushions he sat, and the Rani a step beneath him; and she said, raising her lotus eyes:-

"Speak, Aryaputra, (son of a noble father)-what hath befallen?"

And he, looking upon her beauty with fear, replied,-

"It is thy beauty, 0 wife, that brings disaster."

"And how is this?" she asked very earnestly.

For a moment he paused, regarding her as might a stranger, as one who considers a beauty in which he hath no part; and, drawn by this strangeness, she rose and knelt beside him, pillowing her head upon his heart.

"Say on," she said in her voice of music.

He unfurled a scroll that he had crushed in his strong right hand, and read aloud:-

"'Thus says Allah-u-Din, Shadow of God, Wonder of the Age, Viceregent of Kings. We have heard that in the Treasury of Chitor is a jewel, the like of which is not in the Four Seas - the work of the hand of the Only God, to whom be praise! This jewel is thy Queen, the Lady Padmini. Now, since the sons of the Prophet are righteous, I desire but to look upon this jewel, and ascribing glory to the Creator, to depart in peace. Granted requests are the bonds of friendship; therefore lay the head of acquiescence in the dust of opportunity and name an auspicious day.'"

He crushed it again and flung it furiously from him on the marble.

"The insult is deadly. The soor! son of a debased mother! Well he knows that to the meanest Rajput his women are sacred, and how much more the daughters and wives of the Kings! The jackals feast on the tongue that speaks this shame! But it is a threat, Beloved - a threat! Give me thy counsel that never failed me yet."

For the Rajputs take counsel with their women who are wise.

They were silent, each weighing the force of resistance that could be made; and this the Rani knew even as he.

"It cannot be," she said; "the very ashes of the dead would shudder to hear. Shall the Queens of India be made the sport of the barbarians?"

Her husband looked upon her fair face. She could feel his heart labor beneath her ear.

"True, wife; but the barbarians are strong. Our men are tigers, each one, but the red dogs of the Dekkan can pull down the tiger, for they are many, and he alone."

Then that great Lady, accepting his words, and conscious of the danger, murmured this, clinging to her husband:-

"There was a Princess of our line whose beauty made all other women seem as waning moons in the sun's splendour. And many great Kings sought her, and there was contention and war. And, she, fearing that the Rajputs would be crushed to powder between the warring Kings, sent unto each this message: 'Come on such and such a day, and thou shalt see my face and hear my choice.' And they, coming, rejoiced exceedingly, thinking each one that he was the Chosen. So they came into the great Hall, and there was a table, and somewhat upon it covered with a gold cloth; and an old veiled woman lifted the gold, and the head of the Princess lay there with the lashes like night upon her cheek, and between her lips was a little scroll, saying this: `I have chosen my Lover and my Lord, and he is mightiest, for he is Death.' - So the Kings went silently away. And there was Peace."

The music of her voice ceased, and the Rana clasped her closer.

"This I cannot do. Better die together. Let us take counsel with the ancient Brahman, thy guru [teacher], for he is very wise."

She clapped her hands, and the maidens returned, and, bowing, brought the venerable Prabhu Narayan into the Presence, and again those roses retired.

Respectful salutation was then offered by the King and the Queen to that saint, hoary with wisdom - he who had seen her grow into the loveliness of the sea-born Shri, yet had never seen that loveliness; for he had never raised his eyes above the chooris about her ankles. To him the King related his anxieties; and he sat rapt in musing, and the two waited in dutiful silence until long minutes had fallen away; and at the last he lifted his head, weighted with wisdom, and spoke.

"0 King, Descendant of Rama! this outrage cannot be. Yet, knowing the strength and desire of this obscene one and the weakness of our power, it is plain that only with cunning can cunning be met. Hear, therefore, the history of the Fox and the Drum.

"A certain Fox searched for food in the jungle, and so doing beheld a tree on which hung a drum; and when the boughs knocked upon the parchment, it sounded aloud. Considering, he believed that so round a form and so great a voice must portend much good feeding. Neglecting on this account a fowl that fed near by, he ascended to the drum. The drum being rent was but air and parchment, and meanwhile the fowl fled away. And from the eye of folly he shed the tear of disappointment, having bartered the substance for the shadow. So must we act with this budmash [scoundrel]. First, receiving his oath that he will depart without violence, hid him hither to a great feast, and say that he shall behold the face of the Queen in a mirror. Provide that some fair woman of the city show her face, and then let him depart in peace, showing him friendship. He shall not know he hath not seen the beauty he would befoul."

After consultation, no better way could be found; but the heart of the great Lady was heavy with foreboding.

(A hi! that Beauty should wander a pilgrim in the ways of sorrow!)

To Allah-u-Din therefore did the King dispatch this letter by swift riders on mares of Mewar.

After salutations - "Now whereas thou hast said thou wouldest look upon the beauty of the Treasure of Chitor, know it is not the custom of the Rajputs that any eye should light upon their treasure. Yet assuredly, when requests arise between friends, there cannot fail to follow distress of mind and division of soul if these are ungranted. So, under promises that follow, I bid thee to a feast at my poor house of Chitor, and thou shalt see that beauty reflected in a mirror, and so seeing, depart in peace from the house of a friend."

This being writ by the Twice-Born, the Brahman, did the Rana sign with bitter rage in his heart. And the days passed.

III

On a certain day found fortunate by the astrologers - a day of early winter, when the dawns were pure gold and the nights radiant with a cool moon - did a mighty troop of Moslems set their camp on the plain of Chitor. It was as if a city had blossomed in an hour. Those who looked from the walls muttered prayers to the Lord of the Trident; for these men seemed like the swarms of the locust - people, warriors all, fierce fighting-men. And in the ways of Chitor, and up the steep and winding causeway from the plains, were warriors also, the chosen of the Rajputs, thick as blades of corn hedging the path.

(Ahi! that the blossom of beauty should have swords for thorns!)

Then, leaving his camp, attended by many Chiefs, - may the mothers and sires that begot them be accursed! - came Allah-u-Din, riding toward the Lower Gate, and so upward along the causeway, between the two rows of men who neither looked nor spoke, standing like the carvings of war in the Caves of Ajunta. And the moon was rising through the sunset as he came beneath the last and seventh gate. Through the towers and palaces he rode with his following, but no woman, veiled or unveiled, - no, not even an outcast of the city, - was there to see him come; only the men, armed and silent. So he turned to Munim Khan that rode at his bridle, saying,-

"Let not the eye of watchfulness close this night on the pillow of forgetfulness!"

And thus he entered the palace.

Very great was the feast in Chitor, and the wines that those accursed should not drink (since the Outcast whom they call their Prophet forbade them) ran like water, and at the right hand of Allah-u-Din was set the great crystal Cup inlaid with gold by a craft that is now perished; and he filled and refilled it - may his own Prophet curse the swine!

But because the sons of Kings eat not with the outcasts, the Rana entered after, clothed in chain armor of blue steel, and having greeted him, bid him to the sight of that Treasure. And Allah-u-Din, his eyes swimming with wine, and yet not drunken, followed, and the two went alone.

Purdahs [curtains] of great splendour were hung in the great Hall that is called the Raja's Hall, exceeding rich with gold, and in front of the opening was a kneeling-cushion, and an a gold stool before it a polished mirror.

(Ahi! for gold and beauty, the scourges of the world!)

And the Rana was pale to the lips.

Now as the Princes stood by the purdah, a veiled woman, shrouded in white so that no shape could he seen in her, came forth from within, and kneeling upon the cushion, she unveiled her face bending until the mirror, like a pool of water, held it, and that only. And the King motioned his guest to look, and he looked over her veiled shoulder and saw. Very great was the bowed beauty that the mirror held, but Allah-u-Din turned to the Rana.

"By the Bread and the Salt, by the Guest-Right, by the Honour of thy House, I ask - is this the Treasure of Chitor?"

And since the Sun-Descended cannot lie, no, not though they perish, the Rana answered, flushing darkly, - "This is not the Treasure. Wilt thou spare?"

But he would not, and the woman slipped like a shadow behind the purdah and no word said.

Then was heard the tinkling of chooris, and the little noise fell upon the silence like a fear, and, parting the curtains, came a woman veiled like the other. She did not kneel, but took the mirror in her hand, and Allah-u-Din drew up behind her back. From her face she raised the veil of gold Dakka webs, and gazed into the mirror, holding it high, and that Accursed stumbled back, blinded with beauty, saying this only,- "I have seen the Treasure of Chitor."

So the purdah fell about her.

The next day, after the Imaum of the Accursed had called them to prayer, they departed, and Allah-u-Din, paying thanks to the Rana for honours given and taken, and swearing friendship, besought him to ride to his camp, to see the marvels of gold and steel armor brought down from the passes, swearing also safe-conduct. And because the Rajputs trust the word even of a foe, he went.

(A hi! that honour should strike hands with traitors!)

IV

The hours went by, heavy-footed like mourners. Padmini the Rani knelt by the window in her tower that overlooks the plains. Motionless she knelt there, as the Goddess Uma lost in her penances, and she saw her Lord ride forth, and the sparkle of steel where the sun shone on them, and the Standard of the Cold Disk on its black ground. So the camp of the Moslem swallowed them up, and they returned no more. Still she knelt and none dared speak with her; and as the first shade of evening fell across the hills of Rajasthan, she saw a horseman spurting over the flat; and he rode like the wind, and, seeing, she implored the Gods.

Then entered the Twice-Born, that saint of clear eyes, and he bore a scroll; and she rose and seated herself, and he stood by her, as her ladies cowered like frightened doves before the woe in his face as he read.

"To the Rose of Beauty, The Pearl among Women, the Chosen of the Palace. Who, having seen thy loveliness, can look on another? Who, having tasted the wine of the Houris, but thirsts forever? Behold, I have thy King as hostage. Come thou and deliver him. I have sworn that he shall return in thy place."

And from a smaller scroll, the Brahman read this:-

"I am fallen in the snare. Act thou as becomes a Rajputni."

Then that Daughter of the Sun lifted her head, for the thronging of armed feet was heard in the Council Hall below. From the floor she caught her veil and veiled herself in haste, and the Brahman with bowed head followed, while her women mourned aloud. And, descending, between the folds of the purdah she appeared white and veiled, and the Brahman beside her, and the eyes of all the Princes were lowered to her shrouded feet, while the voice they had not heard fell silvery upon the air, and the echoes of the high roof repeated it.

"Chief of the Rajputs, what is your counsel?" And he of Marwar stepped forward, and not rais- ing his eyes above her feet, answered,-

"Queen, what is thine?"

For the Rajputs have ever heard the voice of their women.

And she said,-

"I counsel that I die and my head be sent to him, that my blood may quench his desire."

And each talked eagerly with the other, but amid the tumult the Twice-Born said,-

"This is not good talk. In his rage he will slay the King. By my yoga, I have seen it. Seek another way."

So they sought, but could determine nothing, and they feared to ride against the dog, for he held the life of the King; and the tumult was great, but all were for the King's safety.

Then once more she spoke.

"Seeing it is determined that the King's life is more than my honour, I go this night. In your hand I leave my little son, the Prince Ajeysi. Prepare my litters, seven hundred of the best, for all my women go with me. Depart now, for I have a thought from the Gods."

Then, returning to her bower, she spoke this letter to the saint, and he wrote it, and it was sent to the camp.

After salutations - "Wisdom and strength have attained their end. Have ready for release the Rana of Chitor, for this night I come with my ladies, the prize of the conqueror."

When the sun sank, a great procession with torches descended the steep way of Chitor - seven hundred litters, and in the first was borne the Queen, and all her women followed.

All the streets were thronged with women, weeping and beating their breasts. Very greatly they wept, and no men were seen, for their livers were black within them for shame as the Treasure of Chitor departed, nor would they look upon the sight. And across the plains went that procession; as if the stars had fallen upon the earth, so glittered the sorrowful lights of the Queen.

But in the camp was great rejoicing, for the Barbarians knew that many fair women attended on her.

Now, before the entrance to the camp they had made a great shamiana [tent] ready, hung with shawls of Kashmir and the plunder of Delhi; and there was set a silk divan for the Rani, and beside it stood the Loser and the Gainer, Allah-u-Din and the King, awaiting the Treasure.

Veiled she entered, stepping proudly, and taking no heed of the Moslem, she stood before her husband, and even through the veil he could feel the eyes he knew.

And that Accursed spoke, laughing.

"I have won-I have won, 0 King! Bid farewell to the Chosen of the Palace - the Beloved of the Viceregent of Kings!"

Then she spoke softly, delicately, in her own tongue, that the outcast should not guess the matter of her speech.

"Stand by me. Stir not. And when I raise my arm, cry the cry of the Rajputs. NOW!"

And she flung her arm above her head, and instantly, like a lion roaring, he shouted, drawing his sword, and from every litter sprang an armed man, glittering in steel, and the bearers, humble of mien, were Rajput knights, every one.

And Allah-u-Din thrust at the breast of the Queen; but around them surged the war, and she was hedged with swords like a rose in the thickets.

Very full of wine, dull with feasting and lust and surprised, the Moslems fled across the plains, streaming in a broken rabble, cursing and shouting like low-caste women; and the Rajputs, wiping their swords, returned from the pursuit and laughed upon each other.

But what shall be said of the joy of the King and of her who had imagined this thing, in- structed of the Goddess who is the other half of her Lord?

So the procession returned, singing, to Chitor with those Two in the midst; but among the dogs that fled was Allah-u-Din, his face blackened with shame and wrath, the curses choking in his foul throat.

(Aid! that the evil still walk the ways of the world!)

V

So the time went by and the beauty of the Queen grew, and her King could see none but hers. Like the moon she obscured the stars, and every day he remembered her wisdom, her valour, and his soul did homage at her feet, and there was great content in Chitor.

It chanced one day that the Queen, looking from her high window that like an eagle's nest overhung the precipice, saw, on the plain beneath, a train of men, walking like ants, and each carried a basket on his back, and behind them was a cloud of dust like a great army. Already the city was astir because of this thing, and the rumours came thick and the spies were sent out.

In the dark they returned, and the Rana entered the bower of Padmini, his eyes burning like coal with hate and wrath, and he flung his arm round his wife like a shield.

"He is returned, and in power. Counsel me again, 0 wife, for great is thy wisdom!"

But she answered only this,-

"Fight, for this time it is to the death."

Then each day she watched bow the baskets of earth, emptied upon the plain at first, made nothing, an ant heap whereat fools might laugh. But each day as the trains of men came, spilling their baskets, the great earthworks grew and their height mounted. Day after day the Rajputs rode forth and slew; and as they slew it seemed that all the teeming millions of the earth came forth to take the places of the slain. And the Rajputs fell also, and under the pennons the thundering forces returned daily, thinned of their best.

(A hi! that Evil rules the world as God!)

And still the earth grew up to the heights, and the protection of the hills was slowly withdrawn from Chitor, for on the heights they made they set their engines of war.

Then in a red dawn that great saint Narayan came to the Queen, where she watched by her window, and spoke.

"0 great lady, I have dreamed a fearful dream. Nay, rather have I seen a vision."

With her face set like a sword, the Queen said,-

"Say on."

"In a light red like blood, I waked, and beside me stood the Mother, - Durga, - awful to see, with a girdle of heads about her middle; and the drops fell thick and slow from That which she held in her hand, and in the other was her sickle of Doom. Nor did she speak, but my soul heard her words."

"Narrate them."

"She commanded: `Say this to the Rana: "In Chitor is My altar; in Chitor is thy throne. If thou wouldest save either, send forth twelve crowned Kings of Chitor to die."'"

As he said this, the Rana, fore-spent with fighting, entered and heard the Divine word.

Now there were twelve princes of the Rajput blood, and the youngest was the son of Padmini. What choice had these most miserable but to appease the dreadful anger of the Goddess? So on each fourth day a King of Chitor was crowned, and for three days sat upon the throne, and on the fourth day, set in the front, went forth and died fighting. So perished eleven Kings of Chitor, and now there was left but the little Ajeysi, the son of the Queen.

And that day was a great Council called.

Few were there. On the plains many lay dead; holding the gates many watched; but the blood was red in their hearts and flowed like Indus in the melting of the snows. And to them spoke the Rana, his hand clenched on his sword, and the other laid on the small dark head of the Prince Ajeysi, who stood between his knees. And as he spoke his voice gathered strength till it rang through the hall like the voice of Indra when he thunders in the heavens.

"Men of the Rajputs, this child shall not die. Are we become jackals that we fall upon the weak and tear them? When have we put our women and children in the forefront of the war? I - I only am King of Chitor. Narayan shall save this child for the time that will surely come. And for us - what shall we do? I die for Chitor!"

And like the hollow waves of a great sea they answered him,-

"We will die for Chitor."

There was silence and Marwar spoke.

"The women?"

"Do they not know the duty of a Rajputni?" said the King. "My household has demanded that the caves be prepared."

And the men clashed stew joy with their swords, and the council dispersed.

Then that very great saint, the Twice-Born, put off the sacred thread that is the very soul of the Brahman. In his turban he wound it secretly, and he stained his noble Aryan body until it resembled the Pariahs, foul for the pure to see, loathsome for the pure to touch, and he put on him the rags of the lowest of the earth, and taking the Prince, he removed from the body of the child every trace of royal and Rajput birth, and he appeared like a child of the Bhils - the vile forest wanderers that shame not to defile their lips with carrion. And in this guise they stood before the Queen; and when she looked on the saint, the tears fell from her eyes like rain, not for grief for her son, nor for death, but that for their sake the pure should be made impure and the glory of the Brahman-hood be defiled. And she fell at the old man's feet and laid her head on the ground before him.

"Rise, daughter!" he said, "and take comfort! Are not the eyes of the Gods clear that they should distinguish? - and this day we stand before the God of Gods. Have not the Great Ones said, `That which causes life causes also decay and death'? Therefore we who go and you who stay are alike a part of the Divine. Embrace now your child and bless him, for we depart. And it is on account of the sacrifice of the Twelve that he is saved alive."

So, controlling her tears, she rose, and clasping the child to her bosom, she bade him be of good cheer since he went with the Gods. And that great saint took his hand from hers, and for the first time in the life of the Queen he raised his aged eyes to her face, and she gazed at him; but what she read, even the ascetic Visravas, who saw all by the power of his yoga, could not tell, for it was beyond speech. Very certainly the peace thereafter possessed her.

So those two went out by the secret ways of the rocks, and wandering far, were saved by the favour of Durga.

VI

And the nights went by and the days, and the time came that no longer could they hold Chitor, and all hope was dead.

On a certain day the Rana and the Rani stood for the last time in her bower, and looked down into the city; and in the streets were gathered in a very wonderful procession the women of Chitor; and not one was veiled. Flowers that had bloomed in the inner chambers, great ladies jewelled for a festival, young brides, aged mothers, and girl children clinging to the robes of their mothers who held their babes, crowded the ways. Even the low-caste women walked with measured steps and proudly, decked in what they had of best, their eyes lengthened with soorma, and flowers in the darkness of their hair.

The Queen was clothed in a gold robe of rejoicing, her bodice latticed with diamonds and great gems, and upon her bosom the necklace of table emeralds, alight with green fire, which is the jewel of the Queens of Chitor. So she stood radiant as a vision of Shri, and it appeared that rays encircled her person.

And the Rana, unarmed save for his sword, had the saffron dress of a bridegroom and the jeweled cap of the Rajput Kings, and below in the hall were the Princes and Chiefs, clad even as he.

Then, raising her lotus eyes to her lord, the Princess said,-

"Beloved, the time is come, and we have chosen rightly, for this is the way of honour, and it is but another link forged in the chain of existence; for until existence itself is ended and rebirth destroyed, still shall we meet in lives to come and still be husband and wife. What room then for despair?"

And he answered,-

"This is true. Go first, wife, and I follow. Let not the door swing to behind thee. But oh, to see thy beauty once more that is the very speech of Gods with men! Wilt thou surely come again to me and again be fair?"

And for all answer she smiled upon him, and at his feet performed the obeisance of the Rajput wife when she departs upon a journey; and they went out together, the Queen unveiled.

As she passed through the Princes, they lowered their eyes so that none saw her; but when she stood on the steps of the palace, the women all turned eagerly toward her like stars about the moon, and lifting their arms, they began to sing the dirge of the Rajput women.

So they marched, and in great companies they marched, company behind company, young and old, past the Queen, saluting her and drawing courage from the loveliness and kindness of her unveiled face.

In the rocks beneath the palaces of Chitor are very great caves - league long and terrible, with ways of darkness no eyes have seen; and it is believed that in times past spirits have haunted them with strange wailings. In these was prepared great store of wood and oils and fragrant matters for burning. So to these caves they marched and, company by company, disappeared into the darkness; and the voice of their singing grew faint and hollow, and died away, as the men stood watching their women go.

Now, when this was done and the last had gone, the Rani descended the steps, and the Rana, taking a torch dipped in fragrant oils, followed her, and the Princes walked after, clad like bridegrooms but with no faces of bridal joy. At the entrance of the caves, having lit the torch, he gave it into her hand, and she, receiving it and smiling, turned once upon the threshold, and for the first time those Princes beheld the face of the Queen, but they hid their eyes with their hands when they had seen. So she departed within, and the Rana shut to the door and barred and bolted it, and the men with him flung down great rocks before it so that none should know the way, nor indeed is it known to this day; and with their hands on their swords they waited there, not speaking, until a great smoke rose between the crevices of the rocks, but no sound at all.

(Ashes of roses - ashes of roses! . . Ahi! for beauty that is but touched and remitted!)

The sun was high when those men with their horses and on foot marched down the winding causeway beneath the seven gates, and so forth into the plains, and charging unarmed upon the Moslems, they perished every man. After, it was asked of one who had seen the great slaughter,-

"Say how my King bore himself."

And he who had seen told this:-

"Reaper of the harvest of battle, on the bed of honour he has spread a carpet of the slain! He sleeps ringed about by his enemies. How can the world tell of his deeds? The tongue is silent."

When that Accursed, Allah-u-Din, came up the winding height of the hills, he found only a dead city, and his heart was sick within him.

Now this is the Sack of Chitor, and by the Oath of the Sack of Chitor do the Rajputs swear when they bind their honour.

But it is only the ascetic Visravas who by the power of his yoga has heard every word, and with his eyes beheld that Flame of Beauty, who, for a brief space illuminating the world as a Queen, returns to birth in many a shape of sorrowful loveliness until the Blue-throated God shall in his favour destroy her rebirths.

Salutation to Ganesa the Elephant-Headed One, and to Shri the Lady of Beauty!

THE BUILDING OF THE TAJ MAHAL

In the Name of God, the Compassionate, the Merciful- the Smiting! A day when the soul shall know what it has sent on or kept back. A day when no soul shall control aught for another. And the bidding belongs to God.

THE KORAN.

I

Now the Shah-in-Shah, Shah Jahan, Emperor in India, loved his wife with a great love. And of all the wives of the Mogul Emperors surely this Lady Arjemand, Mumtaz-i-Mahal - the Chosen of the Palace - was the most worthy of love. In the tresses of her silk-soft hair his heart was bound, and for none other had he so much as a passing thought since his soul had been submerged in her sweetness. Of her he said, using the words of the poet Faisi, -

"How shall I understand the magic of Love the Juggler? For he made thy beauty enter at that small gate the pupil of my eye, And now - and now my heart cannot contain it!"

But who should marvel? For those who have seen this Arjemand crowned with the crown the Padishah set upon her sweet low brows, with the lamps of great jewels lighting the dimples of her cheeks as they swung beside them, have most surely seen perfection. lie who sat upon the Peacock Throne, where the outspread tail of massed gems is centred by that great ruby, "The Eye of the Peacock, the Tribute of the World," valued it not so much as one Jock of the dark and perfumed tresses that rolled to her feet. Less to him the twelve throne columns set close with pearls than the little pearls she showed in her sweet laughter. For if this lady was all beauty, so too she was all goodness; and from the Shah-in-Shah to the poorest, all hearts of the world knelt in adoration, before the Chosen of the Palace. She was, indeed, an extraor- dinary beauty, in that she had the soul of a child, and she alone remained unconscious of her power; and so she walked, crowned and clothed with humility.

Cold, haughty, and silent was the Shah-in-Shah before she blessed his arms - flattered, envied, but loved by none. But the gift this Lady brought with her was love; and this, shining like the sun upon ice, melted his coldness, and he became indeed the kingly centre of a kingly court May the Peace be upon her!

Now it was the dawn of a sorrowful day when the pains of the Lady Arje-mand came strong and terrible, and she travailed in agony. The hakims (physicians) stroked their beards and reasoned one with another; the wise women surrounded her, and remedies many and great were tried; and still her anguish grew, and in the hall without sat the Shah-in-Shah upon his divan, in anguish of spirit yet greater. The sweat ran on his brows, the knotted veins were thick on his temples, and his eyes, sunk in their caves, showed as those of a maddened man. He crouched on his cushions and stared at the purdah that divided him from the Lady; and all day the people came and went about him, and there was silence from the voice he longed to hear; for she would not moan, lest the sound should slay the Emperor. Her women besought her, fearing that her strong silence would break her heart; but still she lay, her hands clenched in one another, enduring; and the Emperor endured without. The Day of the Smiting!

So, as the time of the evening prayer drew nigh, a child was born, and the Empress, having done with pain, began to sink slowly into that profound sleep that is the shadow cast by the Last. May Allah the Upholder have mercy on our weakness! And the women, white with fear and watching, looked upon her, and whispered one to another, "It is the end."

And the aged mother of Abdul Mirza, standing at her head, said, "She heeds not the cry of the child. She cannot stay." And the newly wed wife of Saif Khan, standing at her feet, said, "The voice of the beloved husband is as the Call of the Angel. Let the Padishah be summoned."

So, the evening prayer being over (but the Emperor had not prayed), the wisest of the hakims, Kazim Sharif, went before him and spoke:-

"Inhallah! May the will of the Issuer of Decrees in all things be done! Ascribe unto the Creator glory, bowing before his Throne."

And he remained silent; but the Padishah, haggard in his jewels, with his face hidden, answered thickly, "The truth! For Allah has forgotten his slave."

And Kazim Sharif, bowing at his feet and veiling his face with his hands, replied:

"The voice of the child cannot reach her, and the Lady of Delight departs. He who would speak with her must speak quickly."

Then the Emperor rose to his feet unsteadily, like a man drunk with the forbidden juice; and when Kazim Sharif would have supported him, be flung aside his hands, and he stumbled, a man wounded to death, as it were, to the marble chamber where she lay.

In that white chamber it was dusk, and they had lit the little cressets so that a very faint light fell upon her face. A slender fountain a little cooled the hot, still air with its thin music and its sprinkled diamonds, and outside, the summer lightnings were playing wide and blue on the river; but so still was it that the dragging footsteps of the Emperor raised the hair on the flesh of those who heard, So the women who should, veiled themselves, and the others remained like pillars of stone.

Now, when those steps were heard, a faint colour rose in the cheek of the Lady Arjemand; but she did not raise the heavy lashes, or move her hand. And he came up beside her, and the Shadow of God, who should kneel to none, knelt, and his head fell forward upon her breast; and in the hush the women glided out like ghosts, leaving the husband with the wife excepting only that her foster-nurse stood far off, with eyes averted.

So the minutes drifted by, falling audibly one by one into eternity, and at the long last she slowly opened her eyes and, as from the depths of a dream, beheld the Emperor; and in a voice faint as the fall of a rose-leaf she said the one word, "Beloved!"

And he from between his clenched teeth, answered, "Speak, wife."

So she, who in all things had loved and served him, - she, Light of all hearts, dispeller of all gloom, - gathered her dying breath for consolation, and raised one hand slowly; and it fell across his, and so remained.

Now, her beauty had been broken in the anguish like a rose in storm; but it returned to her, doubtless that the Padishah might take comfort in its memory; and she looked like a houri of Paradise who, kneeling beside the Zemzem Well, beholds the Waters of Peace. Not Fatmeh herself, the daughter of the Prophet of God, shone more sweetly. She repeated the word, "Beloved"; and after a pause she whispered on with lips that scarcely stirred, "King of the Age, this is the end."

But still he was like a dead man, nor lifted his face.

"Surely all things pass. And though I go, in your heart I abide, and nothing can sever us. Take comfort."

But there was no answer.

"Nothing but Love's own hand can slay Love. Therefore, remember me, and I shall live."

And he answered from the darkness of her bosom, "The whole world shall remember. But when shall I be united to thee? 0 Allah, how long wilt thou leave me to waste in this separation?"

And she: "Beloved, what is time? We sleep and the night is gone. Now put your arms about me, for I sink into rest. What words are needed between us? Love is enough."

So, making not the Profession of Faith, - and what need, since all her life was worship, - the Lady Arjemand turned into his arms like a child. And the night deepened.

Morning, with its arrows of golden light that struck the river to splendour! Morning, with its pure breath, its sunshine of joy, and the koels fluting in the Palace gardens! Morning, divine and new from the hand of the Maker! And in the innermost chamber of marble a white silence; and the Lady, the Mirror of Goodness, lying in the Compassion of Allah, and a broken man stretched on the ground beside her. For all flesh, from the camel-driver to the Shah-in- Shah, is as one in the Day of the Smiting.

II

For weeks the Emperor lay before the door of death; and had it opened to him, he had been blessed. So the months went by, and very slowly the strength returned to him; but his eyes were withered and the bones stood out in his cheeks. But he resumed his throne, and sat upon it kingly, black-bearded, eagle-eyed, terribly apart in his grief and his royalty; and so seated among his Usbegs, he declared his will.

"For this Lady (upon whom be peace), departed to the mercy of the Giver and Taker, shall a tomb-palace be made, the Like of which is not found in the four corners of the world. Send forth therefore for craftsmen like the builders of the Temple of Solomon the Wise; for I will build."

So, taking counsel, they sent in haste into Agra for Ustad Isa, the Master-Builder, a man of Shiraz; and he, being presented before the Padishah, received his instructions in these words:-

"I will that all the world shall remember the Flower of the World, that all hearts shall give thanks for her beauty, which was indeed the perfect Mirror of the Creator. And since it is abhorrent of Islam that any image be made in the likeness of anything that has life, make for me a palace-tomb, gracious as she was gracious, lovely as she was lovely. Not such as the tombs of the Kings and the Conquerors, but of a divine sweetness. Make me a garden on the banks of Jumna, and build it there, where, sitting in my Pavilion of Marble, I may see it rise."

And Ustad Isa, having heard, said, "Upon my head and eyes!" and went out from the Presence.

So, musing upon the words of the Padishah, he went to his house in Agra, and there pondered the matter long and deeply; and for a whole day and night he refused all food and secluded himself from the society of all men; for he said:-

"This is a weighty thing, for this Lady (upon whom be peace) must visibly dwell in her tomb- palace on the shore of the river; and how shall I, who have never seen her, imagine the grace that was in her, and restore it to the world? Oh, had I but the memory of her face! Could I but see it as the Shah-in-Shah sees it, remembering the past! Prophet of God, intercede for me, that I may look through his eyes, if but for a moment!"

That night he slept, wearied and weakened with fasting; and whether it were that the body guarded no longer the gates of the soul, I cannot say; for, when the body ails, the soul soars free above its weakness. But a strange marvel happened.

For, as it seemed to him, he awoke at the mid-noon of the night, and he was sitting, not in his own house, but upon the roof of the royal palace, looking down on the gliding Jumna, where the low moon slept in silver, and the light was alone upon the water; and there were no boats, but sleep and dream, hovering hand-in-hand, moved upon the air, and his heart was dilated in the great silence.

Yet he knew well that he waked in some supernatural sphere: for his eyes could see across the river as if the opposite shore lay at his feet; and he could distinguish every leaf on every tree, and the flowers moon-blanched and ghost-like. And there, in the blackest shade of the pippala boughs, he beheld a faint light like a pearl; and looking with unspeakable anxiety, he saw within the light, slowly growing, the figure of a lady exceedingly glorious in majesty and crowned with a rayed crown of mighty jewels of white and golden splendour. Her gold robe fell to her feet, and - very strange to tell - her feet touched not the ground, but hung a span's length above it, so that she floated in the air.

But the marvel of marvels was her face - not, indeed, for its beauty, though that transcended all, but for its singular and compassionate sweetness, wherewith she looked toward the Palace beyond the river as if it held the heart of her heart, while death and its river lay between.

And Ustad Isa said:- "0 dream, if this sweetness be but a dream, let me never wake! Let me see forever this exquisite work of Allah the Maker, before whom all the craftsmen are as children! For my knowledge is as nothing, and I am ashamed in its presence."

And as he spoke, she turned those brimming eyes on him, and he saw her slowly absorbed into the glory of the moonlight; but as she faded into dream, he beheld, slowly rising, where her feet had hung in the blessed air, a palace of whiteness, warm as ivory, cold as chastity, domes and cupolas, slender minars, arches of marble fretted into sea-foam, screen within screen of purest marble, to hide the sleeping beauty of a great Queen - silence in the heart of it, and in every line a harmony beyond all music. Grace was about it - the grace of a Queen who prays and does not command; who, seated in her royalty yet inclines all hearts to love. And he saw that its grace was her grace, and its soul her soul, and that she gave it for the consolation of the Emperor.

And he fell on his face and worshipped the Master-Builder of the Universe, saying,- "Praise cannot express thy Perfection. Thine Essence confounds thought. Surely I am but the tool in the hand of the Builder."

And when he awoke, he was lying in his own secret chamber, but beside him was a drawing such as the craftsmen make of the work they have imagined in their hearts. And it was the Palace of the Tomb.

Henceforward, how should he waver? He was as a slave who obeys his master, and with haste he summoned to Agra his Army of Beauty.

Then were assembled all the master craftsmen of India and of the outer world. From Delhi, from Shiraz, even from Baghdad and Syria, they came. Muhammad Hanif, the wise mason, came from Kandahar, Muhammad Sayyid from Mooltan. Amanat Khan, and other great writers of the holy Koran, who should make the scripts of the Book upon fine marble. Inlayers from Kanauj, with fingers like those of the Spirits that bowed before Solomon the King, who should make beautiful the pure stone with inlay of jewels, as did their forefathers for the Rajah of Mewar; mighty dealers with agate, cornelian, and lapis lazuli. Came also, from Bokhara, Ata Muhammad and Shakri Muhammad, that they might carve the lilies of the field, very glorious, about that Flower of the World. Men of India, men of Persia, men of the outer lands, they came at the bidding of Ustad Isa, that the spirit of his vision might be made manifest.

And a great council was held among these servants of beauty. so they made a model in little of the glory that was to be, and laid it at the feet of the Shah-in-Shah; and he allowed it, though not as yet fully discerning their intent. And when it was approved, Ustad Isa called to him a man of Kashmir; and the very hand of the Creator was upon this man, for he could make gardens second only to the Gardens of Paradise, having been born by that Dal Lake where are those roses of the earth, the Shalimar and the Nishat Bagh; and to him said Ustad Isa,-

"Behold, Rain Lal Kashmiri, consider this design! Thus and thus shall a white palace, exquisite in perfection, arise on the banks of Jumna. Here, in little, in this model of sandalwood, see what shall be. Consider these domes, rounded as the Bosom of Beauty, recalling the mystic fruit of the lotus flower. Consider these four minars that stand about them like Spirits about the Throne. And remembering that all this shall stand upon a great dais of purest marble, and that the river shall be its mirror, repeating to everlasting its loveliness, make me a garden that shall be the throne room to this Queen."

And Ram Lal Kashmiri salaamed and said, "Obedience!" and went forth and pondered night and day, journeying even over the snows of the Pir Panjal to Kashmir, that he might bathe his eyes in beauty where she walks, naked and divine, upon the earth. and he it was who imagined the black marble and white that made the way of approach.

So grew the palace that should murmur, like a seashell, in the ear of the world the secret of love.

Veiled had that loveliness been in the shadow of the palace; but now the sun should rise upon it and turn its ivory to gold, should set upon it and flush its snow with rose. The moon should lie upon it like the pearls upon her bosom, the visible grace of her presence breathe about it, the music of her voice hover in the birds and trees of the garden. Times there were when Ustad Isa despaired lest even these mighty servants of beauty should miss perfection. Yet it grew and grew, rising like the growth of a flower.

So on a certain day it stood completed, and beneath the small tomb in the sanctuary, veiled with screens of wrought marble so fine that they might lift in the breeze, - the veils of a Queen, - slept the Lady Arjemand; and above her a narrow coffer of white marble, enriched in a great script with the Ninety-Nine Wondrous Names of God. And the Shah-in-Shah, now grey and worn, entered and, standing by her, cried in a loud voice, - "I ascribe to the Unity, the only Creator, the perfection of his handiwork made visible here by the hand of mortal man. For the beauty that was secret in my Palace is here revealed; and the Crowned Lady shall sit forever upon the banks of the Jumna River. It was love that commanded this Tomb."

And the golden echo carried his voice up into the high dome, and it died away in whispers of music.

But Ustad Isa standing far off in the throng (for what are craftsmen in the presence of the mighty?), said softly in his beard, "It was Love also that built, and therefore it shall endure."

Now it is told that, on a certain night in summer, when the moon is full, a man who lingers by the straight water, where the cypresses stand over their own image, may see a strange marvel - may see the Palace of the Taj dissolve like a pearl, and so rise in a mist into the moonlight; and in its place, on her dais of white marble, he shall see the Lady Arjemand, Mumtaz-i-Mahal, the Chosen of the Palace, stand there in the white perfection of beauty, smiling as one who hath attained unto the Peace. For she is its soul.

And kneeling before the dais, he shall see Ustad Isa, who made this body of her beauty; and his face is hidden in his hands.

"HOW GREAT IS THE GLORY OF KWANNON!"
A JAPANESE STORY

(0 Lovely One-O thou Flower! With Thy beautiful face, with Thy beautiful eyes, pour light upon the world! Adoration to Kwannon.)

In Japan in the days of the remote Ancestors, near the little village of Shiobara, the river ran through rocks of a very strange blue colour, and the bed of the river was also composed of these rocks, so that the clear water ran blue as turquoise gems to the sea.

The great forests murmured beside it, and through their swaying boughs was breathed the song of Eternity. Those who listen may hear if their ears are open. To others it is but the idle sighing of the wind.

Now because of all this beauty there stood in these forests a roughly built palace of unbarked wood, and here the great Emperor would come from City-Royal to seek rest for his doubtful thoughts and the cares of state, turning aside often to see the moonlight in Shiobara. He sought also the free air and the sound of falling water, yet dearer to him than the plucked strings of sho and biwa. For he said;

"Where and how shall We find peace even for a moment, and afford Our heart refreshment even for a single second?"

And it seemed to him that he found such moments at Shiobara.

Only one of his great nobles would His Majesty bring with him - the Dainagon, and him be chose because he was a worthy and honorable person and very simple of heart.

There was yet another reason why the Son of Heaven inclined to the little Shiobara. It had reached the Emperor that a Recluse of the utmost sanctity dwelt in that forest. His name was Semimaru. He had made himself a small hut in the deep woods, much as a decrepit silkworm might spin his last Cocoon and there had the Peace found him.

It had also reached His Majesty that, although blind, be was exceedingly skilled in the art of playing the biwa, both in the Flowing Fount manner and the Wood-pecker manner, and that, especially on nights when the moon was full, this aged man made such music as transported the soul. This music His Majesty desired very greatly to hear.

Never had Semimaru left his hut save to gather wood or seek food until the Divine Emperor commanded his attendance that he might soothe his august heart with music.

Now on this night of nights the moon was full and the snow heavy on the pines, and the earth was white also, and when the moon shone through the boughs it made a cold light like dawn, and the shadows of the trees were black upon it.

The attendants of His Majesty long since slept for sheer weariness, for the night was far spent, but the Emperor and the Dainagon still sat with their eyes fixed on the venerable Semimaru. For many hours he had played, drawing strange music from his biwa. Sometimes it had been like rain blowing over the plains of Adzuma, sometimes like the winds roaring down the passes of the Yoshino Mountains, and yet again like the voice of far cities. For many hours they listened without weari-ness, and thought that all the stories of the ancients might flow past them in the weird music that seemed to have neither beginning nor end.

"It is as the river that changes and changes not, and is ever and ever the same," said the Emperor in his own soul.

And certainly had a voice announced to His Augustness that centuries were drifting by as he listened, he could have felt no surprise.

Before them, as they sat upon the silken floor cushions, was a small shrine with a Buddha shelf, and a hanging picture of the Amida Buddha within it - the expres-sion one of rapt peace. Figures of Fugen and Fudo were placed before the curtain doors of the shrine, looking up in adoration to the Blessed One. A small and aged pine tree was in a pot of grey porcelain from Chosen - the only ornament in the chamber.

Suddenly His Majesty became aware that the Dainagon also had fallen asleep from weariness, and that the recluse was no longer playing, but was speaking in a still voice like a deeply flowing stream. The Emperor had observed no change from music to speech, nor could he recall when the music had ceased, so that it altogether resembled a dream.

"When I first came here - "the Venerable one continued-" it was not my intention to stay long in the forest. As each day dawned, I said; `In seven days I go.' And again - 'In seven.' Yet have I not gone. The days glided by and here have I attained to look on the beginnings of peace. Then wherefore should I go? - for all life is within the soul. Shall the fish weary of his pool? And I, who through my blind eyes feel the moon illuming my forest by night and the sun by day, abide in peace, so that even the wild beasts press round to hear my music. I have come by a path overblown by autumn leaves. But I have come."

Then said the Divine Emperor as if unconsciously;

"Would that I also might come! But the august duties cannot easily be laid aside. And I have no wife - no son."

And Semimaru, playing very softly on the strings of his biwa made no other answer, and His Majesty, collecting his thoughts, which had become, as it were, frozen with the cold and the quiet and the strange music, spoke thus, as if in a waking dream;

"Why have I not wedded? Because I have desired a bride beyond the women of earth, and of none such as I desire has the rumor reached me. Consider that Ancestor who wedded Her Shining Majesty! Evil and lovely was she, and the passions were loud about her. And so it is with women. Trouble and vexation of spirit, or instead a great weariness. But if the Blessed One would vouchsafe to my prayers a maiden of blossom and dew, with a heart calm as moonlight, her would I wed. 0, honorable One, whose wisdom surveys the world, is there in any place near or far - in heaven or in earth, such a one that I may seek and find?"

And Semimaru, still making a very low music on his biwa, said this;

"Supreme Master, where the Shiobara River breaks away through the gorges to the sea, dwelt a poor couple - the husband a wood-cutter. They had no children to aid in their toil, and daily the woman addressed her prayers for a son to the Bodhisattwa Kwannon, the Lady of Pity who looketh down for ever upon the sound of prayer. Very fervently she prayed, with such offerings as her poverty allowed, and on a certain night she dreamed this dream. At the shrine of the Senju Kwannon she knelt as was her custom, and that Great Lady, sitting enthroned upon the Lotos of Purity, opened Her eyes slowly from Her divine contemplation and heard the prayer of the wood-cutter's wife. Then stooping like a blown willow branch, she gathered a bud from the golden lotos plant that stood upon her altar, and breathing upon it it became pure white and living, and it exhaled a perfume like the flowers of Paradise, This flower the Lady of Pity flung into the bosom of her petitioner, and closing Her eyes returned into Her divine dream, whilst the woman awoke, weeping for joy.

But when she sought in her bosom for the Lotos it was gone. Of all this she boasted loudly to her folk and kin, and the more so, when in due time she perceived herself to be with child, for, from that august favour she looked for nothing less than a son, radiant with the Five Ornaments of riches, health, longevity, beauty, and success. Yet, when her hour was come, a girl was born, and blind."

"Was she welcomed?" asked the dreaming voice of the Emperor.

"Augustness, but as a household drudge. For her food was cruelty and her drink tears. And the shrine of the Senju Kwannon was neglected by her parents because of the disappointment and shame of the unwanted gift. And they believed that, lost in Her divine contemplation, the Great Lady would not perceive this neglect. The Gods however are known by their great memories."

"Her name?"

"Majesty, Tsuyu-Morning Dew. And like the morning dew she shines in stillness. She has repaid good for evil to her evil parents, serving them with unwearied service."

"What distinguishes her from others?"

"Augustness, a very great peace. Doubtless the shadow of the dream of the Holy Kwannon. She works, she moves, she smiles as one who has tasted of content."

"Has she beauty?"

"Supreme Master, am I not blind? But it is said that she has no beauty that men should desire her. Her face is flat and round, and her eyes blind."

"And yet content?"

"Philosophers might envy her calm. And her blindness is without doubt a grace from the excelling Pity, for could she see her own exceeding ugliness she must weep for shame. But she sees not. Her sight is inward, and she is well content."

"Where does she dwell?"

"Supreme Majesty, far from here - where in the heart of the woods the river breaks through the rocks."

"Venerable One, why have you told me this? I asked for a royal maiden wise and beautiful, calm as the dawn, and you have told me of a wood-cutter's drudge, blind and ugly."

And now Semimaru did not answer, but the tones of the biwa grew louder and clearer, and they rang like a song of triumph, and the Emperor could hear these words in the voice of the strings.

"She is beautiful as the night, crowned with moon and stars for him who has eyes to see. Princess Splendour was dim beside her; Prince Fireshine, gloom! Her Shining Majesty was but a darkened glory before this maid. All beauty shines within her hidden eyes."

And having uttered this the music became wordless once more, but it still flowed on more and more softly like a river that flows into the far distance.

The Emperor stared at the mats, musing - the light of the lamp was burning low. His heart said within him;

"This maiden, cast like a flower from the hand of Kwannon Sama, will I see."

And as he said this the music had faded away into a thread-like smallness, and when after long thought he raised his august head, he was alone save for the Dainagon, sleeping on the mats behind him, and the chamber was in darkness. Semimaru had departed in silence, and His Majesty, looking forth into the broad moonlight, could see the track of his feet upon the shining snow, and the music came back very thinly like spring rain in the trees. Once more he looked at the whiteness of the night, and then, stretching his august person on the mats, he slept amid dreams of sweet sound.

The next day, forbidding any to follow save the Dainagon, His Majesty went forth upon the frozen snow where the sun shone in a blinding whiteness. They followed the track of Semimaru's feet far under the pine trees so heavy with their load of snow that they were bowed as if with fruit. And the track led on and the air was so still that the cracking of a bough was like the blow of a hammer, and the sliding of a load of snow from a branch like the fall of an avalanche. Nor did they speak as they went. They listened, nor could they say for what.

Then, when they had gone a very great way, the track ceased suddenly, as if cut off, and at this spot, under the pines furred with snow, His Majesty became aware of a perfume so sweet that it was as though all the flowers of the earth haunted the place with their presence, and a music like the biwa of Semimaru was heard in the tree tops. This sounded far off like the whispering of rain when it falls in very small leaves, and presently it died away, and a voice followed after, singing, alone in the woods, so that the silence appeared to have been created that such a music might possess the world. So the Emperor stopped instantly, and the Dainagon behind him and he heard these words.

> "In me the Heavenly Lotos grew,
> The fibres ran from head to feet,
> And my heart was the august Blossom.
> Therefore the sweetness flowed through the veins of my flesh,
> And I breathed peace upon all the world,
> And about me was my fragrance shed
> That the souls of men should desire me."

Now, as he listened, there came through the wood a maiden, bare - footed, save for grass sandals, and clad in coarse clothing, and she came up and passed them, still singing.

And when she was past, His Majesty put up his hand to his eyes, like one dreaming, and said;

"What have you seen?"

And the Dainagon answered;

"Augustness, a country wench, flat - faced, ugly and blind, and with a voice like a crow. Has not your Majesty seen this?"

The Emperor, still shading his eyes, replied;

"I saw a maiden so beautiful that her Shining Majesty would be a black blot beside her. As she went, the Spring and all its sweetness blew from her garments. Her robe was green with small gold flowers. Her eyes were closed, but she resembled a cherry tree, snowy with bloom and dew. Her voice was like the singing flowers of Paradise."

The Dainagon looked at him with fear and compassion;

"Augustness, how should such a lady carry in her arms a bundle of firewood?"

"She bore in her hands three lotos flowers, and where each foot fell I saw a lotos bloom and vanish."

They retraced their steps through the wood; His Majesty radiant as Prince Fireshine with the joy that filled his soul; the Dainagon darkened as Prince Firefade with fear, believing that the strange music of Semimaru had bewitched His Majesty, or that the maiden herself might possibly have the power of the fox in shape-changing and bewildering the senses.

Very sorrowful and careful was his heart for he loved his Master.

That night His Majesty dreamed that he stood before the kakemono of the Amida Buddha, and that as he raised his eyes in adoration to the Blessed Face, he beheld the images of Fugen and Fudo, rise up and bow down before that One Who Is. Then, gliding in, before these Holinesses stood a figure, and it was the wood-cutter's daughter homely and blinded. She stretched her hands upward as though invoking the supreme Buddha, and then turning to His Majesty she smiled upon him, her eyes closed as in bliss unutterable. And he said aloud.

"Would that I might see her eyes!" and so saying awoke in a great stillness of snow and moonlight.

Having waked, he said within himself

"This marvel will I wed and she shall be my Empress were she lower than the Eta, and whether her face be lovely or homely. For she is certainly a flower dropped from the hand of the Divine."

So when the sun was high His Majesty, again followed by the Dainagon, went through the forest swiftly, and like a man that sees his goal, and when they reached the place where the maiden went by, His Majesty straitly commanded the Dainagon that he should draw apart, and leave him to speak with the maiden; yet that he should watch what befell.

So the Dainagon watched, and again he saw her come, very poorly clad, and with bare feet that shrank from the snow in her grass sandals, bowed beneath a heavy load of wood upon her shoulders, and her face flat and homely like a girl of the people, and her eyes blind and shut.

And as she came she sang this.

"The Eternal way lies before him,
The way that is made manifest in the Wise.
The Heart that loves reveals itself to man.
For now he draws nigh to the Source.
The night advances fast,
And lo! the moon shines bright."

And to the Dainagon it seemed a harsh crying nor could he distinguish any words at all.

But what His Majesty beheld was this. The evening had come on and the moon was rising. The snow had gone. It was the full glory of spring, and the flowers sprang thick as stars upon the grass, and among them lotos flowers, great as the wheel of a chariot, white and shining with the luminance of the pearl, and upon each one of these was seated an incarnate Holiness, looking upward with joined hands. In the trees were the voices of the mystic Birds that are the utterance of the Blessed One, proclaiming in harmony the Five Virtues, The Five Powers, the Seven Steps ascending to perfect Illumination, the Noble Eightfold Path, and all the Law. And, bearing, in the heart of the Son of Heaven awoke the Three Remembrances - the Remembrance of Him who is Blessed, Remembrance of the Law, and Remembrance of the Communion of the Assembly.

So, looking upward to the heavens, he beheld the Infinite Buddha, high and lifted up in a great raying glory. About Him were the exalted Bodhisattwas, the mighty Disciples, great Arhats all, and all the countless Angelhood. And these rose high into the infinite until they could be seen but as a point of fire against the moon. With this golden multitude beyond all numbering was He.

Then, as His Majesty had seen in the dream of the night, the wood-cutter's daughter, moving through the flowers like one blind that gropes his way, advanced before the Blessed Feet, and uplifting her hands, did adoration, and her face he could not see, but his heart went with her, adoring also the infinite Buddha seated in the calms of boundless Light.

Then enlightenment entered at his eyes, as a man that wakes from sleep, and suddenly he beheld the Maiden crowned and robed and terrible in beauty, and her feet were stayed upon an open lotos, and his soul knew the Senju Kwannon Herself, myriad-armed for the helping of mankind.

And turning, she smiled as in the vision, but his eyes being now clear her blinded eyes were opened, and that glory who shall tell as those living founts of Wisdom rayed upon him their ineffable light? In that ocean was his being drowned, and so, bowed before the Infinite Buddha, he received the Greater Illumination.

How great is the Glory of Kwannon!

When the radiance and the vision were withdrawn and only the moon looked over the trees, His Majesty rose upon his feet, and standing on the snow, surrounded with calm, he called to the Dainagon, and asked this;

"What have you seen?"

"Augustness, nothing but the country wench and moon and snow."

"And heard?"

"Augustness, nothing but the harsh voice of the wood-cutter's daughter."

"And felt?"

"Augustness, nothing but the bone-piercing cold." So His Majesty adored that which cannot be uttered, saying;

"So Wisdom, so Glory encompass us about, and we see them not for we are blinded with illusion. Yet every stone is a jewel and every clod is spirit and to the hems of the Infinite Buddha all cling. Through the compassion of the Supernal Mercy that walks the earth as the Bodhisattwa Kwannon, am I admitted to wisdom and given sight and hearing. And what is all the world to that happy one who has beheld Her eyes!"

And His Majesty returned through the forest.

When, the next day, he sent for the venerable Semimaru that holy recluse had departed and none knew where. But still when the moon is full a strange music moves in the tree tops of Shiobara.

Then His sacred Majesty returned to City-Royal, having determined to retire into the quiet life, and there, abandoning the throne to a kinsman wise in greatness, he became a dweller in the deserted hut of Semimaru.

His life, like a descending moon approaching the hill that should hide it, was passed in meditation on that Incarnate Love and Compassion whose glory had augustly been made known to him, and having cast aside all save the image of the

Divine from his soul, His Majesty became even as that man who desired enlightenment of the Blessed One.

For he, desiring instruction, gathered precious flowers, and journeyed to present them as an offering to the Guatama Buddha. Standing before Him, he stretched forth both his hands holding the flowers.

Then said the Holy One, looking upon his petitioner's right hand;

"Loose your hold of these."

And the man dropped the flowers from his right hand. And the Holy One looking upon his left hand, said;

"Loose your hold of these."

And, sorrowing, he dropped the flowers from his left hand. And again the Master said;

"Loose your hold of that which is neither in the right nor in the left"

And the disciple said very pitifully;

"Lord, of what should I loose my hold for I have nothing left?"

And He looked upon him steadfastly.

Therefore at last understanding he emptied his soul of all desire, and of fear that is the shadow of desire, and being enlightened relinquished all burdens.

So was it also with His Majesty. In peace he dwelt, and becoming a great Arhat, in peace he departed to that Uttermost Joy where is the Blessed One made manifest in Pure Light.

As for the parents of the maiden, they entered after sore troubles into peace, having been remembered by the Infinite. For it is certain that the enemies also of the Supreme Buddha go to salvation by thinking on Him, even though it be against Him.

And he who tells this truth makes this prayer to the Lady of Pity;

"Grant me, I pray,   One dewdrop from Thy willow spray,   And in the double Lotos keep   My hidden heart asleep."

How great is the Glory of Kwannon!

THE ROUND-FACED BEAUTY
A STORY OF THE CHINESE COURT

In the city of Chang-an music filled the palaces, and the festivities of the Emperor were measured by its beat. Night, and the full moon swimming like a gold-fish in the garden lakes, gave the signal for the Feather Jacket and Rainbow Skirt dances. Morning, with the rising sun, summoned the court again to the feast and wine-cup in the floating gardens.

The Emperor Chung Tsu favored this city before all others. The Yen Tower soaring heavenward, the Drum Towers, the Pearl Pagoda, were the only fit surroundings of his magnificence; and in the Pavilion of Tranquil Learning were held those discussions which enlightened the world and spread the fame of the Jade Emperor far and wide. In all respects he adorned the Dragon Throne - in all but one; for Nature, bestowing so much, withheld one gift, and the Imperial heart, as precious as jade, was also as hard, and he eschewed utterly the company of the Hidden Palace Flowers.

Yet the Inner Chambers were filled with ladies chosen from all parts of the Celestial Empire - ladies of the most exquisite and torturing beauty, moons of loveliness, moving coquettishly on little feet, with all the grace of willow branches in a light breeze. They were sprinkled with perfumes, adorned with jewels, robed in silks woven with gold and embroidered with designs of flowers and birds. Their faces were painted and their eyebrows formed into slender and perfect arches whence the soul of man might well slip to perdition, and a breath of sweet odor followed each wherever she moved. Every one might have been the Empress of some lesser kingdom; but though rumours reached the Son of Heaven from time to time of their charms, - especially when some new blossom was added to the Imperial bouquet,- he had dismissed them from his august thoughts, and they languished in a neglect so complete that the Great Cold Palaces of the Moon were not more empty than their hearts. They remained under the supervision of the Princess of Han, August Aunt of the Emperor, knowing that their Lord considered the company of sleeve-dogs and macaws more pleasant than their own. Nor had he as yet chosen an Empress, and it was evident that without some miracle, such as the intervention of the Municipal God, no heir to the throne could be hoped for.

Yet the Emperor one day remembered his imprisoned beauties, and it crossed the Imperial thoughts that even these inferior creatures might afford such interest as may be found in the gambols of trained fleas or other insects of no natural attainments.

Accordingly, he commanded that the subject last discussed in his presence should be transferred to the Inner Chambers, and it was his Order that the ladies should also discuss it, and their opinions be engraved on ivory, bound together with red silk and tassels and thus presented at the Dragon feet. The subject chosen was the following:-

Describe the Qualities of the Ideal Man

Now when this command was laid before the August Aunt, the guardian of the Inner Chambers, she was much perturbed in mind, for such a thing was unheard of in all the annals of the Empire. Recovering herself, she ventured to say that the discussion of such a question might raise very disquieting thoughts in the minds of the ladies, who could not be supposed to have any opinions at all on such a subject. Nor was it desirable that they should have. To every woman her husband and no other is and must be the Ideal Man. So it was always in the past; so it must ever be. There are certain things which it is dangerous to question or discuss, and how can ladies who have never spoken with any other man than a parent or a brother judge such matters?

"How, indeed," asked this lady of exalted merit, "can the bat form an idea of the sunlight, or the carp of the motion of wings? If his Celestial Majesty had commanded a discussion on the Superior Woman and the virtues which should adorn her, some sentiments not wholly unworthy might have been offered. But this is a calamity. They come unexpectedly, springing up like mushrooms, and this one is probably due to the lack of virtue of the inelegant and unintellectual person who is now speaking."

This she uttered in the presence of the principal beauties of the Inner Chambers. They sat or reclined about her in attitudes of perfect loveliness. Two, embroidering silver pheasants, paused with their needles suspended above the stretched silk, to hear the August Aunt. One, threading beads of jewel jade, permitted them to slip from the string and so distended the rose of her mouth in surprise that the small pearl-shells were visible within. The Lady Tortoise, caressing a scarlet and azure macaw, in her agitation so twitched the feathers that the bird, shrieking, bit her finger. The Lady Golden Bells blushed deeply at the thought of what was required of them; and the little Lady Summer Dress, youngest of all the assembled beauties, was so alarmed at the prospect that she began to sob aloud, until she met the eye of the August Aunt and abruptly ceased.

"It is not, however, to be supposed," said the August Aunt, opening her snuff-bottle of painted crystal, "that the minds of our deplorable and unattractive sex are wholly incapable of forming opinions. But speech is a grave matter for women, naturally slow-witted and feeble-minded as they are. This unenlightened person recalls the Odes as saying:-

> `A flaw in a piece of white jade
> May be ground away,
> But when a woman has spoken foolishly
> Nothing can be done-'

a consideration which should make every lady here and throughout the world think anxiously before speech." So anxiously did the assembled beauties think, that all remained mute as fish in a pool, and the August Aunt continued:-

"Let Tsu-ssu be summoned. It is my intention to suggest to the Dragon Emperor that the virtues of women be the subject of our discourse, and I will myself open and conclude the discussion."

Tsu-ssu was not long in kotowing before the August Aunt, who despatched her message with the proper ceremonial due to its Imperial destination; and meanwhile, in much agitation, the beauties could but twitter and whisper in each other's ears, and await the response like condemned prisoners who yet hope for reprieve.

Scarce an hour had dripped away on the water-clock when an Imperial Missive bound with yellow silk arrived, and the August Aunt, rising, kotowed nine times before she received it in her jewelled hand with its delicate and lengthy nails ensheathed in pure gold and set with gems of the first water. She then read it aloud, the ladies prostrating themselves.

To the Princess of Han, the August Aunt, the Lady of the Nine Superior Virtues:-

"Having deeply reflected on the wisdom submitted, We thus reply. Women should not be the judges of their own virtues, since these exist only in relation to men. Let Our Command therefore be executed, and tablets presented before us seven days hence, with the name of each lady appended to her tablet."

It was indeed pitiable to see the anxiety of the ladies! A sacrifice to Kwan-Yin, the Goddess of Mercy, of a jewel from each, with intercession for aid, was proposed by the Lustrous Lady; but the majority shook their heads sadly. The August Aunt, tossing her head, declared that, as the Son of Heaven had made no comment on her proposal of opening and closing the discussion, she should take no part other than safeguarding the interests of propriety. This much increased the alarm, and, kneeling at her feet, the swan-like beauties, Deep-Snow and Winter Moon implored her aid and compassion. But, rising indignantly, the August Aunt sought her own apartments, and for the first time the inmates of the Pepper Chamber saw with regret the golden dragons embroidered on her back.

It was then that the Round-Faced Beauty ventured a remark. This maiden, having been born in the far-off province of Ssuch-uan, was considered a rustic by the distinguished elegance of the Palace and, therefore, had never spoken unless decorum required. Still, even her detractors were compelled to admit the charms that had gained her her name. Her face had the flawless outline of the pearl, and like the blossom of the plum was the purity of her complexion, upon which the darkness of her eyebrows resembled two silk-moths alighted to flutter above the brilliance of her eyes - eyes which even the August Aunt had commended after a banquet of unsurpassed variety. Her hair had been compared to the crow's plumage; her waist was like a roll of silk, and her discretion in habiting herself was such that even the Lustrous Lady and the Lady Tortoise drew instruction from the splendours of her robes. It created, however, a general astonishment when she spoke.

"Paragons of beauty, what is this dull and opaque. witted person that she should speak?"

"What, indeed!" said the Celestial Sister. "This entirely undistinguished person cannot even imagine."

A distressing pause followed, during which many whispered anxiously. The Lustrous Lady broke it.

"It is true that the highly ornamental Round-Faced Beauty is but lately come, yet even the intelligent Ant may assist the Dragon; and in the presence of alarm, what is decorum? With a tiger behind one, who can recall the Book of Rites and act with befitting elegance?"

"The high-born will at all times remember the Rites!" retorted the Celestial Sister. "Have we not heard the August Aunt observe: `Those who understand do not speak. Those who speak do not understand'?"

The Round-Faced Beauty collected her courage.

"Doubtless this is wisdom; yet if the wise do not speak, who should instruct us? The August Aunt herself would be silent."

All were confounded by this dilemma, and the little Lady Summer-Dress, still weeping, entreated that the Round-Faced Beauty might be heard. The Heavenly Blossoms then prepared to listen and assumed attitudes of attention, which so disconcerted the Round-Faced Beauty that she blushed like a spring tulip in speaking.

"Beautiful ladies, our Lord, who is unknown to us all, has issued an august command. It cannot be disputed, for the whisper of disobedience is heard as thunder in the Imperial Presence. Should we not aid each other? If any lady has formed a dream in her soul of the Ideal Man, might not such a picture aid us all? Let us not be `say-nothing-do-nothing,' but act!"

They hung their heads and smiled, but none would allow that she had formed such an image. The little Lady Tortoise, laughing behind her fan of sandalwood, said roguishly: "The Ideal Man should be handsome, liberal in giving, and assuredly he should appreciate the beauty of his wives. But this we cannot say to the Divine Emperor."

A sigh rustled through the Pepper Chamber. The Celestial Sister looked angrily at the speaker.

"This is the talk of children," she said. "Does no one remember Kung-fu-tse's

[Confucius] description of the Superior Man?"

Unfortunately none did - not even the Celestial Sister herself.

"Is it not probable," said the Round-Faced Beauty, "that the Divine Emperor remembers it him- self and wishes-"

But the Celestial Sister, yawning audibly, summoned the attendants to bring rose-leaves in honey, and would hear no more.

The Round-Faced Beauty therefore wandered forth among the mossy rocks and drooping willows of the Imperial Garden, deeply considering the matter. She ascended the bow-curved bridge of marble which crossed the Pool of Clear Weather, and from the top idly observed the reflection of her rose-and-gold coat in the water while, with her taper fingers, she crumbled cake for the fortunate gold-fish that dwelt in it. And, so doing, she remarked one fish, four-tailed among the six-tailed, and in no way distinguished by elegance, which secured by far the largest share of the crumbs dropped into the pool. Bending lower, she observed this singular fish and its methods.

The others crowded about the spot where the crumbs fell, all herded together. In their eagerness and stupidity they remained like a cloud of gold in one spot, slowly waving their tails. But this fish, concealing itself behind a miniature rock, waited, looking upward, until the crumbs were falling, and then, rushing forth with the speed of an arrow, scattered the stupid mass of fish, and bore off the crumbs to its shelter, where it instantly devoured them.

"This is notable," said the Round-Faced Beauty. "Observation enlightens the mind. To be apart - to be distinguished - secures notice!" And she plunged into thought again, wandering, herself a flower, among the gorgeous tree peonies.

On the following day the August Aunt commanded that a writer among the palace attendants should, with brush and ink, be summoned to transcribe the wisdom of the ladies. She requested that each would give three days to thought, relating the following anecdote. "There was a man who, taking a piece of ivory, carved it into a mulberry leaf, spending three years on the task. When finished it could not be told from the original, and was a gift suitable for the Brother of the Sun and Moon. Do likewise!"

"But yet, 0 Augustness!" said the Celestial Sister, "if the Lord of Heaven took as long with each leaf, there would be few leaves on the trees, and if-"

The August Aunt immediately commanded silence and retired. On the third day she seated herself in her chair of carved ebony, while the attendant placed himself by her feet and prepared to record her words.

"This insignificant person has decided," began her Augustness, looking round and unscrewing the amber top of her snuff-bottle, "to take an unintelligent part in these proceedings. An example should be set. Attendant, write!"

She then dictated as follows: "The Ideal Man is he who now decorates the Imperial Throne, or he who in all humility ventures to resemble the incomparable Emperor. Though he may not hope to attain, his endeavor is his merit. No further description it needed."

With complacence she inhaled the perfumed snuff, as the writer appended the elegant characters of her Imperial name.

If it is permissible to say that the faces of the beauties lengthened visibly, it should now be said. For it had been the intention of every lady to make an illusion to the Celestial Emperor and depict him as the Ideal Man. Nor had they expected that the August Aunt would take any part in the matter.

"Oh, but it was the intention of this commonplace and undignified person to say this very thing!" cried the Lustrous Lady, with tears in the jewels of her eyes. "I thought no other high-minded and distinguished lady would for a moment think of it"

"And it was my intention also!" fluttered the little Lady Tortoise, wringing her hands! "What now shall this most unlucky and unendurable person do? For three nights has sleep forsaken my unattractive eyelids, and, tossing and turning on a couch deprived of all comfort, I could only repeat, `The Ideal Man is the Divine Dragon Emperor!'"

"May one of entirely contemptible attainments make a suggestion in this assemblage of scintillating wit and beauty?" inquired the Celestial Sister. "My superficial opinion is that it would be well to prepare a single paper to which all names should be appended, stating that His Majesty in his Dragon Divinity comprises all ideals in his sacred Person."

"Let those words be recorded," said the August Aunt. "What else should any lady of discretion and propriety say? In this Palace of Virtuous Peace, where all is consecrated to the Son of Heaven, though he deigns not to enter it, what other thought dare be breathed? Has any lady ventured to step outside such a limit? If so, let her declare herself!"

All shook their heads, and the August Aunt proceeded: "Let the writer record this as the opinion of every lady of the Imperial Household, and let each name be separately appended."

Had any desired to object, none dared to confront the August Aunt; but apparently no beauty so desired, for after three nights' sleepless meditation, no other thought than this had occurred to any.

Accordingly, the writer moved from lady to lady and, under the supervision of the August Aunt, transcribed the following: "The Ideal Man is the earthly likeness of the Divine Emperor. How should it be otherwise?" And under this sentence wrote the name of each lovely one in succession. The papers were then placed in the hanging sleeves of the August Aunt for safety.

By the decree of Fate, the father of the Round-Faced Beauty had, before he became an ancestral spirit, been a scholar of distinction, having graduated at the age of seventy-two with a composition commended by the Grand Examiner. Having no gold and silver to give his daughter, he had formed her mind, and had presented her with the sole jewel of his family-a pearl as large as a bean. Such was her sole dower, but the accomplished Aunt may excel the indolent Prince.

Yet, before the thought in her mind, she hesitated and trembled, recalling the lesson of the gold-fish; and it was with anxiety that paled her roseate lips that, on a certain day, she had sought the Willow Bridge Pavilion. There had awaited her a palace attendant skilled with the brush, and there in secrecy and dire affright, hearing the footsteps of the August Aunt in every rustle of leafage, and her voice in the call of every crow, did the Round-Faced Beauty dictate the following composition:-

"Though the sky rain pearls, it cannot equal the beneficence of the Son of Heaven. Though the sky rain jade it cannot equal his magnificence. He has commanded his slave to describe the qualities of the Ideal Man. How should I, a mere woman, do this? I, who have not seen the Divine Emperor, how should I know what is virtue? I, who have not seen the glory of his countenance, how should I know what is beauty? Report speaks of his excellencies, but I who live in the dark know not. But to the Ideal Woman, the very vices of her husband are virtues. Should he exalt another, this is a mark of his superior taste. Should he dismiss his slave, this is justice. To the Ideal Woman there is but one Ideal Man - and that is her lord. From the day she crosses his threshold, to the day when they clothe her in the garments of Immortality, this is her sole opinion. Yet would that she might receive instruction of what only are beauty and virtue in his adorable presence."

This being written, she presented her one pearl to the attendant and fled, not looking behind her, as quickly as her delicate feet would permit.

On the seventh day the compositions, engraved on ivory and bound with red silk and tassels, were presented to the Emperor, and for seven days more he forgot their existence. On the eighth the High Chamberlain ventured to recall them to the Imperial memory, and the Emperor glancing slightly at one after another, threw them aside, yawning as he did so. Finally, one arrested his eyes, and reading it more than once he laid it before him and meditated. An hour passed in this way while the forgotten Lord Chamberlain continued to kneel. The Son of Heaven, then raising his head, pronounced these words: "In the society of the Ideal Woman, she to whom jealousy is unknown, tranquillity might possibly be obtained. Let prayer be made before the Ancestors with the customary offerings, for this is a matter deserving attention."

A few days passed, and an Imperial attendant, escorted by two mandarins of the peacock- feather and crystal-button rank, desired an audience of the August Aunt, and, speaking before the curtain, informed her that his Imperial Majesty would pay a visit that evening to the Hall of Tranquil Longevity. Such was her agitation at this honour that she immediately swooned; but, reviving, summoned all the attendants and gave orders for a banquet and musicians.

Lanterns painted with pheasants and exquisite landscapes were hung on all the pavilions. Tap- estries of rose, decorated with the Five-Clawed Dragons, adorned the chambers; and upon the High Seat was placed a robe of yellow satin embroidered with pearls. All was hurry and excitement. The Blossoms of the Palace were so exquisitely decked that one grain more of powder would have made them too lily-like, and one touch more of rouge, too rosecheeked. It was indeed perfection, and, like lotuses upon a lake, or Asian birds, gorgeous of plumage, they stood ranged in the outer chamber while the Celestial Emperor took his seat.

The Round-Faced Beauty wore no jewels, having bartered her pearl for her opportunity; but her long coat of jade-green, embroidered with golden willows, and her trousers of palest rose left nothing to be desired. In her hair two golden peonies were fastened with pins of kingfisher work. The Son of Heaven was seated upon the throne as the ladies approached, marshaled by the August Aunt. He was attired in the Yellow Robe with the Flying Dragons, and upon the Imperial Head was the Cap, ornamented with one hundred and forty-four priceless gems. From it hung the twelve pendants of strings of pearls, partly concealing the august eyes of the Jade Emperor. No greater splendour can strike awe into the soul of man.

At his command the August Aunt took her seat upon a lesser chair at the Celestial Feet. Her mien was majestic, and struck awe into the assembled beauties, whose names she spoke aloud as each approached and prostrated herself. She then pronounced these words:

"Beautiful ones, the Emperor, having considered the opinions submitted by you on the subject of the Superior Man, is pleased to express his august commendation. Dismiss, therefore, anxiety from your minds, and prepare to assist at the humble concert of music we have prepared for his Divine pleasure."

Slightly raising himself in his chair, the Son of Heaven looked down upon that Garden of Beauty, holding in his hand an ivory tablet bound with red silk.

"Lovely ladies," he began, in a voice that assuaged fear, "who among you was it that laid before our feet a composition beginning thus - 'Though the sky rain pearls'?"

The August Aunt immediately rose.

"Imperial Majesty, none! These eyes supervised every composition. No impropriety was permitted."

The Son of Heaven resumed: "Let that lady stand forth."

The words were few, but sufficient. Trembling in every limb, the Round-Faced Beauty separated herself from her companions and prostrated herself, amid the breathless amazement of the Blossoms of the Palace. He looked down upon her as she knelt, pale as a lady carved in ivory, but lovely as the lotus of Chang-Su. He turned to the August Aunt. "Princess of Han, my Imperial Aunt, I would speak with this lady alone."

Decorum itself and the custom of Palaces could not conceal the indignation of the August Aunt as she rose and retired, driving the ladies before her as a shepherd drives his sheep.

The Hall of Tranquil Longevity being now empty, the Jade Emperor extended his hand and beckoned the Round-Faced Beauty to approach. This she did, hanging her head like a flower surcharged with dew and swaying gracefully as a wind-bell, and knelt on the lowest step of the Seat of State.

"Loveliest One," said the Emperor, "I have read your composition. I would know the truth. Did any aid you as you spoke it? Was it the thought of your own heart?"

"None aided, Divine," said she, almost fainting with fear. "It was indeed the thought of this illiterate slave, consumed with an unwarranted but uncontrollable passion."

"And have you in truth desired to see your Lord?"

"As a prisoner in a dungeon desires the light, so was it with this low person."

"And having seen?"

"Augustness, the dull eyes of this slave are blinded with beauty."

She laid her head before his feet.

"Yet you have depicted, not the Ideal Man, but the Ideal Woman. This was not the Celestial command. How was this?"

"Because, 0 versatile and auspicious Emperor, the blind cannot behold the sunlight, and it is only the Ideal Woman who is worthy to comprehend and worship the Ideal Man. For this alone is she created."

A smile began to illuminate the Imperial Countenance. "And how, 0 Round-Faced Beauty, did you evade the vigilance of the August Aunt?"

She hung her head lower, speaking almost in a whisper. "With her one pearl did this person buy the secrecy of the writer; and when the August Aunt slept, did I conceal the paper in her sleeve with the rest, and her own Imperial hand gave it to the engraver of ivory."

She veiled her face with two jade-white hands that trembled excessively. On hearing this statement the Celestial Emperor broke at once into a very great laughter, and he laughed loud and long as a tiller of wheat. The Round-Faced Beauty heard it demurely until, catching the Imperial eye, decorum was forgotten and she too laughed uncontrollably. So they continued, and finally the Emperor leaned back, drying the tears in his eyes with his august sleeve, and the lady, resuming her gravity, hid her face in her hands, yet regarded him through her fingers.

When the August Aunt returned at the end of an hour with the ladies, surrounded by the attendants with their instruments of music, the Round-Faced Beauty was seated in the chair that she herself had occupied, and on the whiteness of her brow was hung the chain of pearls, which had formed the frontal of the Cap of the Emperor.

It is recorded that, advancing from honour to honour, the Round-Faced Beauty was eventually chosen Empress and became the mother of the Imperial Prince. The celestial purity of her mind and the absence of all flaws of jealousy and anger warranted this distinction. But it is also recorded that, after her elevation, no other lady was ever exalted in the Imperial favour or received the slightest notice from the Emperor. For the Empress, now well acquainted with the Ideal Man, judged it better that his experiences of the Ideal Woman should be drawn from herself alone. And as she decreed, so it was done. Doubtless Her Majesty did well.

It is known that the Emperor departed to the Ancestral Spirits at an early age, seeking, as the August Aunt observed, that repose which on earth could never more be his. But no one has asserted that this lady's disposition was free from the ordinary blemishes of humanity.

As for the Celestial Empress (who survives in history as one of the most astute rulers who ever adorned the Dragon Throne), she continued to rule her son and the Empire, surrounded by the respectful admiration of all.

The Codes Of Hammurabi And Moses
W. W. Davies

QTY

The discovery of the Hammurabi Code is one of the greatest achievements of archaeology, and is of paramount interest, not only to the student of the Bible, but also to all those interested in ancient history...

Religion   **ISBN:** *1-59462-338-4*   **Pages:132**
MSRP $12.95

The Theory of Moral Sentiments
Adam Smith

QTY

This work from 1749. contains original theories of conscience amd moral judgment and it is the foundation for systemof morals.

Philosophy   **ISBN:** *1-59462-777-0*   **Pages:536**
MSRP $19.95

Jessica's First Prayer
Hesba Stretton

QTY

In a screened and secluded corner of one of the many railway-bridges which span the streets of London there could be seen a few years ago, from five o'clock every morning until half past eight, a tidily set-out coffee-stall, consisting of a trestle and board, upon which stood two large tin cans, with a small fire of charcoal burning under each so as to keep the coffee boiling during the early hours of the morning when the work-people were thronging into the city on their way to their daily toil...

Childrens   **ISBN:** *1-59462-373-2*   **Pages:84**
MSRP $9.95

My Life and Work
Henry Ford

QTY

Henry Ford revolutionized the world with his implementation of mass production for the Model T automobile. Gain valuable business insight into his life and work with his own auto-biography... "We have only started on our development of our country we have not as yet, with all our talk of wonderful progress, done more than scratch the surface. The progress has been wonderful enough but..."

Biographies/   **ISBN:** *1-59462-198-5*   **Pages:300**
MSRP $21.95

The Art of Cross-Examination
Francis Wellman

QTY

I presume it is the experience of every author, after his first book is published upon an important subject, to be almost overwhelmed with a wealth of ideas and illustrations which could readily have been included in his book, and which to his own mind, at least, seem to make a second edition inevitable. Such certainly was the case with me; and when the first edition had reached its sixth impression in five months, I rejoiced to learn that it seemed to my publishers that the book had met with a sufficiently favorable reception to justify a second and considerably enlarged edition. ..

Pages:412

Reference   **ISBN: *1-59462-647-2***   *MSRP $19.95*

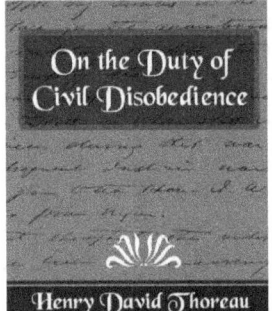

On the Duty of Civil Disobedience
Henry David Thoreau

QTY

Thoreau wrote his famous essay, On the Duty of Civil Disobedience, as a protest against an unjust but popular war and the immoral but popular institution of slave-owning. He did more than write—he declined to pay his taxes, and was hauled off to gaol in consequence. Who can say how much this refusal of his hastened the end of the war and of slavery ?

Law   **ISBN: *1-59462-747-9***

Pages:48

MSRP $7.45

Dream Psychology Psychoanalysis for Beginners
Sigmund Freud

QTY

Sigmund Freud, born Sigismund Schlomo Freud (May 6, 1856 - September 23, 1939), was a Jewish-Austrian neurologist and psychiatrist who co-founded the psychoanalytic school of psychology. Freud is best known for his theories of the unconscious mind, especially involving the mechanism of repression; his redefinition of sexual desire as mobile and directed towards a wide variety of objects; and his therapeutic techniques, especially his understanding of transference in the therapeutic relationship and the presumed value of dreams as sources of insight into unconscious desires.

Pages:196

Psychology   **ISBN: *1-59462-905-6***   *MSRP $15.45*

The Miracle of Right Thought
Orison Swett Marden

QTY

Believe with all of your heart that you will do what you were made to do. When the mind has once formed the habit of holding cheerful, happy, prosperous pictures, it will not be easy to form the opposite habit. It does not matter how improbable or how far away this realization may see, or how dark the prospects may be, if we visualize them as best we can, as vividly as possible, hold tenaciously to them and vigorously struggle to attain them, they will gradually become actualized, realized in the life. But a desire, a longing without endeavor, a yearning abandoned or held indifferently will vanish without realization.

Pages:360

Self Help   **ISBN: *1-59462-644-8***   *MSRP $25.45*

www.bookjungle.com *email: sales@bookjungle.com fax: 630-214-0564 mail: Book Jungle PO Box 2226 Champaign, IL 61825*

QTY

The Rosicrucian Cosmo-Conception Mystic Christianity *by Max Heindel*   ISBN: *1-59462-188-8* **$38.95**
The Rosicrucian Cosmo-conception is not dogmatic, neither does it appeal to any other authority than the reason of the student. It is: not controversial, but is: sent forth in the, hope that it may help to clear...   *New Age/Religion Pages 646*

Abandonment To Divine Providence *by Jean-Pierre de Caussade*   ISBN: *1-59462-228-0* **$25.95**
"The Rev. Jean Pierre de Caussade was one of the most remarkable spiritual writers of the Society of Jesus in France in the 18th Century. His death took place at Toulouse in 1751. His works have gone through many editions and have been republished...   *Inspirational/Religion Pages 400*

Mental Chemistry *by Charles Haanel*   ISBN: *1-59462-192-6* **$23.95**
Mental Chemistry allows the change of material conditions by combining and appropriately utilizing the power of the mind. Much like applied chemistry creates something new and unique out of careful combinations of chemicals the mastery of mental chemistry...   *New Age/Business Pages 422*

The Letters of Robert Browning and Elizabeth Barret Barrett 1845-1846 vol II   ISBN: *1-59462-193-4* **$35.95**
by Robert Browning and Elizabeth Barrett   *Biographies Pages 596*

Gleanings In Genesis (volume I) *by Arthur W. Pink*   ISBN: *1-59462-130-6* **$27.45**
Appropriately has Genesis been termed "the seed plot of the Bible" for in it we have, in germ form, almost all of the great doctrines which are afterwards fully developed in the books of Scripture which follow...   *Religion/Inspirational Pages 420*

The Master Key *by L. W. de Laurence*   ISBN: *1-59462-001-6* **$30.95**
In no branch of human knowledge has there been a more lively increase of the spirit of research during the past few years than in the study of Psychology, Concentration and Mental Discipline. The requests for authentic lessons in Thought Control, Mental Discipline and...   *New Age/Business Pages 422*

The Lesser Key Of Solomon Goetia *by L. W. de Laurence*   ISBN: *1-59462-092-X* **$9.95**
This translation of the first book of the "Lernegton" which is now for the first time made accessible to students of Talismanic Magic was done, after careful collation and edition, from numerous Ancient Manuscripts in Hebrew, Latin, and French...   *New Age/Occult Pages 92*

Rubaiyat Of Omar Khayyam *by Edward Fitzgerald*   ISBN:*1-59462-332-5* **$13.95**
Edward Fitzgerald, whom the world has already learned, in spite of his own efforts to remain within the shadow of anonymity, to look upon as one of the rarest poets of the century, was born at Bredfield, in Suffolk, on the 31st of March, 1809. He was the third son of John Purcell...   *Music Pages 172*

Ancient Law *by Henry Maine*   ISBN: *1-59462-128-4* **$29.95**
The chief object of the following pages is to indicate some of the earliest ideas of mankind, as they are reflected in Ancient Law, and to point out the relation of those ideas to modern thought.   *Religion/History Pages 452*

Far-Away Stories *by William J. Locke*   ISBN: *1-59462-129-2* **$19.45**
"Good wine needs no bush, but a collection of mixed vintages does. And this book is just such a collection. Some of the stories I do not want to remain buried for ever in the museum files of dead magazine-numbers an author's not unpardonable vanity..."   *Fiction Pages 272*

Life of David Crockett *by David Crockett*   ISBN: *1-59462-250-7* **$27.45**
"Colonel David Crockett was one of the most remarkable men of the times in which he lived. Born in humble life, but gifted with a strong will, an indomitable courage, and unremitting perseverance...   *Biographies/New Age Pages 424*

Lip-Reading *by Edward Nitchie*   ISBN: *1-59462-206-X* **$25.95**
Edward B. Nitchie, founder of the New York School for the Hard of Hearing, now the Nitchie School of Lip-Reading, Inc, wrote "LIP-READING Principles and Practice". The development and perfecting of this meritorious work on lip-reading was an undertaking...   *How-to Pages 400*

A Handbook of Suggestive Therapeutics, Applied Hypnotism, Psychic Science   ISBN: *1-59462-214-0* **$24.95**
by Henry Munro   *Health/New Age/Health/Self-help Pages 376*

A Doll's House: and Two Other Plays *by Henrik Ibsen*   ISBN: *1-59462-112-8* **$19.95**
Henrik Ibsen created this classic when in revolutionary 1848 Rome. Introducing some striking concepts in playwriting for the realist genre, this play has been studied the world over.   *Fiction/Classics/Plays 308*

The Light of Asia *by sir Edwin Arnold*   ISBN: *1-59462-204-3* **$13.95**
In this poetic masterpiece, Edwin Arnold describes the life and teachings of Buddha. The man who was to become known as Buddha to the world was born as Prince Gautama of India but he rejected the worldly riches and abandoned the reigns of power when...   *Religion/History/Biographies Pages 170*

The Complete Works of Guy de Maupassant *by Guy de Maupassant*   ISBN: *1-59462-157-8* **$16.95**
"For days and days, nights and nights, I had dreamed of that first kiss which was to consecrate our engagement, and I knew not on what spot I should put my lips..."   *Fiction/Classics Pages 240*

The Art of Cross-Examination *by Francis L. Wellman*   ISBN: *1-59462-309-0* **$26.95**
Written by a renowned trial lawyer, Wellman imparts his experience and uses case studies to explain how to use psychology to extract desired information through questioning.   *How-to/Science/Reference Pages 408*

Answered or Unanswered? *by Louisa Vaughan*   ISBN: *1-59462-248-5* **$10.95**
Miracles of Faith in China   *Religion Pages 112*

The Edinburgh Lectures on Mental Science (1909) *by Thomas*   ISBN: *1-59462-008-3* **$11.95**
This book contains the substance of a course of lectures recently given by the writer in the Queen Street Hall, Edinburgh. Its purpose is to indicate the Natural Principles governing the relation between Mental Action and Material Conditions...   *New Age/Psychology Pages 148*

Ayesha *by H. Rider Haggard*   ISBN: *1-59462-301-5* **$24.95**
Verily and indeed it is the unexpected that happens! Probably if there was one person upon the earth from whom the Editor of this, and of a certain previous history, did not expect to hear again...   *Classics Pages 380*

Ayala's Angel *by Anthony Trollope*   ISBN: *1-59462-352-X* **$29.95**
The two girls were both pretty, but Lucy who was twenty-one who supposed to be simple and comparatively unattractive, whereas Ayala was credited, as her Bombwhat romantic name might show, with poetic charm and a taste for romance. Ayala when her father died was nineteen...   *Fiction Pages 484*

The American Commonwealth *by James Bryce*   ISBN: *1-59462-286-8* **$34.45**
An interpretation of American democratic political theory. It examines political mechanics and society from the perspective of Scotsman James Bryce   *Politics Pages 572*

Stories of the Pilgrims *by Margaret P. Pumphrey*   ISBN: *1-59462-116-0* **$17.95**
This book explores pilgrims religious oppression in England as well as their escape to Holland and eventual crossing to America on the Mayflower, and their early days in New England...   *History Pages 268*

www.bookjungle.com *email: sales@bookjungle.com fax: 630-214-0564 mail: Book Jungle PO Box 2226 Champaign, IL 61825*

QTY

The Fasting Cure by *Sinclair Upton*   ISBN: *1-59462-222-1*   **$13.95**
In the Cosmopolitan Magazine for May, 1910, and in the Contemporary Review (London) for April, 1910, I published an article dealing with my experiences in fasting. I have written a great many magazine articles, but never one which attracted so much attention... New Age/Self Help/Health Pages 164

Hebrew Astrology by *Sepharial*   ISBN: *1-59462-308-2*   **$13.45**
In these days of advanced thinking it is a matter of common observation that we have left many of the old landmarks behind and that we are now pressing forward to greater heights and to a wider horizon than that which represented the mind-content of our progenitors...   Astrology Pages 144

Thought Vibration or The Law of Attraction in the Thought World   ISBN: *1-59462-127-6*   **$12.95**

by *William Walker Atkinson*   *Psychology/Religion Pages 144*

Optimism by *Helen Keller*   ISBN: *1-59462-108-X*   **$15.95**
Helen Keller was blind, deaf, and mute since 19 months old, yet famously learned how to overcome these handicaps, communicate with the world, and spread her lectures promoting optimism. An inspiring read for everyone...   Biographies/Inspirational Pages 84

Sara Crewe by *Frances Burnett*   ISBN: *1-59462-360-0*   **$9.45**
In the first place, Miss Minchin lived in London. Her home was a large, dull, tall one, in a large, dull square, where all the houses were alike, and all the sparrows were alike, and where all the door-knockers made the same heavy sound...   Childrens/Classic Pages 88

The Autobiography of Benjamin Franklin by *Benjamin Franklin*   ISBN: *1-59462-135-7*   **$24.95**
The Autobiography of Benjamin Franklin has probably been more extensively read than any other American historical work, and no other book of its kind has had such ups and downs of fortune. Franklin lived for many years in England, where he was agent...   Biographies/History Pages 332

Name	
Email	
Telephone	
Address	
City, State ZIP	

☐ **Credit Card**   ☐ **Check / Money Order**

Credit Card Number	
Expiration Date	
Signature	

Please Mail to: *Book Jungle*
PO Box 2226
Champaign, IL 61825
or Fax to: *630-214-0564*

ORDERING INFORMATION

web: *www.bookjungle.com*
email: *sales@bookjungle.com*
fax: *630-214-0564*
mail: *Book Jungle PO Box 2226 Champaign, IL 61825*
or PayPal *to sales@bookjungle.com*

Please contact us for bulk discounts

DIRECT-ORDER TERMS

**20% Discount if You Order
Two or More Books**
Free Domestic Shipping!
Accepted: Master Card, Visa,
Discover, American Express